A Million to Stay

A Million to Blow Series
Book 2

BLUE SAFFIRE

Perceptive Illusions Publishing, Inc.
Bay Shore, New York

Blue Saffire/Perceptive Illusions Publishing, Inc.
PO BOX 5253
Bay Shore, New York 11706
www.BlueSaffire.com

Publisher's Note: This is a work of fiction. Names, characters, places, and incidents are a product of the author's imagination. Locales and public names are sometimes used for atmospheric purposes. Any resemblance to actual people, living or dead, or to businesses, companies, events, institutions, or locales is completely coincidental.

Ordering Information:
Quantity sales. Special discounts are available on quantity purchases by corporations, associations, and others. For details, contact the "Special Sales Department" at the address above.

A Million To Stay Book 2/ Blue Saffire—2nd ed.
ISBN 978-1-941924-17-4

*Never walk away if you don't mean it. Making your way
back is never guaranteed.*

–BLUE SAFFIRE

The Call

Gregor

I sit in this hotel room warring with what to do. Looking around at the opulence and luxury, I question walking away from the only life I've ever known.

However, I don't know if the comfort of this lifestyle overrides my happiness and control over my own life. I'm tired of my father trying to control me and all my decisions. I don't want to go into politics, and I don't love working for him, I tolerate it.

However, I'm not sure I'm ready for what Clayton has planned out. To walk away and start over—is that what I want at thirty-three? My thoughts go to Chloe as the sound of her splashing in the bathtub reaches me.

If starting over means we can be together, it may just be what I need to do. My heart races. I'm truly going to ask her to do this with me. I'm going to start my life over. I'll have nothing and I'll be no one. Will she still want me?

My phone rings, pulling me out of my thoughts. I pick it up and see it's my father. I've been avoiding his calls. I get the feeling he's about to force my hand. He wants to start my campaign.

"Hello, Father," I say into the phone.

"Clooney, I know about the girl. What are you thinking? You need to end things." Just like him to get to the point of what he wants. Always what *he* wants.

Annoyed with him calling me by my first name, I bite into my cheek and try to feign innocence when I speak. "What are you talking about, Dad?"

"Don't play games with me, Clooney. The girl has to go, now. She's not the one for you. I want it over."

I feel sick to my stomach. I'm thirty-three, not a child. Yet he has so much power over my life. I'm not this man. I can't live with ties holding me back. I'm no one's puppet.

Clay's voice in my ear starts to grow louder, whispering about breaking free. I could take Chloe and start over. When this week is over, we can board a plane and be off.

It's in this moment I make my decision. I will be my own man at whatever cost.

CHAPTER ONE

Why

Brodi

A week later...

"You have to understand. I'm doing what's best for you," I sigh in frustration.

"You said that last time. I'm so stupid. Why do I keep letting you do this to me?" Chloe sobs.

Her words and tears rip right through my soul. I've never wanted to hurt her. She's the only woman I've ever loved.

Well, she's a woman now. The first time our worlds collided, I had no business being with her. She was so young and naive.

"Come on, Cee," I say, releasing a breath. "That's not fair."

I've never been able to truly walk away from her. She should know this. This is why we're here.

The shit I've done to be with her. Internally, I give a bitter laugh. She doesn't even know my real name.

I've never told it to her for fear of how it could ruin me. I know I'm a bastard. I've only thought of myself when pursuing Chloe.

My needs have always been first. My need to know her name, my need to hear her voice, my need to see her—it's always been about my needs, not hers. My needs are what blinded me in the first place.

I should've acknowledged from the beginning that it wouldn't work. My father has his eyes on the governor's seat. He's been grooming me for it since I was a little boy.

Well before I could walk or talk, my father had plans for my life. None of those plans have ever included a girl eight years younger than me. His call earlier in the week only solidified that.

The media would have a field day if it ever got out I once dated a seventeen-year-old, while I'd been twenty-five. I knew Chloe was younger when I met her. I just didn't know she was *that* young.

In my defense, she lied to me for the first six months. By the time I learned the truth, it was too late. I was already in love with her.

Thank God we hadn't had sex. I had loved the thrill of the chase. At least, I thought it was a chase. Chloe was so gorgeous and intelligent. I thought her playing hard to get in the bedroom was a total turn-on.

"It's the truth," she tosses back at me.

"The truth… the truth. Do you remember how I found out?" I ask, letting my words hang in the air, my temper flaring just a little.

I found out about her age because I wanted to surprise her for her birthday. However, I was the one who was truly surprised. As I sat outside of the high school I'd learned to be the one she attended—not the college campus I'd gone to earlier in the day before the truth made its way to me—I watched her be a teenager.

I felt like an idiot. It was so clear to see it. Watching her with her friends, I had no doubts everything I'd learned an hour before was true. My little Cee was turning eighteen, not twenty-two.

"I never meant for that to happen," she whispers after a few moments of silence.

But it had and I felt betrayed and lost. I was so angry with her and myself. More so myself, because even as I sat there and watched, I knew.

I knew she was the only one for me. She'd carved a spot in my heart and made herself a home. Still, I couldn't let it continue.

I had a career to think about. My initial worries and concerns about us as a couple were nothing compared to the truth that faced me. I broke things off right away.

Now here we are again. Chloe is a brilliant young woman at twenty-five. She has so much going for her future. I won't ask her to throw it all away and I've yet to tell my father that I don't want to follow the path he has placed before me.

Seeing Chloe is a problem for so many reasons. She's a distraction. There are things I must do, and I must do them now.

She's a distraction because I'm always so concerned about my father finding out about her. Now I know he knows. He'll ruin her life to keep her away from me.

I could never allow that to happen. Yet, I'm not in the position to prevent it and that just won't do. When I leave, I'm declaring

war. Since I now know I can't take her with me, I can't leave her
as a pawn.

"Baby," I try, but she turns her back on me. "I'm doing this
for your own good. Before was different—"

"Different how?" She turns back around and yells at me. "You
broke my heart then and you're doing it all over again."

"You lied to me," I bellow, letting my control slip.

I close my eyes as my jaw tics. I've been furious with her for
years. The last time wasn't on me. She was too young. There was
nothing I could do.

"I knew it, I knew when I walked into that restaurant I
should've run back out." She shakes her head. "You came for me,
Brodi. Why? Why come for me if you knew you couldn't stay?"

"I had only planned to talk to you. To see how your life was,"
I choke out.

"Yeah right, you found me, so you could fuck me. It was the
one thing you never got to do. You needed to settle the score,"
she hisses at me. "Hope it was worth it."

I close the small distance between us so fast she jumps back,
startled. I bend until we're nose to nose. My chest heaves with my
own anger.

"I've never fucked you," I retort, placing my hands on her slim
yet curvy hips. "Every time I touch you, I make love to you."

I place my forehead to hers, trying to calm myself. I lick my
lips, lifting my head once more. Her hazel eyes lock with mine
and I hate what I see there. I move my hands to cup her pretty
face, wanting nothing more than to get lost in kissing every single
one of her freckles.

They're so faint and uniquely hers. Like cinnamon dust was blown over her eyelids and just above her upper lip. I groan when my eyes fall to her full mouth.

I thought she was a knockout when I first met her at seventeen. Now, Chloe is drop-dead gorgeous. She commands a room when she enters.

"I promise, this time, I'll stay away." The words burn my tongue as they come out. "I leave the country tonight. I won't drag you into my mess. I could lose everything. I have nothing to offer you. My brothers and I, we're making a bold statement with our actions." I pause and sigh. "I can't protect you from my world like this."

I hear the pain in my voice. It's my job as her man to protect her. I can't do that if I take this course. I just don't know if I can guarantee it.

Chloe has done well for herself. The way her eyes light up when she talks about work, makes me so proud of her. I didn't see that until this week.

I'd brought her here so I could spend time with her. I had every intention of asking her to start over with me but... I can't.

Chloe has Ally to take care of. Her best friend Sidney means the world to her. She has a life outside of me. For once, I'm not being a selfish man. I've thought this through.

I don't want to give Chloe up, but I can't keep hurting her and she can't just drop her life for me. I have too many unknown variables in my life. At thirty-three, I'm starting over.

I thought Clayton to be crazy when he suggested defying my father on such a level. Yet, I know if anyone could pull this off it would be Clayton. My little brother is one determined little SOB. Neither of us wants to live under our father's thumb.

Cane, my youngest brother, is the good son. The one who listens and toes the line. Well, when it comes to what meets the eye.

Clayton and I know him better. We know the truth when it comes to Cane. He seeks the adrenaline rush that gives a sense of control. The Hennessey men are known for their control and their need for it.

It's why I have to do this. I have to let Chloe go. I want to plead with her not to give up on me, not to let me go. I want to promise I'll be back for her, but I don't know that I can make that promise.

My father could make our lives hell, prevent us from making a way for ourselves. It's the reason I choose to leave the country. Clayton will do what needs to be done here.

I'll build our fortune overseas. It's all a part of the plan. Chloe was never a part of the plan. I wasn't supposed to go after her. I was supposed to leave her be.

"I don't need protection from your world. I only need it from you," she whispers, pulling from my hold on her face.

I let my hands fall and watch helplessly as she grabs her bags. When the week started, I hadn't planned for her to leave with those bags without me. Had I made the choice to follow through with the plan, I had all intentions of boarding a plane with her by my side.

This is the right thing to do.

I keep telling myself that as the door slams shut behind her. I'm losing her again. I nearly fucked up my entire life the first time.

My father was furious with me. He couldn't understand what triggered the mess I had become. He sent me off to stay with my ornery uncle.

Uncle Devin grunted at me for weeks about getting my life in order. His wife, Raven, spent most of her time trying to pull me out of my funk. Then, one night he found me drowning in my own sorrows. I spilled my guts without thinking.

"She's the love of my life. How could she be so young?" I slurred.

"You do know your grandmother is ten years your grandfather's junior?" my uncle asked.

"Shit like that made sense back then. It will be just one more thing against us in my world," I grumbled.

"This pity party is beneath you. Suck it up, Bro-di," he drew out my nickname.

Clayton started calling me the name. For the life of me, I still don't know how he got Brodi from Gregor. Mom says it's because he was trying to say brother. The shit stuck and the entire family calls me Brodi. All except for my father.

"I didn't ask you to join," I said dryly.

"She's underage for now. You're a Hennessy, this will not stop you forever." Uncle Devin sighed.

"Her age is just one of our problems." I rubbed my forehead.

"Now you're making excuses. You sound like a pussy. Sink or swim, Gregor. Be your own man. One day you will learn, you have to be in control of your own destiny." He patted my shoulder.

I scoffed at his words. I've never controlled a thing about my life. I think that's what drew me to Chloe. She went with what I said, what I wanted. Had I known it was because of her age, I would have thought differently.

"I'm to be governor," I snorted. "My destiny is written."

"I don't believe that bullshit any more than you do, son. Your father has dreams, but someday you will find your own and pursue them. You will see." He nodded and left me to my thoughts.

His words stuck with me from that night. I'm letting Chloe go again because I need to pursue my own dreams. She has her own life to live and family that needs her.

"I'm so sorry, baby," I whisper to the air because the woman I love is long gone.

CHAPTER TWO

The Decision

Chloe

A month later...

I sit in my room, balled up on my bed. I feel so stupid. This is all my fault.

I was so happy to have the assistant of a private client contact me for a meeting. Sidney and I have been climbing the ladder in the financial district. My girl is doing her thing, but I'm hot on her heels.

A big client was just what I needed to get things going for me. I needed the chance to show what I can do. Taking a lunch wasn't unusual.

What should have tipped me off just a little was the fact it was my favorite restaurant, from when I dated *him*. Second, I should have noted the private room.

Brodi had spoiled me back then. I always felt bad for lying to him. I was just in such disbelief someone his age was interested in me.

Someone his age who looked so freaking gorgeous. With his strawberry-blond waves, gray eyes, those full lips, and his height, he was what dreams were made of. Brodi has always towered over me, even now, at five-eleven, he's half a foot taller than me.

Back then he made me feel like a god had fallen from the heavens and chosen me. I was so eager to please him and had told him I was twenty-one before I could stop myself. I never dreamed he'd believe me or that we would date for so long.

I knew back then Brodi was wealthy and out of my league. We met in a coffee shop of all places. I'd been on a coffee run for the managers at the summer internship I had landed. All junior year, Sidney and I had sold candy bars in the neighborhood to earn money to go to Century 21 for our summer internship attire.

We'd been proud of the looks we pulled together on a budget. Gaining Brodi's attention had only been the icing on the cake. I still own the red pumps, black slacks, and cream blouse I wore that day.

"You have a beautiful smile," he whispered in my ear as I looked down at a text Sidney sent me from the cheap phones we pooled together to get on a shared plan.

When I looked up, I felt my breath whoosh from my lungs. He was gorgeous. Something about those eyes. They were an arresting gray, sucking me right in.

"Thank you." I blushed and wanted to kick myself.

"I was just leaving." He held up his cup for me to see. "But I couldn't leave without knowing your name and asking for your number."

My heart hammered and my palms started to sweat. I wanted to squeal. My mind screamed for me to tell him I was in high school, but my heart told me to do whatever was necessary to hold his attention. He looked older, not in a time roughen way, but I knew he wasn't in high school.

"My name is Chloe and I'll take your number instead," I purred like I was all grown up.

When he gave me a crooked smile from those full lips, my knees threatened to give. He sauntered over to the counter, murmuring something to the pretty barista. She smiled back at him, handing over a pen. He retrieved a napkin, then jotted something down on it.

When he stood before me once more, his long fingers held the napkin out to me. "I'll be waiting for your call at eight." He winked. "Don't be late."

I called at eight on the dot. I couldn't believe the incredible conversations I'd been able to hold with him. I knew I fell in love with him. I was so in awe that he had fallen in love with me as well.

When he learned the truth, I could see the hurt and anger in his eyes. It tore right through me. My heart was broken when he said we could no longer be together.

I never thought I'd see him again. *Never.* When I walked into that private room—those gray eyes taking me in—my heart was torn from my chest all over again.

However, he had healed it. For another six months, I had Brodi in my life to heal that old pain. We fell right back into our relationship, like nothing ever happened.

Brodi wined and dined me. He showered me with expensive gifts, but what was most precious to me was his words of love. We never had an encounter without him telling me how much he loved me or how much he missed me during our time apart.

"I love you, Cee. You have no idea how much I love you," he'd *whisper.*

I, on the other hand, held back this time. So afraid to get hurt and lost in him. I wouldn't dare let myself open up. I dripped pieces of me into our relationship.

The more comfortable I became the more I gave. I've always known Brodi had his own secrets. He never talked about his life, despite asking me about mine.

No, that's a lie. Brodi shared about the pressure his dad placed on him. It seemed to be the one thing in his life that stressed him.

He had shared with me a time or two how the pressure made him feel. Then, there are the few times he's mentioned one of his brothers. Never by name and he always changed the subject when he caught himself.

Yup, Brodi has had as many secrets as I had. Yet, I decided to lay my bones bare on that trip. I gave him everything I am.

"After my mom passed, I had to do everything. It's been so rough taking care of Ally," I told him.

"I became a mother to Ally overnight. At least, that's how I feel now," I had said.

I shared with him about Sidney being my best friend. My best friend who helped me claw my way out of despair. Sidney helped me get a new apartment in a better neighborhood for Ally.

"I would've never been able to afford it if she hadn't moved in with us," I confided in him.

We worked together to keep my teenage sister in line as she moved through junior high into high school. We're still working together to keep her on track to graduate and get into the conservatory she's been dreaming about.

"I'm in awe of you. You've always been so mature for your age," Brodi said while looking into my eyes.

My heart swelled. I believed his words. For a week, I talked and talked, sharing my life with him. Never once did I think that at the end of the week, when it was time to go home, he would devastate my world all over again.

I've barely been holding my shit together in the last month since I walked out of that hotel suite. Now this.

I could never ask Sid to see me through this. I have Ally to worry about, I made a promise. My career is still so new. I'm so fucked, and I didn't know what else to do.

"I hate you, Brodi. You made me a killer," I sob as I wrap my middle with my arms and curl into a tighter ball. "I never want to see you again."

CHAPTER THREE

The Ultimatum

Gregor

Five and a half years later...

Steam is coming out of my ears as I ride up in the elevator of the penthouse building my brothers and I own. This was one of Cane's better ideas. A place where we could be close to one another and have each other's backs.

We've always been close because we grew up in the same bullshit environment. I'd do anything for my brothers. At thirty-eight, I'm the oldest. I have Clay by two years and Cane by ten, but you would think Clay was the oldest.

He took to the role of protector early in life. He hated when Dad would chastise me. As small as he was, he would talk back to Dad before he had any real words to speak.

Leave Brodi. Good boy.

The memory of Clay's defiant phase brings a smile to my lips for the first time in weeks. However, it's short lived as the elevator dings and the doors open. I step off and loosen my tie as I move forward.

It looks like we're heading into battle again with dear old Dad. The man doesn't know how to concede defeat. We earned the right to be the men we are. He's wrong for this.

"You want me to wait out here?" Ethan asks as we get to the front door of Clay's penthouse.

I nod at my head of security. "You can head down to your level. I don't think I'm heading out again tonight."

He pats me on my shoulder and returns the nod. I've known Ethan since junior high school. He's as close to me as one of my brothers. He knows all my secrets, even the ones I'm too embarrassed and ashamed to tell my family.

I pull the key card for my brother's place and open the door. When I step into Clay's living room, I find Cane standing in front of the fireplace with a scowl on his face. Clay is sprawled out on the couch with his head back. He runs a hand through his thick red locks before lifting his head and locking eyes with me.

I stare into gray eyes just like mine. The only real difference in looks between me and my brothers is our hair. I'm the only strawberry blond. Both Clay and Cane have dark-red hair. They both took after Dad.

Clay stands, blowing out a breath. "Let's head into my office. I have everything in there," he says and grabs his tumbler of brandy from the coffee table.

I grunt and start after him as Cane brings up the rear. He's surprisingly silent given the circumstances. At twenty-eight, I don't think he's any more ready to get married and run Dad's company than we are.

I work my jaw as I take a wide stance and stand in front of Clay's desk as he takes a seat behind it. He closes the file that's always on top of his desk. The one on Sidney James.

Moving it aside, he pushes forward what looks like the same docs that were delivered to me. I glare at the pages, picking them up. The terms are the same as the ones given to me.

This can't be happening. Clooney Hennessy is one relentless old bastard. We should have seen this coming.

"How the fuck did he pull this off?" I seethe as I look down at the copy of the papers my father's lawyers served me.

"He's best friends with the devil. Who the fuck knows?" Clay mutters. "I'm not folding to this. We worked too hard. I'll figure a way out."

I groan and close my eyes. Rage consumes me. I've sacrificed way too much for my father to pull this now.

His timing is totally fucked. I've already got so much going on. I need to find answers to my problem in Dubai. Everyone is out to control me in some way. I'm tired of this shit.

"Fuck, I don't need this right now. This is total bullshit."

Cane snorts as he leans against the bookshelves. I turn to glare at him. I spot right away something is different about him.

"Why are you so calm about this?"

"Because Dad seems to be giving him grace. Unlike you and me, he's been given an extra year and a half to meet the terms," Clay says bitterly.

"You'll have this figured out by then," Cane says. It's a statement, not a question.

"The old man started this, but I'll be the one to finish it," Clay seethes.

His anger fills the room, matching my own. It took me five and a half years to get where I am. Five and a half years to stand on my own two feet, without my father's help or his name.

When I left for Morocco, I left the Hennessy name behind, along with the childish Brodi I'd become. I couldn't bring myself to be called by the name my brother once used as an endearment. I was too embarrassed to hear the five letters my love once cried out in my ear.

I'm a different man from the one I left behind. The man I left behind has regrets, he failed to find solutions. He walked out on the woman he loved to rebuild his life. For five and a half years, I've tried to convince myself I did what was right.

"Clay, he doesn't get to win. Not like this. Not after what I've given up."

"He won't, but we might have to play his game. Luckily, Cane has time. That might work to our advantage. Only the two of us have to look like we're going through with this."

My heart pulses like an open wound. This is the last thing I need. I can't be forced into another thing in my life.

I won't survive it. I'm already shredded from the cages I've busted through. The vise grip I'm in is threatening to crush me as it is.

I tell myself over and over, I left because Chloe had a life of her own. She had responsibilities I couldn't drag her away from. Yet, for five and a half years I've had a hole in my chest. Now this.

"Play his game," I seethe. "Clay, the man is trying to force us into marriage. He wants to control our future. This isn't right.

This is our empire. We built every single thing we have. We've out-earned anything that has the Hennessy name on it."

"How dare he try this shit? I'm not marrying some woman of his choosing just to please him," I bellow.

"Then don't. It doesn't say we have to marry who he wants. Just that we have to marry and take over the family business. Once we're engaged, he'll back off. Then I can find us a way out of this."

I work my jaw as I think over his words. I'm thirty-eight and never married because there's only one woman for me. If I can't have Chloe, I'll die alone. I've tried to move on only to have it blow up in my face.

I know for a fact it's Chloe or nothing. I could have come for her sooner. I almost did, but I promised her that I'd never bother her again.

I tried. I tried to stay away. The woman is just my weakness. I stay away from New York as much as I can because her presence is too much of a temptation.

I'm proud of her. She hasn't reached the level she talked about, but I see she's worked her ass off. I know she'll do it in time.

I often wonder what happened to set her back. She was neck and neck with Sidney, but somehow, Sidney James became a star and Chloe has been coasting. She's hardworking, but still, something seems to be holding her back.

"Are you suggesting what I think you are?"

"Yes, I'm ready to go after Sidney. This is an open door. I need her and she could use me. May the chips fall where they may," he replies. "I think a million dollars will make this all the more appealing."

"What?" Cane chokes out. "You're not serious. Do you always offer so much?"

"Never, but Sidney is different. I'll do what's necessary."

"What do you know about her? About the people in her life? Clay, you have so much more at stake now."

My anger rises. Chloe is a part of Sidney's life. Cane knows nothing about her, but his comment still sets me off. Clay's decision will bring Chloe into my world one way or another.

"I've been studying Sidney and her life for almost a year and a half. I know all about her and the people in her life. You just focus on getting lost so Dad doesn't speed up your time line," Clayton replies. "Gregor, this is what we need to do."

I shake my head. This is all nuts. I have no right to do this, but now the idea is rooted in my brain. I release a breath.

"That's easy for you to say. My options aren't as promising. Honestly, you really think I should offer someone a million dollars to marry me?"

"Make it promising. What's a million to you? Make an offer. It's less than we stand to lose if we don't do something. For now, it's a proposal. I know you have someone in mind."

That I do. I've wondered not once if Chloe's lack of progress has anything to do with me, with us. I noticed the change when I left. Yes, I've kept an eye on her all these years. As soon as I was able to, I started to keep tabs on her.

I was frustrated those first few months, not knowing, not having the means to be sure she was okay. It was what I feared most, not being there for her if she needed me.

There had been a point where I didn't think my brothers and I would pull it off. Then Clayton closed a deal that yielded us millions. Things seemed to catch fire from there. I sealed the deals I was working on, and we were building our net worth hand over fist.

I wanted to run home and claim my woman, but I'd hurt her, and I couldn't bring myself to see that hurt again. So, I've suffered. I've held so much regret.

Not anymore. I'm getting older and I want more out of life. I'm no longer wet behind the ears, wishing I could be my own man. I've become my own man and I want the one woman who has always owned a part of my soul.

Do I think this is going to be easy? Fuck, no. Chloe has a temper, and she has a right to it when it comes to me. I also know I have the right touch to smooth the feathers I plan to ruffle.

"Okay." I nod toward the closed files on Clay's desk. "Her, it's her. Make the contract. I'm in."

Clayton smiles at me and I swear in this moment he looks just like our father. Anger rises inside me. I can't believe the old bastard is forcing our hands like this.

"I'll take care of everything. It's only an engagement. I'll make the agreement for six months. I should be able to figure things out before time is up," he says.

"I think we've both lost our minds." I pull a hand down my face.

"You damn sure have." Cane snorts and storms from the office.

Clay waves him off. This is typical Cane behavior. Clayton catches my gaze and holds it. My little brother sees too much sometimes. I shut down before he reaches for the secrets I'm not ready to share.

He opens the file with the information on Sidney and everyone close to her, including my Chloe. Picking up the photo of Chloe, he holds it up, facing me.

"I don't know your story with her, but I know this is the way to get what we want," he murmurs into his glass of brandy. He takes a sip. "At least this is how to get what I want."

He drops the photo and picks up the one of Sidney. I knew Clayton had plans to go after Sidney James. I also knew about the money he planned to offer.

At first it was half a million, not his usual quarter of a mill. A million is the most he's ever offered in one of his arrangements. Which tells me that my brother for once in his life, may not be thinking clearly.

"You really think tossing a million dollars at this woman is going to get you what you want?" I ask, nodding at the picture in his hand.

He drops the photo and leans back in his chair, eyeing me on the other side of his desk. I sit back in my own chair, pondering my little brother. His darker-red hair gives him more of a brooding look, but he's still as handsome as I am.

I honestly don't get why he's going this route. I tilt my head to the side and change my mind. I do know why he's choosing this course.

My brother is in love with the chase. The chase is what caused him to step out from under Dad. He worked hard to build something more than what Clooney Hennessy Sr. has.

Clayton was willing to chase down every lead, contact, connection, and resource he needed to complete his goal and he excelled at it. He lives for the chase. Being the middle child, Clayton has always sought to control his environment.

Then there's his secret. The one thing that almost destroyed his youth. It could have ruined his life. My brother has been cautious of the company he keeps since.

It totally makes sense. I haven't seen him date without a contract in place. Again, bringing me back to the fact that this happens to be the largest compensation I've ever seen him offer.

He doesn't intend to fail. Yes, I get him. This is about more than my father for him. He's just using his resources.

Clayton lifts a brow at me and shrugs. "I have my reasons, just as you have yours. It's not the money that will make this work, it's the circumstances. It will work."

"But why her? Why do you think it will work with her?" He nods at the folder on his desk.

I saw the curiosity in his eyes when he looked at Chloe's picture. I always date redheads, I have ever since the first time I lost Chloe. I've just never dated a Black redhead outside of her.

Chloe will forever be the goddess of my life. Staring at another who reflects her beauty and all the traits that draw me to her would cripple me.

I hadn't planned to go about things this way. It was my intention to leave her alone. However, if I'm going to be forced to marry. Chloe is the one. Deal or no deal, she's it.

A few months back when I saw Chloe in one of the images my brother had been staring at, I started to demand answers. I wasn't that surprised by what Clayton revealed. However, my interest was piqued by the mention of the love of my life's best friend being the source of his obsession.

"It won't, but I owe her so much. As you said, the circumstances will bring her to me. If you're right about Sidney's pending problem and your involvement, this will line things up.

"In addition, Dad has our backs against the wall in the midst of all of this, but I will have to put in a lot of work to get her to stay," I huff.

Clayton studies me. "Who is she to you?"

"We both know you already know the answer to that," I grumble underneath my breath.

When I don't respond further to appease his curiosity, Clayton releases a low whistle. His eyes light with recognition. "Are you sure you want to do this with her? Is this—"

"You know nothing about it, Clay. Just have the damn contract drawn. If we're going to beat the old man at his game, let's do that. My patience has run out. It's time. If we're going to do this, let's do it," I snap and stand to leave the room.

CHAPTER FOUR

The Envelope

Gregor

A year and six months later…

I wake to my phone ringing by my head. Placing a hand on my head, I groan. I didn't get any sleep last night.

For hours, I turned over what Clay and I plan to finally set in motion. After a year and a half, the time is right. Opportunity is in our favor.

I've had more than enough time to back out, but with each day that passes, I know I won't. Time is running out and I'm anxious to finally have Cee in my arms. Once those invitations go out today, there's no turning back.

However, it's been eighteen months since Dad started this shit and we still have no other solutions. It makes the most sense to do this Clay's way. Not to mention my life has gotten more complicated. I only want to deal with people I can trust.

"Hello," I breathe into the phone after a deep inhale.

"Good morning, sir. Have you checked your email this morning?"

"Good morning, Eric. No, I haven't," I say to my assistant.

"I think you might want to. I know you're in New York, but this is going to need your attention."

I sit up and place the phone on speaker as I go through my emails. I furrow my brows. Of all the times, this would happen now. I worked on this deal for months. All they had to do was sign the paperwork today.

"What the fuck is going on?"

"I don't know, sir, and they won't talk to anyone but you."

"Fuck, fine. I'll call and see what I can do."

I don't have time for this. I wasn't expecting Clay's call last night to tell me he was setting things in motion now, but he doesn't know about the shit I have going on. I'm supposed to be on my way to Dubai.

It was a trip I had planned to get some answers and to see to my responsibilities there. I don't plan to be gone long.

I wish I could disappear like Cane and act like this isn't happening. He has dodged this bullet and still has two years to get out of it. I can only imagine why that is. My little brother still has some growing up to do.

"Sir, I'm sorry. That's not going to do. They want to talk to you in person. They're insisting."

"Are you shitting me?" I seethe.

"I guess they feel they have all the bargaining chips here. They're making demands because they're threatening to pull out."

"I get that, Eric. Fuck. Listen, get the jet ready for me. I'm heading your way now."

"And Dubai?"

"You leave me to worry about that," I growl.

I hang up and start a text to Clay and David. I need to make this trip, but I don't want to change a thing with Chloe. If she finds out this is coming from me before she agrees to the contract, I'm fucked. I need Clay to come through for me.

Me: *Emergency in Georgia. Move forward as planned.*

I go to put my phone down, but it rings. Looking at the name on the screen, I groan. The dull headache in my head starts to throb.

I don't need this shit right now. I send the call to voice mail. I'll deal with that crap when I've had some coffee.

Chloe

"Hey, Jerry," I call to the doorman of my building as I walk through the door he's holding open for me.

I've come a long way from the projects in East New York. I think my mom would be so proud. I know she'd be proud of Sid. My girl is teflon strong.

It's been a long day. My girl, Sid, has been through hell and back in the last year and a half. I never thought this shit would end.

I've been by her side every step of the way. Those assholes at the firm really think I give a fuck who speaks to me and who doesn't. Sid is my family. She has been my ride or die since day one.

I wasn't going to turn my back on her. Even if it costs me my job. I have some money saved. Just barely, Ally's tuition has been kicking my ass, but I've made do. I would never tell Sidney that things are a little tighter since we decided to move into our own apartments.

I was the one to push the decision. I thought having her own place would cause her to start to date again. It hasn't, I can't say I blame her.

Sid has had some really shitty boyfriends in the past. I just wish she would try to date a little. Especially after all this bullshit.

She could really use a good release. I know I could. I frown at the thought.

It's been so long since I've had sex. I may talk shit to Sid, but my heart hasn't allowed me to move forward much. I honestly would love a good fuck.

I look into the mirror beside the elevator in my apartment building. I've still got it. Guys hit on me all the time.

I just haven't found one who makes me want to throw caution to the wind and lose control. That's what I need. I need someone to lose control with.

I can't remember the last time I got to be reckless. I've made my life about Ally after almost ruining everything for us. I don't have time to be a silly ho.

Maybe, just maybe, once Ally graduates college, I'll find me a dick to ride the fuck out of. I sigh at my thoughts, running a hand through my hair.

The girl at my salon does wonders. I can never get my unruly red hair this sleek and shiny. She earns her tip every time.

"Ms. Sinclair?" My name is called from behind me.

Looking into the mirror's reflection, I see a tall guy standing behind me. I turn, lifting a brow as I slowly roll my eyes over him. He's dressed in a sharp suit and his dark hair is neatly combed back away from his face. His brown eyes are boring, but he's handsome, nonetheless.

"Yes?" I reply expectantly.

"I'm the executive assistant of Clayton Hennessy. I was asked to deliver this package to you, personally. Inside you will find a letter for you and the other is for a Ms. James. There are also instructions inside." He holds out a large black envelope to me.

I wrinkle my brows. Clayton Hennessy is that deal, for real. He runs shit around the East and West Coast. His name is known throughout the financial district and business sec altogether. You want to have connections to just about anyone and anything, you make nice with Clayton Hennessy and the world is yours.

I lick my lips at the thought of the doors and opportunities, knowing someone like Clayton could offer. All this shit with Sidney was like watching a witch hunt. There may be a verdict on her case, but I don't trust what they'll try from here.

She says she's done with the district, but I know Sid. She loves the thrill. She'll find her way back one way or another.

Clayton has the kind of power to make sure she can. The Hennessy name rings all types of bells. He could help Sid. With that thought, I quickly take the envelope.

Hennessy is embossed on the outside of the large black stock envelope. I reach inside and pull out two black, smaller envelopes. Our names are embossed in the same fancy silver writing, on the outside of each thick black envelope. I open the one addressed to me. My heartbeat pounding.

I'm both excited and nervous at the same time. What if this is another attack on my best friend? I frown at that thought and start to read the letter.

Dear Chloe,

It has come to my attention that you and I both have a few topics of common interest. Sidney James being one of them. In light of her recent victory, I'd like to reach out to celebrate. As you know, my team had a hand in seeing to it things went Sidney's way. I have a proposal to offer you both.

I'm a man of resources and I'd like to use mine to help you both find a little enjoyment in your lives. I'm well aware that Ms. James may not be on board with this, but I was wondering if you would be so kind as to persuade her to join you for an evening at my club.

Please ensure she receives the letter I've sent. I insist the two of you join me. One does not work without the other. I will see you both, tomorrow evening at Club Dream. Rest assured; I will make it worth both of your time.

Sincerely,
Clayton Hennessey

I can't help the sly grin that takes over my face. Sid needs this, a night out to forget her troubles. Heck, from the rumors I've heard, Clayton is a fine-ass man. It may be more than worth our wild to show up to this invitation.

Clooney Hennessy is also a known figure in the business world. Although, his son tends to be more of a mystery. Clayton stays out of the limelight.

I once heard there are other sons, but they too remain hidden. If they, in fact, exist, the rumor mill never has complete facts. You have to take what you hear with a grain of salt. I've learned to check facts for myself in the financial circuit. People talk and they never get the story right.

I've heard talk of an older son who had a falling-out or something with the dad. I want to see this Clayton with my own eyes. Call me a myth buster, my interest is piqued.

"You can tell your boss we'll be there," I purr to the assistant still standing before me.

He nods. "Thank you. I'll be certain to do so," he says with a shy smile.

"Oh, yes, Sid, we're going to get you laid and paid. Hennessy has all the connections we need. Things are starting to look up," I say to myself as I get into the elevator.

CHAPTER FIVE

The Surprise

Chloe

As soon as I open my apartment door, the silence and loneliness sets in. I miss Ally and Sid. This place feels so empty without them. There's no music playing, no one dancing or laughing through the place.

"You need to get a life, Chlo," I murmur to myself.

I think about dating and wince. I'm not ready for that life. Yet, I don't know if I can do the casual sex thing. Yup, I'm all talk. I've only ever been with one guy.

Not that I haven't thought about changing that. I'm just not ready to sign up for that disappointment. My vagina deserves better.

I kick off my shoes and start to strip out of my clothes as I move through the quiet space. Once in my panties and bra, I flop down on my bed and stare up at the ceiling.

My thoughts turn to Sid. She dodged a huge bullet. I truly think this meeting with Clayton will be good for her. Sidney has sacrificed so much for me. I only want to see her happy.

She has such a kind heart. Yet it's guarded. She's been even more guarded since the indictment. I have to be cautious about how I sell tomorrow night to her.

I tap my lip in thought. I snap my fingers as I think of how to spring this on her. Jumping up from the bed, I go to grab the envelope from the table by the door, where I left it.

Envelope and phone in hand, I pad to the kitchen for a glass of wine and then head back into my room. I dial Sid as I sit on the bed and fold my legs in front of me. Sid picks up as I take a sip from my glass.

"Hey, Chloe, what's up?"

"Hey, girl. How are you holding up?"

"I'm fine. Thinking about going shopping tomorrow for some retail therapy."

I snort. Just like Sid, she's a shopaholic. I bet that's how she plans to celebrate her victory. Not on my watch.

"Well, I think we should celebrate. I'm taking you out tomorrow. No arguments allowed. You can buy something to wear when you go shopping."

I can almost see her rolling her eyes in my head. I bite my lip to keep in my excitement. I don't want to tip my hand too soon.

To be honest, I'm not even sure why I'm so excited. I don't know if it's for Sid or for me. Maybe it's time I explore dating.

This could be an opportunity for me to get out of this funk and move on with my life.

"Okay, fine. I'll let you take me out, but where are we going?"

"That, my dear, is a surprise. Just make sure you look sexy. I've got the rest."

"Chloe," she groans in warning.

"You'll thank me later."

"Will I really?"

"You make me sound like I'd sell my best friend to the highest bidder. I've got your back, hun."

"It's because you say things like that I worry."

"You love me. You know I've got you. I'm so excited. This is the first time you're going out in a year and a half. We're going to make it a night to remember."

"Okay, I'm in, but let me call you back. I'm trying to get this last blog post of the day up. Love you."

"Love you too, Sid. Later."

CHAPTER SIX

Shock

Chloe

I think I'm still in shock. I can't believe Brodi is pulling this shit. All I want is to go home and crawl in my bed and pull the covers over my head.

Instead, I'm still at this club. I look across the room at Sid as she stands next to Clayton. I would laugh if I weren't so pissed off. She looks totally bewildered. I've never seen her look so frazzled, not even during the trial.

Each time Clayton leans in to kiss her, it's like I'm witnessing more of her brain cells fry. I remember those days. It's a family trait, the ability to hypnotize with a single kiss. I used to have the same goofy lost look.

I take a deep breath and it feels like I've inhaled fire. Looking down, I allow the memories to come through to fuel the resolve I need to start building now, if I'm going to come face-to-face with that man.

Tears build, causing me to ball my fists. A waitress walks by with glasses of the free champagne that has been floating around. I grab two glasses and down one immediately.

"Hey, beautiful. I'd ask to buy you a drink, but they're free tonight." I turn to glare at the person speaking, only to find a handsome, tall guy is the owner of the voice.

I should take this guy to the nearest bathroom and fuck his brains out.

That would serve Brodi right. Even as I think the words, I know I won't. I'm not even sure why I thought I'd go through with that contract before I knew who it was attached to.

You thought you could move on.

I snort at my thoughts. Seven years and I haven't been able to move on. The thought alone burns my belly. Brodi is so wrong for this.

"How about a dance instead?" Handsome gives me a blinding smile that does nothing for me.

"Not this one, buddy. Keep moving." I turn to find Clayton's guard. I think he called him David.

His lips are pursed as he cuts a hand across his throat and shakes his head at the guy. Now this guy looks like he might be able to make me forget Brodi once and for all. However, that thought makes my stomach turn as well.

I down the second glass of champagne. "David, right?" I say as I look up into his eyes.

He looks back at me and nods. "I suggest you let your boss know, if we don't leave soon, I'm fucking the next guy who looks promising."

He lifts a surprised brow and gives me a crooked grin. "I was sent to collect you so we can all leave," he replies.

"Great," I bite out. "Take my ass home."

I push past him and start for the door Clayton and Sidney are walking through. Finally, I can put this night behind me.

CHAPTER SEVEN

Hurting

Chloe

I wish I never agreed to go to that damn club. I wish I never opened that invite to that place. My heart aches so bad, I can feel it in my bones. I was all for that contract a few hours ago, before Clayton said the name Brodi.

How can a single name turn my world upside down? I refuse to go down this road again. He promised he'd stay away. I want to sob in pain as I realize who Brodi truly is.

Gregor fucking Hennessy. The eldest son who I've heard whispers of. The one who had fallen out with his father. For the first time I've ever known, the district's gossip is wildly accurate. Looking at Clayton's gray eyes as he watches Sidney, I don't know how I missed this.

Clayton's hair may be much darker, but the face. He and his brother have so many similar features. The eyes, the nose, and that mouth. Those mouths are made for sin.

Over the years, I've tried to tell myself Brodi was just a dream, none of it ever happened. It's the only way I know how to breathe. I've wiped him from my thoughts and my memory. It's the only way I could stop the bleeding in my heart.

I resent him so much for this. For not staying buried under whichever rock he was under. I turn away from watching Clayton ogle my friend to look out the SUV's window.

I know that look, Sid doesn't stand a chance. If Clayton is anything like his brother, she might as well place her heart in his hands and walk away. It will be useless to her.

She will never own it again. I just hope Clayton takes better care of hers. It's too late for mine. I gave up wanting love or believing in it a long, long time ago.

The SUV stops, pulling me from my musing. I just want to go home and soak in a hot bath. Just the knowledge of Brodi making a reappearance in my life has every single muscle in my body tense. I close my eyes, reaching for my temples to try to release some of the pressure.

"This isn't my home. You told me you would be taking me home," Sid says in a tired voice. I can feel her exhaustion from the back seat where I'm sitting.

She sounds how I feel. My emotions are all over the place. First, the bullshit with Brodi—which I'm still wrapping my head around—then my accounts and Ally's tuition. Oh, let's not forget the warrant for my arrest.

In all honesty, I signed those papers because of Ally. If I didn't have my sister to worry about, Brodi or Gregor, whatever the fuck his name is could kiss my fucking ass.

I don't even know how all of this is supposed to help matters, but I trust Sid with everything I am. If she's willing to do this, then I trust her instincts. She has always had better instincts than I have. Although, when I open my eyes to see her glaring at Clayton, she looks as wary as I feel.

"Yes, I did, and I have. Our New York home," Clayton says.

"Wait, what?" Sid shakes her head slowly.

If I wasn't so pissed, I'd laugh. Clayton reaches to tip her chin up with his fingertips. I shudder in my seat. I've had that exact move done to me more times than I'd like to remember. It must run in the family too.

"I told you to read the contract, Sidney. If you would've read the contract, in its entirety, you would've read that you'll be living with me," he replies to her, placing a kiss on the tip of her nose.

"Excuse me?" Sidney breathes with knitted brows.

I feel for her. I've been there done that. Brodi had me trapped like a charmed rat just like Sid looks right now. Then it hits me. If I'm here and I signed that damn contract… *fuck.*

"Oh, this is priceless," I huff. "I'm guessing I signed up for the same crap."

Clayton has the nerve to chuckle as he moves out of the car. He doesn't answer me, which pisses me off more. I already know the answer, but I'm fuming just the same. Sid turns toward me, but I roll my eyes, turning away from her.

I don't want her to see what I'm barely hiding. I've been trying to hold it together all night. I thought we'd never leave the little engagement party Clayton orchestrated.

I start to climb from the SUV, needing fresh air like I need life. Clayton holds his hand out to help me. I take it and step down. Looking around, I note the opulence of the buildings surrounding us.

I keep my focus straight ahead as Sid takes her time getting out of the car. Wherever I'll be spending the night, I just want to get there and pass out. I can process this all better after I've had some sleep. In the morning, I need to call my sister and see how things are and what I need to do next.

All of our shoes echo across the sparkling floors as we move into the lobby. I've set a brisk pace, causing Clayton to hurry a dazed Sid along. I feel bad, but I need to be alone as soon as possible.

"Good evening, Mr. Hennessy," the doorman greets Clayton, offering me and Sid a big smile.

"George, this is my fiancée, Sidney, and this is my soon-to-be sister-in-law, Chloe," Clayton introduces us.

I whip my head back, Clayton's words slamming into me like a sledgehammer. I physically feel his words punch through my heart. I feel like I'm going to be sick.

I hardly hear the rest of the doorman's words. I only see his lips moving. Clayton replies to him, but I still can't hear anything as my mind rebels against me.

"If you need anything, I'm here most evenings. The other boys are just as helpful." My ears finally process the doorman's last words.

"Thank you," I say at the same time as Sid.

I follow as Clayton leads her to the elevator, climbing inside. I can't help glaring at Clayton. The frown on my face is evident even to me.

I want to throw something at him as he looks back at me with that amused smile on his face. It reminds me too much of his brother.

"You don't like the way I introduced you?" He tilts his head to the side as he looks at me.

"I don't know you, Clayton. So, I will save the words I have to say for your brother," I snap.

"Well, you will need this." He holds out a key card. "We live on the same floor. You can access all three levels from this elevator, but you will need that card. The main entrance is on the top floor. It's the one we prefer to use."

I pluck the card from his fingers, relieved to soon be alone with my feelings and thoughts. I can feel my anger rising. Feelings of hurt and abandonment push to the surface, threatening to choke me.

"I think you should call your brother and warn him to stay away from me," I hiss in warning.

Clayton tries to smother his smile as he nods. There's nothing funny about this. I turn my back to both him and Sid, feeling my anger push through. My shoulders sag as the elevator stops and the doors open.

I can be as angry as I want to be, but he's not here for me to say what I need to. Brodi is the one who I need to unleash all this anger on. I step off the elevator, grateful to soon be able to be alone. I'm ready to crumble.

Clayton murmurs something to Sid behind me. Then he moves to me, guiding me toward the left side of the hall. Again, I take notice of the beauty of this place. Even the front door is something to behold. Thick mahogany wood greets me as I slip the key card into the slot.

"I'll show you around quickly," Clayton says, reaching over my head to push the door open for me.

I drag my tired body through the entrance, only making it a few steps before I freeze. I feel him before I see him. It's the oddest thing.

I can feel his eyes on me. They sear me to my soul. A small whimper leaves my lips as my brain registers his presence.

All the anger I've held for the last seven years roars through me like a fire. It billows up in me like a thick cloud of smoke. I turn my head slightly and that's when I see him.

I lose my breath. He's older, the boyish look is gone from his face, but that hasn't taken away from him being sexy as fuck. His temples are now gray, blending in with his strawberry-blond locks. Instead of making him look old, it adds something regal and scorching to his short thick waves of hair and that chiseled handsome face of his.

His dress shirt hangs loose from his pants and the buttons are all open, leaving his tanned sculpted chest on display. His thick thighs sing of naughty things, within his gray slacks. His bare feet prove that everything about him screams sexy.

Yet, the fire of anger within doesn't blow back. It increases. I reach for the vase closest to me and hurl it at him with all my might, growling when it misses him.

He promised. He knows he's my weakness. I know that's why he made the promise in the first place. I ache so deeply.

"You motherfucker," I scream, tossing a glass bowl—the first thing I'm able to get my hands on. "How dare you?"

Brodi dodges the bowl with ease, holding up a hand in warning to Clayton. I don't even turn to see what Clayton is getting ready to do. My focus is on the man who crushed me seven years ago.

Frustration covers his face, along with a sexy five o'clock shadow. His gray eyes arrest me for the briefest moment. I snap out of it and reach for another expensive-looking vase.

"Stop throwing shit at me and then we can talk," he booms with that deep voice, freezing me yet again. I close my eyes as the sound washes over me.

It shouldn't comfort me. It shouldn't affect me at all, but it does. I hate my body for responding to him. I resent my heart for aching for him.

"Fuck you, Brodi, or Gregor, or whoever the fuck you are," I sob, no longer able to hold it in.

"Go, Clay, I've got it," he commands, not taking his eyes off me. He watches me like a small child he's trying to win favor with. My entire body trembles with my tears as it all comes rushing back to me. "Come here, baby. I know, I'm sorry."

Even as I shake my head, my body betrays me. My feet are carrying me to him before I can get a hold of myself. When his big arms wrap around me, I feel like I've finally come home.

"I hate you," I sob into his chest. I hate him, but I hate myself more.

"I know, but I'll die doing everything I can to fix that," he says into my hair. "I've never stopped loving you, my Chloe. Never."

Gregor

I'm not going to lie. Having Chloe in my arms feels just like coming home. I've waited for this day impatiently. It couldn't feel any better. Yet, her sobs are wrecking me.

Each deep cry from her tears a hole right through my chest. This is what I left behind. I knew it wouldn't be easy, but I didn't think it would be this gut wrenching.

Chloe is weeping like a woman who has lost so much. Indeed, I feel the same way about our love, but I feel her sorrow so deeply. It's in every hitched breath, in each tremble of her body, and the tight grasp she has on my shirt.

I vowed when I decided to come for her that I would fix it. Now, that oath is like the air I need to keep breathing. I couldn't hate myself more for doing this to her.

I don't believe I deserve this woman in my arms, but I need her. I can't see my life without her, not for another minute. It's the reason I cling to her, even as she tries to pull away from my embrace.

I tighten my arm around her waist and continue to rub soothing circles against her back. She drops her hand from her tight hold on me.

I know I'm losing her. I sigh heavily, bracing myself for the fight ahead of me, no matter how long it may be.

"You promised," she gasps out through a hitched sob.

"I know. It is and will always be the only time I ever lie to you," I reply.

"Bullshit," she snorts.

I look down at her, narrowing my eyes. Chloe tries to remain defiant, but it only lasts a few seconds, before she turns her eyes away from me, while she sucks her plump bottom lip into her mouth. I reach for her chin, lifting her face to me.

Her brows wrinkle, her lip releases from her mouth as it begins to tremble. She refuses to give me eye contact, so I wait. I've waited this long for her; I'll wait an eternity.

Her lips begin to move as she finally lifts her eyes and accepts my silent command. I want to know when I've ever lied to her. I've omitted details about my life, but I've never lied to her.

"I thought your name was Brodi," she scoffs. "I've always been a fool for you. The laughs you must have had at my expense."

"First, let me remind you of something. Watch your mouth, I'll allow your tone, because I know you're hurting," I reply tightly.

"Fuck you," she hisses. "You have to be kidding me. You walk out of my life for seven years and you expect... what? What do you expect? I'm not that same girl. What we had... it's gone."

"We will never be over," I bite out. "I made decisions that were best for us. I've never lied to you about anything, other than promising I would stay out of your life.

"I expect for you to be angry. I expect for you to need time, but I also expect to work for your heart again. I expect to do everything in my power to show you I'm the man you need."

"I don't need a man," she hisses at me.

I cup the back of her neck, drawing her to me as I bend to be within inches of her sweet lips. Her chest heaves, but she doesn't resist me. It's just the opposite. She melts into my hold.

I know it's against her will. I can see the frustration on her face. Her mind might want to rebel against me, but her body has a memory of its own. It knows me. I'd put money on it, her body craves mine as much as I crave hers.

"You're right, you don't need a man. You need me. The only man you will ever need. The only man you were ever meant to be with. Fight me all you want, Chloe. All the signs are there. You feel it. I can see you do," I breathe against her parted lips.

However, before I can take her soft mouth with mine, she rips away from my hold. I watch as she backs away, placing a gap between us. I mentally chide myself for pushing too hard, too soon. I can see the wariness in her eyes. I also see so much scorn.

"How can I need someone who I don't even know?" She shakes her head as if saying the words to herself.

"You know me better than anyone does. We know each other better than any two people can know each other. From the beginning, we've been able to finish each other's thoughts. None of that has changed just because of a little distance," I reply.

More tears stream down her cheeks as she laughs like a madwoman. The laugh comes from deep within. It's throaty and sexy, but I push that thought to the back of my mind.

To another, she would look on the verge of losing it, deranged even. To me, she looks gorgeous even in this moment. When her laughter dies down, she looks at me with so much loathing, I feel like I've been punched in the gut.

I feel like shit on the bottom of her shoe. I never thought I'd see those sweet eyes look at me in such a way. For the first time, I question if the love she once had for me is completely gone.

"You don't know me," she seethes with so much salt in her words. "You know nothing about me. How could you? You left me with the world on my shoulders and more hurt than any woman should have from the man of her dreams."

"Baby—" I start, only to have her lift her hand to halt me.

"Don't," she barks. "Show me the direction of the bedrooms. I need a hot bath and a bed. I'm here because of my sister. Whatever you thought this…"—she points between us—"would be, it will never be. I can never feel anything for you again. Don't ask me to. I'll do what the contract asks of me, but you better be able to fix Ally's enrollment and this bullshit with my finances.

"If it weren't for her, I'd say fuck it and test my luck with the shit coming for me. You got lucky, Brodi, but not that fucking lucky."

I hold my tongue from reprimanding her. Flexing my jaw and clenching my fists. I get the eeriest feeling that I'm missing something bigger here.

Her anger is so much greater than I expected. I can literally feel it coming off her. Yes, I knew she would be pissed at me. I even knew she'd give me that sass and fire, but there is something else, something I haven't put my finger on yet.

I rant and rage in my head about the brief time after I left that I have no details of. Chloe was so different from the woman I knew when I finally started to get reports on her. I tried to tell myself that there was something else going on.

I wanted to believe our breakup had nothing to do with how much she had changed. I feel like a coward now for ignoring what was right in front of me. Chloe was hurting more than I wanted to admit.

Now, here she stands, and it's evident that I hurt the woman I love more than I'll ever be able to stomach. I walked out on her. I still believe it was the right thing to do.

I couldn't ask her to leave her life behind, but I would never have become my own man had I remained here under my father's thumb. Our timing has just always been off.

Not this time, this time I'll make it all right for her. This time our hearts will have what they desire most. Which is why I nod my head toward the bedrooms, honoring her request.

"The master is at the end of the hall. Your things are in there," I say tightly.

"Stay away from me," she calls over her shoulder, as she starts for the bedroom.

I run a hand through my hair as I narrow my eyes on her back. For now, yes, I'll stay away. Only because I know if I don't, I'll go after what's mine. I know for a fact; Chloe won't be able to deny us for long. We're a force together.

I see the hurt in her eyes, but I also see the flame for us. It's still there, but I want more than her body. I've come for my woman, mind, body, and soul. I'll take the pieces, the ones I've broken into a million shards. I'll be the one to make them whole again.

"You're going to need a fucking miracle, Gregor," I mutter to myself as Chloe disappears from my sight.

CHAPTER EIGHT

Turmoil

Gregor

After cleaning up the mess from Chloe's outburst, I spent the night on the couch, but I didn't get any sleep. I could've slept in one of the guest rooms, but I didn't want to chance Chloe making a run for it. I know she signed the contract, but last night... it's haunting me.

I finished a bottle of Jack while analyzing every detail. I'm still analyzing her actions and words when my phone pulls me from my thoughts. I lift it from resting on my bare chest and groan.

I was already exhausted before coming home to Chloe last night. The shit I've been dealing with has me ready to tear my hair out. My father couldn't have picked a worst time for his bullshit.

Not only have deals been going awry with the business, but my personal life has been more complicated than I'd like. I made the mistake of letting a business relationship become personal. I just needed a release.

At the time, I had intended to keep my word and stay away from Chloe. Addison was my executive assistant. She had been with me for years.

I trusted that she understood the nature of our relationship. I thought I had made things clear to her. Somewhere along the way, she crossed the line. I watched her become possessive and attached.

Things turned very sour. I broke it off and sent Addison to the Dubai offices to work there. She was a great employee. I just never should have gone there.

The calls started a few months after she settled into her new assignment. First, it started with her begging me to come see her. Then her calls became more desperate. I never expected the bomb she dropped on me when she did get my attention.

I blow out a breath and answer the call. My head is pounding as I bring the phone to my ear. It will probably explode by the time I get off this call.

"Why aren't you here?" Addison starts the call without a greeting or waiting for me to offer one.

"I told you, I had things here that need my attention. I'll be on a plane shortly," I grumble into the line, pinching the bridge of my nose.

"You promised to be here, I—" she begins with her usual griping tone.

"And I will be," I cut her off. I'm not about to get into this. "I have things I need to get settled here."

"Sure, whatever's best for your companies," she huffs. "This isn't fair to—"

"Don't tell me what's fair." My anger starts to rise. "I'll be there soon, just as I said I would."

I hang up the phone, rubbing the tension from the back of my neck. I still can't believe my shit luck. All of this can complicate my plans.

My instincts have told me I need to proceed with caution from the beginning. I'm going to follow my gut. It's done me well over the last few years.

If I would have followed my instincts in the first place, I wouldn't be dealing with this shit. I do have pressing business. A few days ago, before Clayton informed me it was time, I'd planned to sort out the issues with a few new contracts, while on the plane to Dubai. Then I had to make the emergency trip to Georgia.

I made the trip yesterday and straightened things out there, but I just couldn't take off without seeing Chloe first. I felt like I was drowning. I haven't had this feeling in so long.

I needed to anchor myself in her. She has always been a place of calm for me. The thought of her calming presence has my feet moving toward the master bedroom before I can process the fact I'm moving that way.

I turn the knob and grin when I find it unlocked. I half expected her to lock it. Not that I don't have the key.

I push the door open, leaning on the doorjamb. I smile when I see her pink bonnet I had brought in for her resting on the pillow. It brings back so many memories.

"I can't believe I fucked us up," I mutter to myself and shake my head.

Seven years ago, once I found my way back into her life, we spent every moment together that we could. I hadn't liked when she would have to rush home away from me. I hadn't known about Ally at first.

Eventually, I was able to coax her into spending the night a few times a week. It was later when I found out Chloe was getting Sidney to watch her little sister so I could have those nights with her.

I frown at the thought. My behavior always seems so selfish when it comes to Chloe. My frown deepens as thoughts of Addison try to take over my mind.

Maybe it's time I admit to still being a selfish man. Yet I don't think anyone can blame me for my behavior now. Not toward Addison.

With her, it's a matter of control. I went from my father trying to control my life to having Addison dangling her control over me in my face. I rub at my chest, feeling like a bastard as the vision of green eyes fills my head.

I shake the image away. This is getting me nowhere. The tension in my body feels like it's going to shred me to pieces. I need the woman sleeping in my bed.

My grin returns as memories of my favorite way to wake her fills my thoughts. I know just how to make things up to Chloe. I move toward the bed without a second thought.

At the foot of the bed, I peel the covers back gently. A groan nearly rips from my lips as her long brown limbs come into view. I haven't seen such perfection in years. I can almost taste her on my tongue.

I lick my lips, reaching to squeeze my hard cock through my briefs. What I would give to spread her sexy legs and thrust inside of her. Memories of her giving herself to me for the first time surface.

I'm thrown back in time. I remember it like yesterday. The way she smelled, the sound of her voice, every moment that led up to her ultimate trust.

"Thanks, Brodi. That was delicious," she said as we washed the dishes together.

I looked over at her and smiled. She looked gorgeous. The simple black dress accented her toned body and killer curves. The red heels were my weakness. I'd been surprised I hadn't tried to make a move that night.

However, I promised myself I'd take my time with her. When I took Chloe for the first time, I wanted it to be special for her. She'd been so guarded, and I understood why.

"Should I put on some music?" I asked as I flicked my hands over the sink to dry the water off.

She gave me the most adorable smile. Our taste in music clashed sometimes, but when we got it right, we got it right.

"Sure, why not?"

I walked over to my records and smiled as I pulled out the Teddy Pendergrass greatest hits album. I placed the record on the record player and "You're My Latest, My Greatest Inspiration" began to play through the apartment.

I turned and met her back in the kitchen where she watched me with a smile on her face. Pulling her into my arms to dance with me, I looked into her eyes. Willing her to see how much I loved her.

She wrapped her arms around my neck, and I started to sway us in the kitchen. I dipped my head to peck her lips. What was meant to be a soft, tender kiss turned into a passionate kiss as I drank her in, and she lifted on her toes to get closer to me.

"Brodi," she said cautiously.

"Yeah, baby?"

"I... I love you."

I couldn't help the smile on my face. "I love you too, my Cee."

"Then make love to me. I'm ready."

I sucked in a sharp breath. The desire in her eyes punched through my chest. I eased my hands down to her shapely ass as I took her lips and kissed her breathless.

"Are you sure?" I asked, calling on my restraint.

"Yes, I'm ready for you to make me completely yours."

I lifted her in my arms and set her on the kitchen island. I kissed her again as I held on to her waist. She locked her fingers in my hair while tugging me closer. I reached for the zipper on the back of her dress and tugged it down.

When I got it free, I peeled the front of the dress down and drew back to take a look at her. Her smooth skin screamed for me to have a taste. Reaching for her bra straps, I pushed them from her shoulders, before reaching behind her to unclasp the fabric and remove it from her body.

"You're stunning," I murmured before I leaned in to lift one of her breasts into my mouth.

She threw her head back and cried out my name. I almost rushed to have more of her, but I wouldn't ruin this for either of us. I slowly pushed the hem of her dress up. She lifted her hips, allowing me to push the fabric up to her waist.

I ran my hands over her thighs, savoring the feel of her soft skin against my palms. Lowering before her, I tugged her forward to the edge and pulled her panties down her long legs. I looked into her eyes to ensure she was still with me.

She bit her lip and looked at me with pleading eyes. I dove in for my first taste of her pussy. A groan rumbled in my chest.

The gasp that left her lips caused me to look up to catch her eyes, but they were focused on the ceiling. Her lips were parted. It was such a gorgeous sight. Tilting her body back, I placed a hand on her stomach and devoured her pussy. Her first orgasm hit, and I started to finger her as I continued to eat her delicious honey.

"Oh, God, Brodi," she called out. "Baby, I need more."

I groaned as her juices filled my mouth. I knew what she was pleading for. The step that would bond us together for life.

I stood and wrapped my arms around her to carry her into my bedroom. "Love T.K.O." started to play as I placed her on my bed and stood back to strip from my clothes. She eyed me with so much desire in her eyes.

Once naked, I moved to peel her dress down her body. Tossing it over my shoulder, I climbed on the bed with her and scooped her legs over my forearms. My cock bumped up against her wet center as I took her lips for a deep kiss.

I only broke the kiss to look into her eyes. Slowly, I started to slide inside her. She threw her head back and gasped as I pushed all the way in. She was so slick from me eating her pussy and fingering her in the kitchen.

A whimper left her lips as I stilled to allow her to adjust to me. We'd talked about protection a few weeks before and decided not to use it. She was on the pill.

Her tight sex rippled around me. I had to grind my teeth for control. I dropped my forehead to hers, breathing her in.

"I love you so much," I breathed against her lips.

"Brodi, God, I love you too."

I started to pound into her and took things up to the next level of pleasure. I spent an hour diving for the part of me I knew I lost to her.

I come back to the present on a sharp inhale. I ate her innocence up that night. It was a gift I have cherished for all these years.

I climb up the bed, nestling my body between her legs, tugging them gently over my shoulders. I inhale her scent through the thin fabric of her panties. She smells better than I remember. Hooking my fingers into the fabric, I shift it aside and pause.

Visions of the hurt I saw in her eyes last night halts me in my movements. Again, I question if her love for me is still there. I consider the setback I could be throwing us into by doing this.

When Chloe sighs in her sleep, moans my name, and shifts her hips in my face, I forget my doubts. I know we need each other. All questions fade, I'm a man of action.

It's time I start to take more action in my life. Starting with claiming my woman here and now, then fixing the mess I've buried in Dubai.

Chloe

I've tossed and turned all night. I was sure I would cry myself to sleep, but as the tears ran out, my brain was still filled with thoughts of the man somewhere outside my bedroom door. I still can't believe it's him. He still smells the same, his large hands still heat my skin the way they always used to.

I wasn't sure if I wanted to melt into him or strangle him for all the hurt he had caused me. I thought I'd placed that bullshit in a tightly sealed bag. Yet just the sound of his voice plowed through me like a rolling storm, ready to wash away the past and water something that's too willing to bud and bloom.

I feared the threat of that budding feeling. I've never seen myself as a weak woman—I still don't, but when it comes to *him*—I wish I could ignore the pull he has on me. I wish I could blame it on lust.

If I could, then this would only be a matter of the flesh, not my wounded heart. I know I need to shut him out. If only shutting him out was so easy.

I thought of locking the door, but somehow, I convinced myself it wasn't the right thing to do. Then, I obsessed for hours over why I convinced myself it wasn't. Haven't I gotten over him?

Was leaving the door unlocked a sign that I'm willing to welcome him back into my life?

In the end, my exhausted brain reasoned that I'm in a strange place. Locking the door wouldn't be the smartest thing to do. I also went as far as rationalizing it all to, in fact, being blind lust, nothing more.

I guess that's why, when I finally did go to sleep, I've done nothing but dream of him. It started with promises, promises I need to hear.

"I'll never leave you again." His voice vibrates through me. Feeling so real and all-consuming.

I find myself clinging to his words. I need them more than life. Hearing them allows me to breathe through this dream, giving me safety, which I know isn't permitted in real life.

Although, believing his words morphs into me, allowing him to give me something I should never crave again. At least not from this man. Yet, even in my dreams I've made excuses for him.

How could I not, with dreams this strong—who has the strength to deny a man with this type of power? My body shakes and quakes with each stroke of his tongue. It's been so long since I've had sex. It's no wonder my dream is so vivid.

Well, that was my thought, until my fingers tangle in his hair and his deep groan fills my ears. It's too real, all of it. My butt crack is soaked, as are the sheets beneath me. My eyes flutter open.

The room is dark, just the slight light from the hallway filters in. I give my eyes a moment to adjust, while my core continues to pulse with pleasure, coiling with need and anticipation. I'm going to come again, soon, harder than the climax I already had in my so-called dream.

I look down and find a head full of strawberry-blond locks between my legs. A moan escapes my lips, causing his eyes to flicker up to lock on mine. My heart slams in my chest. I look away, not able to stand the words he's trying to say with just those gray orbs.

My hips start to move of their own accord as I plant my feet into the mattress. I don't miss the tight grip he has on my thighs. I've negated sanity.

Somewhere in the back of my brain, there's screaming for me to push the head between my legs away. Yet, the deprived part of my brain that hasn't had the touch of *this* man in years—she's yelling for me to shut the fuck up and ride his face like a cowgirl.

I listen to her and my body that's screaming to finish. I buck my hips up off the bed, rocking against his hungry mouth. He grasps my hips in his big hands, holding me to him as he devours me.

It's too much. I shouldn't have set the challenge, knowing he would accept and deliver. He always does.

I try to back away, but he chases me down until I have nowhere to run. My back is against the headboard, my legs are shaking as I try to wiggle free. He's not having it. In one swift motion, my legs are tossed back over his shoulders and his hands are guiding my core into his waiting face.

I cry out, feeling my soul as it tries to leave my body. This is why I've never tried to replace him. I've heard my friends at work talk of one-night stands that have gone completely wrong, or the guys who have talked shit about their dick game, only to disappoint.

I've never known that type of disappointment. Every touch I've ever received has been one of pure fire and unleashed sensuality that is unmatched. I know nirvana. It's the reason I wouldn't allow him to kiss me last night. One kiss and I would've been putty at his feet.

"Please," I sob out, feeling my peak rush me. "I need. Oh, please... I need."

I shouldn't be begging him for anything, but I never have a single rational thought when it comes to him. If only I could scratch this itch, then tell him to kiss my ass. Yup, that's what I need.

"*Mm*," he murmurs into my center, pushing in deeper with his tongue.

This man's mouth is a place of sin. My chest feels like it bursts open while he eats up every last drop, I gush all over his face and reach up behind me to cling to the headboard.

You would think he would back off once I begin to rain down on him. Nope. He growls into me, taking. I feel his thumbs at the base of my opening, prying me apart for his exploration.

I'm too wrung out to protest. I close my eyes and try to call on my strength to end this. A deep rumble grabs my attention and has my eyes opening once again.

I look down to see those gray eyes on me. This time they hold a fire in them that shows so much determination and frustration. I almost open my mouth to ask him what's wrong.

I halt my concern, chiding myself for it. My senses begin to come back to me. I can't believe I was on the verge of pouncing on him to ride that glorious prize of his. Heck, I was nearly begging for it moments ago.

I try to squeeze my thighs together. Narrowing my eyes as I try to push all the lust from them, but my face is quickly met with the pillow. I'm flipped onto my stomach so fast, the breath whooshes from my lungs.

My hips are in the air and my crack is met with his hard length throbbing against me through the fabric of his briefs.

"Don't," I grate out in warning.

"Never have I taken you without you being with me," he hisses in my ear.

I don't reply. I can't. I should push him away, but I don't.

I'm hit with a ton of emotions—surprisingly to me—the strongest one being my need for him. I hate it. I don't want to admit it, but it's there in the forefront, ripping me to pieces.

As if knowing just how much I need him and in which way, he wraps himself around me. One hand covers my right breast, the other clasping my throat. He doesn't squeeze.

Instead, his thumb caresses the soft flesh behind my ear. My spot. He remembers my triggers.

He hasn't moved to thrust inside me, but I can feel him pulsing against me, hot and heavy. I shiver, my sex squeezing with want for him. It's the soft trail of kisses against my shoulder that causes me to break.

"Please don't," I gasp.

"Shh," he coos. "I need you, but I won't take this any further. I can feel you're not ready."

"Then, get your hands off of me," I bite out, but it sounds feeble, even to my ears.

Instead of releasing me, he flicks my nipple with his thumb and my ear with his tongue. My chest starts to heave, my sex weeps in expectation, and my body trembles. I know the power behind this man's touch. He has yet to show me even an inch of what he's capable of.

"I'm sorry," he murmurs into my ear, placing his forehead against the back of my head.

Silence fills the room as I wait for him to release me. I don't want his apology, so I don't acknowledge it. I hold my tongue. I won't unleash my anger like this. I want to look him in his eyes when I place the final nail in the coffin.

Only, as he continues, I realize he's not apologizing for the past. I stiffen in his hold, holding my breath. His words are a wrecking ball to my resolve.

"I'll never be able to walk away from you. I'm alive when I'm with you. In the last seven years, very little has meant anything to me. I've fought with this for so long.

"You were my greatest sacrifice to build the life I've built for myself. In the end, I realized that none of it has meant a thing without you. Moments that should have been ours together have felt so hollow." He takes a pause, blowing out a breath that fans against my neck and warms my skin.

"I've never stopped loving you. From time to time, I'm going to forget that things aren't the same between us. My mind and heart have to learn the time has passed for when there wasn't a second thought of sliding between your legs and diving deep inside you.

"In my heart, you are forever mine. I apologize now for all the moments that I'll forget things are any different." With that, he tips my head back, covering my lips with a searing kiss.

I can taste myself all over his mouth and tongue. I whimper as he kisses me breathless. If I were a weaker woman, I would reach for his hard dick and guide it inside me, but I'm not.

He may not know or remember the hurt he has caused, but I remember enough for both of us. When he finally releases my lips, I push at his chest, wiggling my way free of his possessive hold. I'm strong enough, but I'm not fool enough to stand in the path of temptation.

I climb from the bed, feeling the shredded fabric of my panties hanging around my waist. I tug down the hem of the T-shirt I took from one of his drawers.

There's a closet filled with things for me, but I wandered into his closet and took this shirt after my bath last night. I hadn't consciously done it, only noticing what I'd done as I climbed into bed. Another thing I questioned myself about most of the night.

"My things still look good on you," he murmurs while giving me a heated stare.

I want to tear the shirt off and toss it at him. Instead, I turn and stomp my way into the bathroom. I need space.

I need space because if he were anyone else, I would've tried to beat the shit out of him for climbing into my bed without my consent and devouring my pussy the way he did.

You needed a release. He gave you one.

The words sound like total BS to my brain. I'm in trouble. I reach for my swollen lips and groan. Big trouble.

I've told myself a huge lie. I could totally lose my heart to him all over again.

Remember. If you let the memories surface this will be easy. You've made bigger sacrifices than he has.

I shake my head. I can't open that box. I can't allow myself to remember the past. It's too much and it will destroy me.

CHAPTER NINE

Regret

Gregor

I fall back onto my ass on the bed, running a hand through my hair. Chloe's body and eyes are saying one thing, but everything else about her screams caution. This is going to be harder than I convinced myself it would be.

Chloe doesn't even know she's a temptress. My greatest weakness. Just tasting her has made me more determined to right this.

This is not going to be easy at all. The timing is totally fucked.

I hear the reminders in my head, but if I think of timing, it will never be right. Chloe and I always have something stacked against us. This time, I'm not going to let anything get in the way of what I know is mine. I won't sacrifice us ever again.

Mind made up; I go out to one of the guest bathrooms to take a shower. I swirl my tongue in my mouth, savoring the lingering flavor of my woman. Memories of our past flood my brain.

I don't know how I've gone this long without her. I make quick work of my shower before I can get too lost in my thoughts. I truly do need to get to Dubai.

I have things to settle and even more to take care of. Things I've kept from everyone. My lips tighten as I think of dinner at my parents' house tonight.

Clay and I were going to introduce the girls to Mom and Dad. I don't think this is the right time for me to reveal my relationship. My father knows me too well.

The man is relentless when he wants to be, but my brothers and I haven't fallen far from the tree. I can't allow my father to get wind of any part of my situation. It would just be fuel for him and his plans, for him to work this all in his favor and against the things I want and need.

"I'm not marrying anyone but Chloe," I bite out as if my father is in the room. I release a heavy breath as I get dressed. My mind takes me all over the place.

My mother is often the silent type. She was devastated when my father refused to speak to me for almost three years. When she finally had enough, she put her foot down.

Mom was the force that drove Dad back into the lives of my brothers and me, which sent him right back to trying to run things his way.

I won't be forced into a life I don't want by anyone. Not my father, not Addison—no one and nothing. Which is why I won't be attending tonight's dinner.

My fiancée and I will be on a plane to Dubai. Things with Chloe are already fragile, but I want her at my side. We can deal with my parents another time.

I need my father to believe that I'm about to marry Chloe. If I take her there at this stage, it will all blow up in my face. I'm going about this the best way. I nod at my thoughts as I pack a suitcase for Chloe.

"What are you doing?" Her voice punches through my thoughts.

I look up to find her watching me cautiously. Her hands on her hips, my bathrobe tucked around her curvy, slender body. Her hair is combed neatly around her shoulders, reminding me of the bonnet she wore in her sleep.

"We'll be leaving after I feed you breakfast," I inform her, returning to my task.

"To go where?"

"Dubai, I have some things I need to attend to there. We also need some time to talk and work things out, so you'll be coming with me," I reply.

"Hold on," she huffs, causing me to look up at her once again. "My life is falling to shit. My sister is being thrown out of school and you want me to just fly away with you?"

"You will have access to my accounts, and I've already placed my black card in your wallet." I fold my arms across my chest as I watch her. "Clay has your sister's situation under control. I texted with him this morning for an update. Things should be resolved by the time we return."

It's just a little bend of the truth. Clayton is handling Ally's situation, just not in the way I know will give Chloe peace of mind. However, I won't give her any of that information.

I need Chloe with me, which means I need her confidence in the way things are being handled concerning her and her sister.

She side-glances me. "By the time we return. When will that be?" she asks cautiously.

"We'll be back in time for our engagement party and the weddings," I say, groaning internally as soon as the words slip free.

I need to pull my shit together. I have too much on my mind. I didn't mean to allow that last part to slide.

Clay had a good point. We need to plan the weddings to keep our father thinking we're going along with his demands. So we've both set dates for when those weddings should take place.

My words don't float over Chloe's head. Her eyes narrow and she mirrors my stance, folding her arms across her ample breasts.

"Weddings?"

I wave her off. "Come, see if there's anything else you would like packed. I need to make a few calls. Breakfast will be waiting when you're ready."

I move from the room before she can quiz me any further. I can feel her anger hurled my way without having to look at her. I'll give her time.

"Well, ain't that a bitch," she huffs at my back.

I want to chuckle, but I don't. The contract was the beginning for me. I have bigger plans.

Chloe doesn't need to know that right now. It will all become clear in time. For now, I need to put distance between us and New York.

If I can change our environment, I can change everything else. I will not fail. Not this time, the stakes are too great.

I will have my woman once and for all.

CHAPTER TEN

Give Me Strength

Chloe

My mind is spinning with so many thoughts. I shouldn't be on this plane. I'm not sure what's going on with my sister and I haven't talked to Sid.

Anything could be going on back home. I tried to call Ally, but her phone went to voice mail, and she hasn't responded to my texts. My little sister is an amazing flutist.

She earned a seat in the summer conservatory program in Europe. She should be enjoying herself and playing her flute, while exploring the Italian and French culture. Sid was so proud of her, she paid for Ally's travel expenses, while I covered the rest.

Never once have I ever worried about paying for Ally's dreams. I've worked my ass off to make sure I never had to. Yes, things have been tight, but I've sacrificed to ensure she has it all.

Now, all of that's just up in the air. If they kick her out of school, she'll have to come home from Europe as well. That alone should've kept my ass from getting on this plane.

However, the man sitting across the aisle from me, reassured me everything was under control, and we needed to go. I put up a fight right until the very end, when he tossed me over his shoulder and carried my ass out of the front door. I'm still pissed and not talking to him.

I can feel his eyes on me, but I refuse to look at him. These clouds have been very entertaining thus far. If I could calm the hell down, I could fall asleep at least.

"You can't spend an entire fourteen-hour flight ignoring me." His voice fills the cabin of the plane.

I still don't turn to face him as the sound of his voice makes my heart squeeze. I purse my lips, narrowing my eyes on the sky outside the window. I harden my resolve. I will not make this... whatever he thinks this will be—easy for him.

"Do you remember our first date?" He chuckles.

I don't respond. I remember it all right. I was so nervous and sure he would figure me out. I didn't think I was mature enough to pull it off but being with him was so easy. It's always been so easy between us when it's not hurting like hell.

"You were the most beautiful woman I'd ever seen," he snorts. "Or at least, I thought you were. Sometimes, I still can't believe I didn't see how young you were."

I shift in my seat, hating the fact that his voice comforts me. It's like a lullaby. I want to hear it over and over, just to soothe the ache away.

My mind travels to the way I woke this morning. I squeeze my thighs together, still feeling the weight of his palms on them. I can feel the heated trail his kisses left across my skin.

"It was always in the way you looked at me." His words bring me back to the present, causing me to focus on his one-sided conversation I refuse to be a part of. "I felt like you understood me in a way no one else ever has. Your eyes looked into my soul."

I scoff, hurting from the truth of his words. I used to think I knew him so well. There was a time when I knew what he wanted before he did before he could say a word to ask for it.

I would finish his thoughts, answer his unspoken questions. I knew when he was stressed most and how to get him to relax. Our relationship seems like it was so long—continuing for years—not six months here and another there.

My heart has always felt like it has known him for an eternity. Even now, it beats to a rhythm meant for him. Though, I'd never let him know that.

"I remember the first time we made love. There I was, a thirty-three-year-old man and yet, I felt like an adolescent boy. I wanted to make it special for you, but you made it amazing for me. Never had I ever had a woman so responsive to me. You... you came alive and brought me to life with you." He sighs heavily.

I'm tempted to turn to look at him. His words tug on a memory I tell myself I would rather have forgotten. I was already under his spell before he ever pushed his way inside of me. After I gave myself to him that first time, I'd as good as signed my soul away.

He gets up to move across the plane to sit beside me. My chest heaves once before I get it under control. His presence takes over as he sits next to me.

His strength and determination seep into my skin, ignoring the invisible barrier I try to place between us. The sound of him placing something on the table before me, causes me to turn my head. A small box now rests on the tabletop.

I look at it for a long moment, gritting my teeth, still refusing to speak. When I say nothing, nor move to reach for the box, he nudges it in my direction.

"What is this?" I say sharply.

"This is your engagement ring. I need you to put it on before we reach our destination," he replies.

I jerk my head to look at him. My jaw is so tight, I think my teeth are going to break. I'm instantly hit with the full force of his eyes. I want to look away, but I'm captured in his gaze.

"I'm not wearing that," I grunt.

He sighs in frustration. I turn back for the window, needing a release from his stare. My reprieve is short lived. He slips his fingers under my chin, turning my face back to his. I avoid his eyes to keep the steam going inside me.

"Don't… come on, look at me, baby," he coaxes me like a snake charmer.

I lift my eyes to his. He searches my face without a word for several moments. I feel like he's looking into the core of who I am, seeing my past.

Fear creeps in as I think of things he can find there. Not fear of his discovery, but fear of having to deal with what's lurking there.

"Unfortunately for you, you signed an agreement to be my fiancée and that includes wearing that ring," he finally murmurs. "You don't owe me anything, but I need you to see this through with me. For reasons I'll explain at another time, I'm asking you to do this."

"Why not explain them now? As a matter of fact, why not explain why me? Why am I here?" I bite out.

"Because I'm still in love with you," he says without taking even a moment to think.

Pulling my face from his hold, I frown, as if tasting something sour. My skin still scorches even after the contact is broken. His eyes remain on me, but he reaches his hand out for the box on the table.

"Why now?" I say just above a whisper.

He shakes his head, this time his eyes drop to the box in his hand. I watch as a wide range of emotions run over his face, faster than I can read them. When his eyes lift to mine again, I see nothing but pain.

"I thought of coming back to you every single day for seven years. At first, I knew I couldn't. For all the reasons I let you go to begin with. I couldn't. Then, I convinced myself to keep a promise I could never keep in the end," he says.

"But you made it," I say louder than I mean to. "They were your words."

"And I knew it to be a lie from the time they left my mouth. Chloe, that's our past. I want to make this right for our future," he says, almost pleading.

I shake my head, turning from him. "I don't think that's possible," I mutter.

He shifts in the seat next to me, leaning in closer. He pauses for a moment before placing his forehead against the side of mine. I close my eyes as I soak in the feel of him.

"I used to think many things were impossible. These last seven years have been one of the worse parts of my life. Yet, I pushed through, secretly hoping that somehow life would bring you back to me. It has and I'm not letting go this time. So, it's possible.

"Just breathe, baby. Let me in enough to show you. Take all the time you need, if that's what you want, but open the door. Let me in. I'll work with that," he whispers against my temple.

Tears soak my lashes. I almost open my mouth to tell him why I can't, but the moment his arms wrap around me—pulling me into his embrace—all I can do is nod. A war rages within me. One I'm not sure I'll survive.

I've needed this hug for so long.

The words whisper in my head, but my heart doesn't want to receive them. Hurt, angry, bitter, all of those describe the woman I've become, but I'm also the woman who has longed for his comfort so desperately—before I became all those things. I know he can't fix it. Yet, I open the door just a crack in hopes that he knows how to stop this pain.

Tell him. Tell him now.

I ignore the voice within because I don't know how or where to begin. For now, I just allow him to hold me. I take the strength he's offering me. I need it more than he will ever know.

"One day at a time," he says gently. "We'll take it one day at a time."

CHAPTER ELEVEN

Hidden Secrets

Addison

I sigh when Gregor's phone goes to voice mail again. If he boarded the plane when I texted him last, he should be here by now. I don't think he understands I need him here.

Gregor thinks I want to control him. At first, I thought that was what I wanted too. I had all the cards and intended to play them. I had every intention of revealing my hand to all the right players.

I did my research. I know everything there is to know about Gregor, even many of the things he believes he hides well. I know his weaknesses.

I know what challenges him. I knew just how I planned to manipulate him, but that time has passed.

I had to give up the grand plan I had. I blame it on karma. She served me a dish and flavored it in shit. I've done many things I can't say I'm proud of, but I never thought I deserved this.

A judgment that has rung so loud it will ripple through the earth long after I'm gone. Two months ago, the final blow was dealt. My hopes and dreams of a turnaround have laughed and abandoned me.

I don't have the energy to be a woman scorned or a vindictive bitch, nor do I have the time. I have to concede to my loss. There was a time when I wanted nothing more than to be Mrs. Clooney Gregor Hennessy Jr.

I thought I was on my way to that prize once. Gregor and I worked side by side for months, years. I was there whenever he needed. I was whatever he needed.

One night, after a gala, I could see he needed to scratch an itch and I was there for it. Gregor had been in one of his moods and we'd both had a lot to drink. I thought I could help him with his brooding disposition.

One thing led to another, and I'd gotten comfortable in his bed. Gregor warned me that he wasn't looking for more. As time went on, it was I who had ignored his warnings. I'd been sure I could get him to want more, but it took too long for me to see he would never want anything more than a warm bed.

When I'd made a play to establish our relationship in public, he was furious and made that fact known. I'd been embarrassed and felt so stupid when he sent me off to Dubai not too long after. It was as clear a blow off as any.

I'd resolve myself to lick my wounds in silence, which I would have. After all, I didn't have much of a choice. I still had my job and benefits when he had every right to throw me out on my ass.

Unfortunately, I had already made my final move with very poor timing—not knowing all the things that were stacked against me. I didn't understand I would tip my hand in the wrong direction so badly.

There was no way I could just fade into the background. Fate had a cruel joke she wanted to play on me. There would be no sulking and moving on.

The Universe had other plans for me. While I was plotting against Gregor, the stars snickered as they plotted against me. Somewhere along the line, I'd lost Gregor's trust, just as I should have.

I played the game poorly and continued to do so. I've kept things from him that he should've known. Now, it's all coming back for me. I've run out of time.

I can hear in his voice his patience is running thin with me. He believes I want to trap him here. That ship has sailed.

I need him. This isn't about wanting the perfect husband and a lavish life. I need Gregor here in Dubai.

Once, I thought it best to try to get him to at least agree to transfer me to the States. Now, that's not even an option. This has nothing to do with me.

Life is so precious. We all make mistakes, but we should never take life for granted. I did once.

I felt entitled to so much. I thought I could take what I wanted because of my beauty and the circles I fought, schemed, and climbed to run in.

Heck, I continued to think I was owed the world, even after I received the bittersweet pill of reality. When faced with the decision to choose what was more important to me, I made the choice that has led me here.

I often question that choice. I don't know if I made the right one, but I can't say that I regret it. My mistake was thinking that I was invincible.

I thought I could wield my feminine power for everything I needed in this life, but life has given me a big slap on the hand. I can't shake my tits and make this one go away. I'll have to pay my penance.

I think back to when I first set my sights on Gregor. He's one of the good ones. I wanted him to fall for me.

I wanted the love I saw in his eyes when he looked at that picture in his desk. The Black girl with the wild red hair and the sparkling eyes. The one in the picture Gregor takes out to stare at when he thinks no one is around to pay attention.

She's a gorgeous woman. The only thing she and I have in common is the color of our red hair. I don't know why I thought that was enough for me to replace her.

"Addison." I turn my sad eyes toward my childhood best friend as she whispers my name.

She's been here in Dubai for the last few months. When I needed someone, she was the one person I knew would drop everything to help me. She was here two days after I called her.

Now, I look into her eyes and see the concern. I turn away, not wanting to see the reflection of truth in her gaze. There's no hiding from the facts any longer.

"He'll be here," I say.

"Yes, but you should be resting," Emma says softly.

A tear rolls down my cheek. I don't want to rest. I need to get my affairs in order. I have to tell the truth, all of the truth. Not that he won't be able to see it on his own.

"Rest will come soon enough," I say tiredly. "Where's Chloe?"

"Resting, like her mother should be," Emma sighs.

I nod my head, looking down at the locket clutched in my fingertips. I flip it open, running my finger over the tiny picture. Her green eyes stare back at me.

"I'm so sorry," I whisper to the picture. "I was so selfish."

CHAPTER TWELVE

Truth Be Told

Gregor

As tension tries to coil within me, Chloe's presence tamps it back down. Just having her in my arms makes all the difference. I haven't released her since she allowed me to pull her into me.

I held her while she slept on the plane. I've had her in my embrace the entire ride to the hotel. Now, my back aches and my arm has gone stiff, but I wouldn't move for anything.

Chloe is exhausted. She's been knocked out for hours. Only murmuring for me to put her down when I lifted her from the car to carry her into the hotel.

Guilt burns my chest. I couldn't just walk into my home, here in Dubai, with Chloe on my arm. We still have much to discuss, but first, I need her to place this ring on her finger. It will be best if I establish who Chloe is in this situation.

I will not hide anything from her. There's just been too much tension for me to broach the subject. Chloe will be the first in my family to know the secrets I've stashed away here in Dubai.

Family.

Yes, I already consider her my family. Chloe is in the core of me. She has influenced so much in my life. Even that which I now hold dear, the reason for all my trips here.

It's been frustrating not being able to be here for months. I've been tied up in deals and acquisitions in the States. Clayton has needed a hand with the growth of our companies in the US.

My overseas team is a well-oiled machine. I've been able to let them run things while I handle business back home.

These last three months have been the longest without me making a trip to Dubai. I thought about bringing my worlds together, but that feeling of something being hidden from me has kept me from making that happen. I need the people around me to be people I can trust for many reasons.

I groan as my phone rings on the nightstand. I should have known Addison wouldn't allow me to rest for long. I can't for the life of me figure out why she's been so impatient. Yes, this has been the longest I've been away, but she's never been this needy and demanding.

I get the feeling she's ready to play that hand she's been holding. It's as if she knows I'm getting ready to make a major change in my life. I have wondered repeatedly if this sudden change is a coincidence or if she has plotted for such a time as this. I shake that thought off.

I've kept Chloe's existence to myself. I never have pillow talk of the woman I love with my lovers—not that there were many. I haven't even shared with my brothers what this woman at my side means to me. I doubt—even as resourceful as Addison is—that she has figured anything out about Chloe.

"Hello." I sigh tiredly into the phone.

"Excuse me, is this Mr. Hennessy?" A woman with a shaky voice sniffles over the line.

It's not Addison's voice, but the caller ID says it's her number. I knit my brows, feeling them pinch in the middle of my forehead. Sitting up, I slip my arm from beneath Chloe and swing my legs over the side of the bed.

"Yes, this is he," I reply cautiously.

"You don't know me. I'm a friend of Addison's, Em… Emma. I found her… I need you to come to the hospital. I can't make any decisions on her behalf, and I don't know what to do… I… I have Chloe," she rambles shakily.

"I'm on my way," I reply, needing to hear nothing further.

The bed shifts behind me and I turn to find hazel eyes watching me with concern. I reach for her hand, squeezing it. It's a gesture more for me than it is for her.

"I'll text the information," Emma whispers.

"Is my daughter okay?" I ask, needing the reassurance before I hang up the line.

There's a gasp the moment the words are out of my mouth. I watch as all the blood drains from Chloe's face. Tears spill over like a dam has broken. I reach to pull her to me, but she backs away as if I'm a flame moving to burn her.

"She's fine, but you need to get here," Emma replies.

"I'll be there," I say and hang up.

"Cee, I will explain everything. I need to get to the hospital," I rush out as I put my shoes back on.

"Is… is your daughter, okay?" Chloe chokes out.

The sound of her words is like a knife being twisted in my chest. It's closer to a sob than actual words. I close my eyes and nod. I didn't want her to find out like this.

"It's her mother. She's in the hospital. I need to get there," I reply when I open my eyes.

"They're here?" she asks with a scowl on her face.

"Yes." I nod.

"Wait, you brought me here, to another country, where you have a family? Have you lost your fu—"

"Don't," I say firmly. "It's not like that and I don't have time to explain right now. My little girl is in a foreign country with a woman I don't know, and her mother was found ill or injured. I don't have details and I'm not about to stand here and fight with you when I need to find out what's going on."

Chloe whips her head back and I feel like shit for talking to her so harshly, but I'm about to lose my mind. So many things could have happened. I need to get to my little girl.

I close my eyes again, my jaw working under my skin. I pinch the bridge of my nose, reining in my control. This is all going to hell in a handbasket.

"Come with me. I'll explain as much as I can on the ride there." I open my eyes and see a broken woman standing before me.

She has her arms wrapped around her waist, hugging herself tightly. Her head is bent as she sways from side to side. I open my mouth to soothe this situation as much as I can, but her next words take my knees out from under me.

"Our child would have been six by now… this year. I often wonder if we would've had a boy or a girl. You left and I did what I thought was best. I couldn't force Sid to help me with a baby and Ally was just a freshman in high school. I was already struggling to care for her.

"There isn't a day I don't ache for my child. You go take care of *your* daughter. When you have your situation straight, I'm going to need you to arrange for me to return home. I'll take my chances with what's coming for me back there," she says in the most detached voice I've ever heard.

I'm literally on my knees as a roar rips from my chest. "*Oh, God.* I didn't know." I sob like a broken man. I tear at my hair as the weight of her words slams into me. "I never knew. I wouldn't have left if I knew."

Now I understand. The time that I had no contact and no way to know what was going on with her. That brief moment when something changed that I didn't have an eye on.

Now, I can see the reason behind the hatred that has flashed in her eyes. I left when she needed me most. When our child needed me to be there.

How the fuck can I ever fix this?

CHAPTER THIRTEEN

Numb

Chloe

Before that call, I may have found it in me to feel sorry for the man who fell to his knees before me. After that call... I'm just numb. I have no feelings, no thoughts, nothing.

I just want to leave. Gregor sat sobbing on the floor for... I don't know how long. I've never seen a grown man cry so hard. I sat on the plush carpet staring at him, unfeeling. I could only watch.

At some point, he stood, turned his back, doing what he does best. He walked out. I'm not hurt. I'm not angry.

I'm just aware of the fact that some time ago he left and hasn't been back since. I've been sitting here on the floor in the same spot. I haven't moved once. I don't know how much time has passed. I don't know when he will return to send me home.

I'm numb.

Tears won't come. I can't move. I'm just waiting to go home.

Gregor

It killed me to have to get up and walk out of that room. I was torn between knowing where I needed to be and knowing where I was expected to be. In the end, I went with expectations.

Staying where I needed to be would get me nowhere. Chloe and I are walking a burning bridge. I loathe myself for what I've done.

I can't number or name the number of times I've watched my daughter playing while envisioning Chloe as her mother. It has always been a subtle burn that my daughter is named after the woman I love. Although, I once thought my little girl would be the only ray of sunlight I would ever have again.

I've warred with myself for two years about having a child that doesn't belong to the woman I belong to. What guts me is the fact that I don't remember the night my daughter was conceived.

I had put distance between myself and Addison. It was time to. I saw the signs.

It was coming. Her public display at my company party was just the final straw. Which is how I missed this.

I didn't see that the mother of my child was sick. I had no clue. When I come to Dubai, it's to see my daughter, not her mother.

In my fury, I asked Addison to give me space when I came for visits. Yes, Addison lives in my home here in Dubai. She takes care of my daughter. As long as my little girl is involved, I make sure that both she and Addison have the best.

However, when I'm here, Addison stays on her side of the house, and I stay on mine. Missing the fact that Addison has been dying hasn't been hard to do at all.

I walk into her hospital room, still reeling from what the doctors have told me. They were waiting for me to fill me in on it all. Her cancer has been in stage four for a year now. She was sick during the pregnancy. It's only been progressing.

"You're here." Her voice comes out so weak, I barely make it out.

"Why did you keep this from me?"

I have a hard time keeping the bitterness out of my voice. I'm so angry, I can't see straight. She's been battling cancer all this time and never said a word. I will never understand her.

She licks her dry lips. "I thought I could beat it," she says hoarsely. "For her, I thought I could."

"They said you should never have gone through with the pregnancy... that you denied treatment to have her," I say tightly.

"She was my hope. I wasn't going to let her go," she replies.

"Hope for what? For us? Please tell me you didn't do this because of me," I say.

"I knew you would be angry." She smiles but starts to cough. I reach for the water on the tray and hold the straw up to her lips. She takes a small sip and continues.

"At first, yes, I had hope for us. I never wanted to admit the hold someone else had on you. I thought... with time you would see... but I was wrong.

"After I saw how much finding out I was pregnant pushed you away, she became my hope." She starts to cough again.

I lift the straw for her to take another sip. I'm filled with so much rage. I still question how this happened. I've never gone without protection with any woman other than Chloe. For the life of me, I still can't remember that night.

I can drink with the best of them. It takes a lot for me to get wasted. I've never gotten so trashed I lose chunks of time and memory. I don't do heavy drugs so that's not a thought in the equation.

Yet, I can't remember that night. I've tried. Once the blood tests came back and confirmed Chloe was mine, I tried to remember when this happened. Addison was the one to fill in the gaps.

It was the last trip she accompanied me on as my assistant. I had no choice but to take her, although reluctantly. Too many things were going wrong, and I needed her there to make sure the deal closed smoothly.

No one else knew the account as well as she did. She'd been by my side as I put the entire thing together myself. There was one night during the trip that I sat talking with a leggy redhead that caught my attention at the bar.

I remember a lot of the conversation, but at some point, I must have cut ties and gone to my room. I woke the next morning with a crushing headache, but I was alone. That I do remember.

According to Addison, we met at the bar, and I ditched the woman for her. This I don't remember. When I asked her about me waking alone, since she has always tried to stay in my bed as long as she could. She told me we had a disagreement and she left.

Yet, things were fine for the rest of the trip. I don't remember there being tension between us. Nor do I remember anything from that night past my conversation with the other woman at the bar. It's not like me, which is why I've had DNA tests run several times.

I've had a team looking into what really happened that night. Footage from the hotel, the log for my room entries, anything that would help me understand how this happened.

"You still don't believe she's yours." Addison's voice pulls me from my thoughts. "She is, Gregor. Please don't hold the things I've done against her."

"Things you've done?" I narrow my eyes at her.

Her words come out sounding cryptic. My hackles go up. Finally, she's going to tell me what I've been feeling in my gut—whatever it is I've felt she's been leaving out for over two years.

"I should've known better," she whispers.

Reaching out a hand, she looks at me hopefully. I drop my gaze to the offered hand. My anger tells me to leave it there. However, the doctor's words encourage me to put my anger aside and comfort her.

I'm not a soulless man. I feel for Addison. Not as a lover, but as someone who knows she's leaving her child behind. She's been in pain this whole time, all while knowing she'd be leaving her little girl.

She opens her mouth as if she's going to speak again, but her lips close. A smile takes over them and her fragile hand in mine goes lifeless.

"Addison," I choke out. "Addison."

I call out over the sound of the machines. I close my eyes against all my emotions. I have so many questions and still no answers. I stand completely lost. The mother of my daughter just passed away right before my eyes.

The bitterness returns. Addison fucked me right to the very end. I don't feel like a bastard for my thoughts. I know Addison has just taken a secret to her grave.

A secret I need to know. I release her hand, turning to walk from the room. I'm numb inside.

I feel hollowed out. After this, I'm going to have two broken Chloes on my hands. Still, I'm fighting to breathe after Cee's earlier words.

I left her behind with our child. I left her with no options. No choice but to get rid of a part of us.

Now this. I'm a man lost. So lost, I don't remember sitting or having my daughter placed in my arms. I don't remember making a phone call until the voice on the other end draws me back to reality.

"Gregor, honey?" My mother brings me out of my thoughts.

Looking at my watch, I twist my lips. It's five in the morning in New York. I can hear the tiredness in her voice. I'm sure she had a late night with hosting the dinner party I cut out on. I clear my throat to make my request.

"I need your help. My world is falling apart. I need someone I trust to help me before it crumbles," I murmur into the phone.

"I'm on my way," she replies without a second thought.

We end the call and I get arrangements in order for her to come and join me. Looking down into my lap, my eyes water. My sleeping daughter rests so trustingly in my arms.

My other child never got to trust me. Why? Because I wasn't trustworthy. I should have found another way. I should have given us a time line before I let her go.

I can't say if I would have come this far or built this life if I had. Once the baby was born, I probably would have run back to my father for help, but at least I would have had my child and my woman.

Now… I don't know what I have. My eyes focus on the small being in my embrace. I pull her to my chest and start to rock. There will be no more hiding this small creature.

I'm not truly sure I want to continue trying to find the missing link to what happened almost three years ago. She's here, she's mine, and she needs me to protect her.

I've failed one child of mine. I can't afford to make that mistake with this little one too. It's not an option.

"Gregor," my best friend and head of security calls my name.

I look up at Ethan. Clayton and I got lucky with friends. Without David and Ethan, we wouldn't have been able to pull any of this off.

"We should go. I gave them my information in case they need anything else. For now, let's get you two out of here," he says.

"Where's that woman?" I ask, my voice breaking.

"She said she was going to the restroom and never returned." He frowns.

"I want her found."

"I'm on it. Come on," he replies.

I blow out a breath.

"Take me to the house. My mother is on her way in. When she arrives, I need you to look after them until I can… I need to start fixing my mess," I say, placing a kiss on my daughter's small head.

Ethan nods. I see the guilt in his eyes. This isn't his fault. His sister died the week in question. I wouldn't have wanted him anywhere other than with his family.

If I got shit-faced and got someone pregnant, that's on me. I've never blamed anyone else for this. I've just had questions. None of them matter now.

She's gone.

CHAPTER FOURTEEN

Here to Mend

Gregor

When I enter the room, Chloe is still sitting on the floor in the exact same spot I left her in. She's still wearing the clothes she had on when we flew in. I didn't think my heart could break anymore today.

Whatever was left just spilled out on the floor before me. She looks as lost as I feel as she stares at the wall. I don't think she's seeing anything. She's just sitting, waiting.

I can't help but wonder if this is how she looked after I abandoned her and our child. Was this how it was after she had to make the choice that will forever haunt us both? I deserve this pain. She doesn't.

I drag my heartless shell over to her. Gathering the last of my strength, I bend and lift her up into my arms. Carrying her limp body into the bathroom, I stand here before the toilet. Holding her up with one arm, I peel her panties down with the other.

Before today, I would have felt nothing but desire as I drag the fabric down her toned thighs. Today, there's nothing sexual about this. She's not responsive at all—no fight, no sass, nothing.

I set her on the toilet as the tears roll down my cheeks. When I hear her start to relieve herself and I'm sure she's not going to fall over, I move to the bathtub and fill it with water. I pour in the bubbles that were left in a basket for us inside.

Checking the temperature, I cut off the water and return to retrieve Chloe. I remove her panties from her ankles and take off her dress and bra. I will her to curse me out and tell me to get out.

Yet, she just stares ahead. I lift her, walking her over to the bath. Gently, I place her in the water.

Making quick work of my own clothes, I climb in behind her. I put my arms around her, locking her in my embrace and bury my face in her hair. Then I break down.

I sob for our past, I sob for our present, I sob for our future. I sob and beg God to show me how to fix this. I've never felt this helpless in my life, even when I had nothing.

"I'm sorry, sweetheart," I say, kissing the top of her head. "I'm so sorry, baby."

When I've cried my voice raw and she begins to chatter in my hold, I release some of the water and add more warm water. This time I wash her quickly before getting us out and toweling her off.

When we're back in the bedroom, I dress her in one of my shirts and tuck her into the bed. I order room service. Although, I'm sure neither of us will eat it.

Once the food arrives, I leave it behind, climbing into bed. I spoon a sobbing Chloe and hold her tightly. I don't know how, but we have to make it through this.

CHAPTER FIFTEEN

Torn in Two

Chloe

It's been two days. He hasn't left my side once. We cry together, we exist together, but we don't speak to each other. Maybe I should say that I don't speak to him.

I have nothing to say. I haven't been able to request to go home. It may say I'm masochistic, but I haven't requested to leave because his care and attention are the only things keeping me together.

I've started going to the restroom on my own, but that's about it. If I were left alone, I wouldn't move to do much more than relieve myself, if that. Brodi has fed me each day, watching me closely to make sure I finish what he places in front of me.

I sleep most of the day. In my dreams, I can trust the arms I lie in. In my dreams, it doesn't hurt so much.

"Chloe," Brodi murmurs as I stare down at the toast and fruit he's placed in front of me.

I don't reply. I can't. I'm afraid of what I'll sound like. I don't want him to hear my hurt. He may be watching it, but if I'm silent, he can't hear it.

"Cee, baby?" he tries again.

I close my eyes against the soothing feel of the nickname he calls me. I loathe the fact that he still has the power to soothe me.

"I have to go out today. I'll come back as soon as I can." He reaches to brush a lock of hair from my face.

I flinch away. My anger returning. It's the first real emotion I've felt in days. I latch on to it and let it loose.

I let my hands fly, connecting with his face. I can see the stunned look when I catch him with an accurate two piece. Anger fills his eyes, but he doesn't react.

I can't stop. I start to pound on his chest. I'm angry he won't fight back or at least try to stop me.

"I hate you, I hate you, I hate you. Get out. Go to your baby mother and your child. Leave me the fuck alone. You stupid piece of shit," I yell at him.

He puts his arms around my waist. When my arms get tired, and I can barely beat them against the hard muscles beneath his shirt, I shove at him tiredly. He presses his lips to my ear.

"She died. Addison was terminally ill. She died in the hospital the other day. Chloe has been with my mother for the last few days. I just wanted to check in," he says.

I snort. "No, I've been here with you. Can't you even keep our names straight?"

He pulls back, his jaw working. His gray eyes darken. I see that his lip is busted, and he'll have a bruise on his cheek.

"Chloe Annie Hennessy. That's my daughter's name," he says through tight lips.

It's like he's torn me in half. I don't know how to feel about any of the information I've received in the last five minutes. It all starts to work through my brain.

"Please go," I whisper.

He nods his head. Stepping back, his eyes remain on me. He looks as conflicted as I feel. As if he wants to stay but needs to go.

I won't be here when he returns. I'm going home with or without his help. It'll hurt more to get over this alone, but I think that's for the best.

"I'll see you later," he says, almost in warning as if he has heard my thoughts.

I don't respond. I turn my back to him, crossing my arms over my chest. I can sense when he stops his retreat. His eyes are on me, burning a hole in the back of my head, but I don't acknowledge him.

"We will talk later," he says, his voice firmer this time.

I flip him the bird. He snorts, but this time I'm left with the chill that enters the room once he's gone. I shove the tray of food to the floor from the little table he placed in front of the bed.

"Son of a bitch," I sob.

My body grows heavy and my knees weak. I climb onto the bed to cry out my tears before I start to figure out a way back home. Unfortunately, I pass out from exhaustion, wrapped in a blanket of my sorrow.

Gregor

"You love this woman?" my mother asks suspiciously as she looks at my bruised face.

"Yes." I sigh. "I've hurt her repeatedly. This is my own doing."

"I can understand her being hurt, but to place her hands on you," my mother replies, pursing her lips.

"I deserve way more than this. She's within her rights, believe me."

"Nothing makes this okay," she says firmly.

"We have a long past..." I pause. I can't tell my mother Chloe and I were having trouble before this. I still need this engagement to look real. "We were working through that... I thought we could... I once left her pregnant, scared, and alone. She had no choice but to abort our child."

I blow out a breath as reality bites in. Hearing the words aloud slices through me. All the money in the world could never replace what I've lost. I continue through my ache.

"I brought her here and within hours of our arrival, everything was turned on its head. She found out I had a child here," I say, the words tasting like acid.

"Oh, Gregor. Did we never talk to you about condoms? I still can't believe you would hide this child from us for so long." My mother takes a pause, her cheeks turning red. "Okay, I think I understand why she hit you."

I grin for the first time in days. At the moment, my mother looks like she's thinking about going upside my head. I know Chloe isn't the only one I've hurt. This has been difficult for my mother to step into.

"Everything is so complicated." I look at my daughter. "I wanted to make sure she was mine. No, no, I think I've always known. There's just something else Addison was hiding. I wanted to find out what before I entangled my family in all of this.

"I don't remember the night we were supposed to have hooked up to conceive my little girl. We had a casual relationship prior, but I ended that sometime before we could have made a baby together," I explain.

"Yet here she is. She looks like you when you were a little boy," she replies.

"Grandma… see baby?" Chloe says as she holds her doll up to my mother.

"Yes, beautiful. She's almost as pretty as you are," my mother coos.

"Pretty baby." Chloe nods. "Daddy, see baby?"

"Yes, sweetheart, I see your pretty baby." I chuckle.

She turns back for her toys, ignoring us once again. She's been occupied with the doll I bought today in hopes of making her smile. She's too little to understand how much her world has changed. I look down at my palms.

"I can't say that I regret her. I love my daughter. I just wish she had the mother I would have chosen," I say.

"The one you have hurting in a hotel room?"

"Yup, the one I'm too selfish to let go of," I snort.

"This isn't an easy thing. You've hurt her deeply. Something I know is so hard for you. You're such a loving person, but I've never known you to give up." She exhales, reaching to lift my chin. "I don't know what happened back then, but I bet every penny I have that your heart was in the right place. Explain things to her. Then, let her decide."

I sit thinking about her words. She's right. I've never explained to Chloe why I did what I did. I just told her things were ending for her good. If I can make her understand… I have to try to make her understand.

"Daddy, I sleepy," Chloe whines, coming to climb into my lap.

I wrap my arms around her and hold her tightly as she falls asleep with her head on my shoulder. I wish my life could be as simple as hers. I kiss the top of her head.

"She adores you," my mother whispers with a smile.

"And I her," I murmur back.

"Gregor, if she's still there when you return, you just might have a shot."

I close my eyes and groan. I just keep digging this hole, but there was no way I was letting Chloe leave without me. I still have things to settle here. We'll return to the States when I wrap things up.

"What have you done?" my mother huffs.

"I gave orders for my men not to let her leave the hotel," I mutter.

"You boys fuss with your father but you're each just like him. Stubborn to the bone and determined to have things your way. The poor girl."

"She's probably going to kick my ass again." I chuckle.

"Yes, just like your father. I think you enjoyed it," she teases. "Give me that little one. You go fix your mess."

CHAPTER SIXTEEN

Who I Am

Chloe

I open my eyes to find gray ones staring back at me. I focus and take in his face as he stands over the bed. The bruise on his cheek and his busted lip bring earlier back to me.

I twist my face up and lift to get dressed. I should have been gone by now. I didn't mean to sleep so long. When I look at the clock, I see I've slept the day away.

"Baby, stop," he calls as I start to slide off the bed.

"Stop calling me that."

"You will always be my baby, Cee," he replies.

"I'm leaving. This time, leave me alone."

"My father had my life mapped out from the womb. I can't remember ever dreaming of wanting to be a fireman or a police officer. I never dreamed of those things because I knew I was going to be governor.

"All roads were leading right for that seat. Until the day I walked into a coffee shop and saw the most beautiful woman I've ever seen in my life. I never imagined you were so young.

"I… I was so fucked up over losing you the first time, but the scandal our relationship would have caused… I had to let you go," he chokes out.

"Why are you telling me this?" I whisper.

"I need you to understand. If, after I tell you things from my side, you decide to leave… I'll try to let you go. It's not going to be easy for me. I've loved you since that first date." He chuckles softly, but his words are filled with pain.

"What's so funny?"

"When I think about it now, I should've known you were too young for me. You were adorable and so nervous, but you were just what I needed. You didn't expect anything from me, and you just let me be," he replies.

"Getting over you was so hard," I say into my lap.

"You're preaching to the choir," he scoffs. "My father couldn't figure out what was wrong with me, so he sent me off to stay with my uncle. I spent most of my time with him drunk."

He climbs onto the bed, sitting with his back to the headboard. Reaching for me, he pulls me between his legs. My back to his front.

I remain stiff. A war rages as I sit in his embrace. Yet, I can't move away and I'm hanging on to every word.

"I told myself… I'd just check on you. See you one last time. You know… see you as a woman and wish you well. But you walked into that room and took my breath away. I knew then, I'd never love another.

"Things were so all over the place. My father was really pushing me to secure my hold on supporters and run for mayor. We were going to make the big leap from there.

"One day, I just stopped. You were in one of my T-shirts, walking around the apartment I kept for us. It felt more real to me than anything else in my life. Clay had this plan. We were going to walk away from my father's money, his connections, everything.

"It wasn't a question of if he would be furious. It was how furious? I couldn't chance him homing in on you and destroying your life—"

"None of that mattered to me. My life was ruined anyway. I... something broke inside," I say softly. "I just couldn't find that...that thing. It was gone."

The tears start again. That time in my life was so hard. I still don't think I've fully gotten my life back together since. I know I haven't.

"I see that." His voice breaks. "Baby, in my mind I was doing the right thing. After you talked about your life all week. I realized you had responsibilities you couldn't walk away from.

"You were so mature for your age. With so much on your shoulders, I couldn't ask you to leave your sister behind and I didn't know if my brother's crazy plan would work. I couldn't afford to take care of you and Ally. It was best if I broke things off," he says hoarsely.

"I would have waited. For you, I would have waited," I sniffle.

"I know, but you were so young, so beautiful. I couldn't ask you to sit around waiting on me. For months, I was destitute. I had nothing. Babe, the shit I had to do to eat." He makes a disgusted sound.

"Don't tell me you were selling your body," I try to joke.

It's my way of dealing with pain when it's too much to bear. This... this is becoming too much. I'm crumbling as I sit here.

"Pretty damn close," he says, disdain coloring his words. "I went to one of those sperm banks. I was desperate. I hadn't eaten in days. Clay was doing well in the States, but I was still hustling to get things done on my end.

"All of my funds went to looking the part to make deals happen. Food was an afterthought. I wasn't about to tell my little brother I was failing and starving."

"Oh," I breathe, my heart aching even more.

The thought of him having more children out there threatens to implode my chest. I start to rock myself and he rocks with me. It's more soothing than I want to admit.

"I caught a break not long after that. Now that I think about it, Addison was one of my first hires. I was focused. I did everything I needed to do to get my life on track.

"But it haunted me that I had to do the things I did. I contacted the bank I'd gone to, praying I was never picked as a donor. I didn't try to make myself sound too flattering on the questionnaire.

"Just so happens, I was never picked. I paid them a nice sum to make sure it was all destroyed. I'm telling you this so you understand. I... I never meant to have a child with anyone.

"I wouldn't even date for the first few years. Addison... she... she caught me on a bad night. Your birthday was a few days before and I was going crazy missing you.

"I had made my mark. I had enough money to take care of you. I just wanted to hold you in my arms, but I made that fucking promise. I had a few drinks and at the time... I just needed to hold someone." He pauses.

I don't speak. I can't. I don't know if I want to hear this, but I feel like I need to.

"I should have ended it after that first time. I let her know I wasn't looking for more than what it was. Things changed... she changed. I saw it becoming a problem, so I started to create distance.

"That wasn't enough, she didn't respect my boundaries. She... I had transferred her here. A few months passed and I found out about the baby. I didn't believe her at first.

"I hadn't touched her or so I thought. When I found out Chloe was mine, I felt like I hit a new low. I hadn't planned to get married or have a family if it wasn't with you.

"My name is Clooney Gregor Hennessey Jr. Brodi is my nickname. Clay couldn't say Gregor when he was little, so he called me Brodi. I never lied. When we met, everyone close to me called me by that name," he says, releasing a long sigh.

"Did you love her?"

"Have you heard a word I've said? Addison was manipulative and drove me insane. I didn't even know she was sick. I found out in the hospital as she lay there dying. If it didn't involve my daughter, I didn't interact with her," he replies.

"Tell me about her," I say like a glutton for punishment.

"Addison?"

"No, Chloe."

Gregor

Hope bloomed when Cee asked about my little girl. I've been rambling about her since. I've told her everything I know about my chubby little angel.

When I notice how silent she's become, I stop. I chide myself for going on and on. This can't be easy for her.

"Please tell me where to start? I was prepared for a different battle, baby. I'm still here to fight for you, but I'm drowning in figuring out how," I breathe.

She's silent still. I hold my breath waiting for her reply. I look down to make sure she's not sleeping. She's staring at her hands.

"I honestly don't think you can. At least, I don't know what or how to tell you. You want me, Brodi, figure it out. You did this. You fix it," she finally says.

"Challenge excepted, Cee. I just need you to be willing to let me try," I murmur.

"Yeah, I'll think about that."

"That's all I'm asking."

CHAPTER SEVENTEEN

Another Mill

Chloe

I lift my lids and sense something is different about the room. My fingertips meet the cool sheets beside me. I know what's missing right away.

I shouldn't feel so disappointed that he's gone. It makes me think of something my mother once told me when I was younger. You always crave the source of your greatest pain.

It's as if you want to show it you can survive it. Sometimes you want to prove to yourself that you can change its outcome. Most times you're just drawn to the high of the pain itself.

When it comes to Brodi, I haven't figured out which category I fall into. I want to hate him for the rest of my life, but he's not making that easy. They say actions speak louder than words.

In this case, they do. I hear everything he has told me. I'm listening to the words, saving them for when I'm ready to dissect them. However, it's his actions that are pulling at my attention.

Brodi is so much bigger than me, but he let me attack him. I know he allowed it. The man I remember from the past wouldn't even allow me to so much as curse in his direction.

However, he stood there and took that ass whipping. I saw the anger in his eyes. I know he could have stopped me if he wanted. Yet, he didn't.

He has taken care of me when I couldn't care to do it for myself. If I'm honest, it felt good to have that. After what I had to do all those years ago, I didn't have an ounce of that same support. I needed it. I just didn't have it.

Still, I'm so afraid of allowing myself to trust him. That's something he has to earn, and it won't be easy. I can see myself on the next episode of *Snapped* if he ever hurts me again.

Then don't give him a chance to.

My cell phone rings. I look around and find it on the nightstand charging. Brodi must have put it there. I've been so out of touch with the world.

I go to answer, but I don't know the number. I think for a few seconds on whether or not I want to pick up. Ally comes to mind, causing me to swipe and place the phone to my ear.

"Hello."

"Is this Ms. Sinclair?"

"Yes, it is," I say cautiously.

"I was instructed to contact you by Mr. Hennessy. Your accounts have been released, but your million dollars is pending delivery. I've set up a trust to provide you access to the funds as early as tomorrow," he says.

My heart sinks. So I can't trust Brodi. He has given up already. I wasn't supposed to get that money until the end of the six months.

Coward.

He couldn't even face me this time. Having someone else call to do his dirty work. Fuck him. I don't need him or his money.

"You can tell Mr. Hennessy to—"

"Why don't you tell me?" Brodi's sleep-roughened voice booms.

I turn to find him in the doorway with two mugs in his hands. His chiseled chest on display. A pair of pajama pants are hanging on to his hips for dear life. He looks good for his age.

Not worth it, Chloe.

"Thank you for the call," I say into the phone and hang up.

"What were you going to tell me?" he asks, lifting a brow.

"I thought... nothing," I mumble.

"Yes, you were supposed to receive the money at the end of the contract. But as I promised last night. I'll do my best to let you go. If that's what you want," he says, walking over to hand me a mug.

I narrow my eyes at him. This is still Brodi. He doesn't play this fair. There's a catch. I know there is.

I take a sip of what I thought to be coffee. A smile tugs at my lips when the taste of hot chocolate bursts in my mouth. Oh, he's here to play hard.

Okay, Brodi. I see you.

If he's trying to prove how much he knows me, he's getting there. I hope he remembers I know him too. At least... enough to know he's up to something.

"So if I want to leave in the morning, you're going to be okay with that?"

"No," he says like something sour just hit his tongue. "I'm not okay with that, but if it's what you want…What if I offer you another million?"

"What?"

I look at him like he's crazy. Placing my mug down, I fold my arms over my chest. This should be good. I think he's lost his damn mind.

"A million to stay. A million to see the slate clean, because we can't wipe away our past. It's too important to me… to us. But… I'm not trying to buy your forgiveness or put a value on our child.

"I want you to stay. Allow me to show you the man I am. I'll never walk away from you again. Let me show you I'll never hurt you again," he says.

The way he says our child stirs all types of shit inside me. I'll admit, a part of me has been wanting to leave the district. It's not the same without Sid. I lost my love for that place a long time ago.

Two million dollars could do so much for me. I can help Ally reach her dreams and still pursue my own. The wheels are in full gear.

"Do you still paint?"

I jerk my head up. I can't believe he remembers that. I haven't dreamed of being an artist since I was a teenage girl, when I first met him.

My heart races as I think of the thrill I used to get from sketching and painting. I've painted some over the years, but I haven't thought about doing it for a living in so long.

On Sundays, I'd sketch and get lost as therapy. Ally would sit playing her flute and I would paint for hours. Actually, I stopped when my sister went to college. It just wasn't the same when she wasn't there.

"I haven't in a while," I answer.

"Never too late to go after your dreams," he says, winking at me.

I look away. I refuse to get caught up in those eyes. They're one of my weaknesses when it comes to him.

"How long do I have to stay?"

"The six months. Fulfill the original contract with me. Help me keep my father from forcing me into a marriage of his choosing and losing everything my brothers and I have built. Someone's still out there trying to expose us and ruin our lives.

"That threat is real. I can still help you and you can help me. I'm only asking that you allow me to try to mend what I've broken in the process," he replies.

Six months, I can do six months. I'll be two million dollars richer, and I can tell him to kiss my ass in the end. That'll work for me.

"It's not like our relationship can last more than six months at a time anyway," I mumble.

He places his mug down, climbing onto the bed until we're face to face, nose to nose. His hot breath fans against my lips. This is the Brodi I know. I can sense his need for dominance right on the surface.

"Only thing standing in the way of me dragging you down an aisle today is the world of hurt I've left you in. I have no questions about who I want to spend the rest of my life with, Cee.

"This time, it's going to take my flesh on fire from the inside out to tear me away from you. Unless…unless I truly can't fix what I've done and that look of hate isn't able to fade.

"Although, I can promise you. I'm here to do whatever it takes. Six months isn't nearly long enough for all of the love I have for you," he breathes.

Run, Chloe. Abort, abort!

I'm getting my shit and running in my head, but my body and heart have me rooted to the bed. His heat has wrapped around me like an embrace. His words are chipping at the ice around my heart.

On this episode of American Greed, *we have Chloe Sinclair. A million dollars wasn't enough. She sold her soul to a sex god for an additional million and lost everything. Including her sanity.*

I swear, I hear the words in the voice of that guy from the show. Still, I know in the depths of my mind it isn't the money—it's my bleeding heart—that causes me to speak my next words.

"The only thing I can promise you, Brodi. There's another ass whipping waiting for you if I so much as try to open my heart to you and you hurt me... not that you'll have a chance. For now, I'll stay, but I don't know about anything else." I shrug.

***

I've stepped into another moment of insanity. I've agreed to stay. I think to call Sid, but I'm too embarrassed to share any of this with her. I've been keeping Brodi a secret from her for years.

My thoughts go to my sister, I've had a few missed calls from her. I need to check in. Especially since it looks like I'm not returning to New York anytime soon. She should at least know I'm not there.

I look at the time. I believe we're three hours ahead of Europe. I pick up my phone and dial Ally, she should be home or maybe out with friends. A smile comes to my face, at least she's young and can make a happy life for herself.

Maybe she'll find herself a nice guy who will treat her the way she deserves. I'll kill him if he doesn't.

"Hey, Chloe. I've been trying to reach you for days. What's going on?"

"I had to take a trip. I'm not sure when I'll be headed back home. Is everything all right? Things worked out with school, right?"

I'll strangle Brodi if he didn't keep his word. Guilt twists in my stomach. I was so wrapped up in my sorrow, I didn't think to check in to make sure everything was okay.

"Well, about that. I'm in New York."

"I'm going to fucking kill him. He can't keep his word on shit."

"Wait, calm down. I'm assuming you're talking about Cane's brother."

"Who the fuck is Cane?"

"Um, Clayton's youngest brother. You're with the oldest one, right?"

I sigh and reach for my temple. I'm too young to allow Ally and Brodi to give me a stroke. I try to relax so I can figure out what's going on.

"Yeah, I am."

"They did take care of everything with school. Clayton found out... well, he got me out of some trouble right on time. I'm here in New York while he cleans everything up for me."

"Ally," I groan.

"It's going to be okay. I promise."

"My head hurts. How's Sid?"

"I haven't seen her much. Clayton keeps her pretty busy. God, that dude is possessive. I didn't know she was dating anyone. That engagement ring is so fire. I wish someone looked at me the way he looks at her."

"Ally, focus," I snap. "So she's fine? You have seen her?"

"A time or two. Yes, she's fine. Chlo, are you going to tell me what's really going on? I appreciate the cavalry you sent in, but how did they know to come?"

I chew on the inside of my mouth. I don't have an answer for her because I don't know what she's talking about. Clayton did seem to be a step ahead that night, but I don't even know what kind of trouble Ally has gotten herself into.

"I'm still filling in blanks, Al, but you can fill in what you've gotten into."

"Hey, Cane wants to head out for something to eat. I'll talk to you later."

"Ally," I growl.

"Love you, sis. Later."

She hangs up in my ear. I look at the phone because I know she didn't just lose her mind and hang up on me. I'm going to kick her ass.

CHAPTER EIGHTEEN

Old Times

Gregor

It's only been a little over a week, eight days to be exact, but this is the first time I've seen her smile since laying eyes on her in my apartment. She looks peaceful. Her hair is pulled up in a ponytail, my T-shirt hangs off one of her shoulders. Her eyes are bright but lost to the task before her.

Music is flowing through the suite. A soundtrack to each stroke of her brush. Her lips are parted and her tongue peeks out as she leans into the canvas.

I chuckle to myself. She's totally engrossed in her task. I love this woman. Everything about her amazes me.

"You know, you can stop watching me so hard. I'm not going to float away. I have a million reasons to stay," she says, with that smile still on her lips.

"I like watching you paint. You look happy," I reply.

She turns her gaze toward me. Tilting her head to the side, she studies me. I watch her, trying to figure out what's going on in her head.

"You don't," she says, her eyes narrow on me. "It's in your eyes."

"Are you painting me in your head, baby? You know all you have to do is ask and I'll pose for you," I say.

I watch as her eyes light up. She looks like I just offered her the world. I rise and start over to the side of the room she's on. Leaning over her, I kiss her forehead.

Her smile falters a bit, but I refuse to let it sting. I have to focus on healing us, not on the pain. Without prompting, I lift my shirt over my head.

Pulling the string on my sweats, I let them fall to the floor. Chloe's mouth falls open. My lips turn up.

I smile harder when she licks her lips before catching herself. Her brows dip as she frowns. I move back into position for her viewing. Standing in my boxer briefs with my legs wide, I clasp my hands behind my back.

"I'm all yours," I croon.

She makes a little sound in the back of her throat and rolls her eyes. I watch as she mumbles to herself while getting fresh supplies set up.

"You're not going to be able to hold that pose," she grumbles at me.

I roll my shoulders back. "Try me," I retort.

"Suit yourself," she mutters.

It only takes her seconds to start sketching. I watch as her face takes on a look of complete concentration. Each time she glances at me, I don't see lust. Instead, I see determination and thoughtfulness.

Time tickles by and my shoulders start to ache a bit, but I don't give in. I stand, offering myself bare. My face is open to my emotions as I get lost in thoughts about my life, our life, all the things Chloe and I have been through.

"What made you return to the States?" Her voice breaks through my musing.

"I accomplished what I set out to do. Clay needed me and… I was homesick, I think. I've been around the world but there's nothing like home. Home is truly where my heart is," I say as I stare back at her.

She dips her head, turning back to the canvas. I love that shy smile, but it's gone as soon as it comes. My own grin falls.

"I guess you never truly made up with your father?"

"My father is an odd man. He wouldn't speak to us for almost three years. Yet, he's always meddling in our lives now," I reply.

I never got to tell her that my father was the one who pushed me to break things off and leave. After some thought, knowing Chloe, I don't think that's something she should know. I still need her to interact with my father when we return.

"He's probably pretty pissed about not having a son as a governor," she says, pulling me from my thoughts.

"Not so much. He wants the seat and control of it. He'll still get it. My cousin, Wade, has been giving my father everything he's dreamed of," I scoff.

"You don't sound too happy about that. Are you having regrets?"

"No, Wade's an asshole," I say flat out.

"Oh." She chuckles.

"Tell me why you never dated?"

Her face tightens and her hand pauses midsketch. I observe as her eyes move toward me slowly. It's clear I've crossed into a hot topic. The light atmosphere and mood shift.

"How would you know I never dated?"

I want to kick myself. However, I did tell her I would never lie to her ever again. Maybe telling her this will show I was never truly able to leave her behind.

"Once I was able to get on my feet, I had the resources to look after you. To make sure you were okay from a distance," I reply.

"You had people snooping into my life," she hisses.

"If you want to put it that way. Yes."

"I don't understand you," she says in a broken whisper.

Placing her pencil down, she stares at the canvas before her. I hate that vacant look. I don't want to lose her again today. Watching her disappear into herself for hours is not an option.

I saunter over to her and tug her from her seat. Her gaze comes to mine slowly. Bringing her arms around my neck, I wrap her waist and start to sway our bodies to the music.

"Let me help you understand me," I say after a few beats. "Communication is our problem. Our lack of sharing the entire truth gets in our way every time. Not this one. Tell me what you're thinking, and I'll answer your confusion."

"You didn't want me. Why watch over me? Why snoop into my life? Is it a power thing for you?"

"I think I need to make something very clear. There has never been a time I haven't wanted you. I've dated women hoping to fill my loneliness, but all I ever see is you.

"Your face, your smile." I pause, reaching to stroke her red hair. "Your laugh. I never see them, only you."

"Then why not be with me?" she says in such a small and hurt voice.

"Because I had nothing for us. Baby, you had so much going on in your life. You had responsibilities of your own. I, as a man, couldn't in good conscience drag you where I knew I was going.

"I thought I was doing the right thing. I didn't know I'd destroy us both. I didn't know that all I needed was the very thing I was leaving behind. Selfishly, I thought I was hurting myself more than I was hurting you," I choke on my last words.

I couldn't have been more wrong. Chloe made all the sacrifices. All I did was exist. My heart breaks all over again, but I know I deserve the pain.

Her eyes fill with tears as she looks up at me. I see her searching. For what? I'm not sure.

She turns her gaze away from me, placing her head on my bare chest. Her hands slide from my neck over my chest and around to my back. I try to will myself not to harden any more than I already have.

"This all feels too right," she whispers.

I rub my hand up and down her back. It does feel right. I close my eyes. I've wanted to have this feeling for so long. I'm willing to fight the world to keep it.

"Chloe—"

"Shh, don't ruin it. Just be. Be who you were before you killed me," she says.

Her words burn a hole through me. I no longer have to fight my growing erection. If anything. I want to place my clothes back on and walk away to wallow in my shame.

Instead, I remain silent, thinking of old times. When I'd dance her around the apartment, making her laughter ring out. I think of when I had her to love.

Just like back then, I dip to kiss the top of her head. Then I move my lips to her ear. I say the words, knowing they won't count, but needing to say them anyway in hopes they eventually will.

"I love you."

Chloe

A shiver runs through me. Foolishly, I've let my guard down in this moment. It feels too right not to. This is the way I remember him.

The sweet moments where I felt like the most loved woman in the world. It's a dangerous game I'm playing. I know it is.

However, a part of me needs this more than I'm willing to admit. I just need to separate reality from the fairy tale.

Keep your heart safe. This isn't real.

I hear the words, but I don't think my heart does. As I sink into the heat of his nearly naked body, I know my body doesn't. I melt into him as if he isn't the flame that burned me once before.

"I love you," he says again.

It's the tenth time he has. I've been counting. With each song that passes, the longer I hold on to him, the more I'm falling down the rabbit hole. His words are like an ice pick.

Turning my face up, I look into his eyes. I release a shuddering breath. Those gray eyes pierce through me.

Reaching up, I caress his face. Aged, but still perfection. His lips are coaxing me in. A temptation I should deny.

He lifts a hand to run his fingertips across my cheek. I close my eyes as that connection tries to hum to life. His simple touch is searing. When I do open my eyes and look into his, I'm taken away to another place.

I move my hand to the back of his head, and I pull him toward me. Our lips nearly join when his phone rings. He squeezes his eyes shut and groans.

I step back as if I've been scorched. Knowing that could be a call about his child almost buckles my knees. I turn and head for the bedroom. I've had enough for today.

I'm only confusing myself. Like I said, my heart is needy, but my mind knows better. This can't happen.

Don't get caught up in the moment.

CHAPTER NINETEEN

Speak Up

Chloe

"What do you have for me, Justin?" Brodi says into the phone.

He's on a conference call. I don't know how he does it. It's like he goes all day. This call is with his Georgia team from what I've overheard. While it's early afternoon for them, it's late into the evening for us.

It hasn't slipped my notice that he's been working from here in the hotel when I'm sure he needs to go into his office. Instead, his assistant Eric—who he flew in from Georgia after one of his employees here fell ill—comes by daily with stacks of paperwork and a tablet he hands off to Brodi and returns to pick up each evening.

When I asked about the tablet, Brodi explained important and classified docs are on it. Things he doesn't quite trust having emailed or transferred through doc shares. I can understand that.

Especially after he explained his father found a way to outsmart him and his brothers to gain controlling interest in their companies and he isn't entirely sure if the person targeting me and Sid is also behind the issues he's been having with some business.

"No, run those numbers by me again," he says into the phone.

I've been trying to paint as quietly as I can. However, his barking orders have proved to be a distraction. He's been going since early this morning.

Giving up on painting, I stand and head into the bedroom, shutting the door behind me. Looking at the time, I think of Ally. We still haven't had a real talk.

Each time I call, she sounds like I've woken her up. I'm starting to call bullshit. My sister thinks I don't know how to calculate time zones. My calls are not waking her from some deep slumber.

Grabbing my phone off the charger, I check for messages. Sid has been texting nonstop. I feel bad about not returning her calls or texts, but I know I'll break down if I speak to her and my mind hasn't been right to compose a text that won't cause alarm.

Instead of replying to her last text, I call Ally. She can let Sid know I'm safe and alive. However, my sister's phone rings several times before her voice mail picks up. This girl is trying me.

"Ally, call me back," I bite out and hang up.

"You know what?" I murmur to myself as I dial her number again. She's taking advantage of this distance. I have to remind myself that she's twenty-two.

Otherwise, Brodi would be sending me home to shake some sense into her. I still don't know why she's home. Something that's been burning my last nerve.

"Hello," she pants into the phone after picking up on the third ring.

"Ally, what the—"

"Listen, I can't talk right now. I'll call you back."

She hangs up and I stand stunned and fuming. She has some damn nerve and why the hell was she panting like that? I go to call her back, but the door opens and Brodi pops his head in.

"I haven't taken a break for dinner. You want to come downstairs with me for a bite at the bar?"

I look up at him. I go to say no, but if I stay here, I'm only going to drive myself crazy over Ally and what's going on in the States.

"What's going on with my sister? I know you and Clayton talk. Has he told you anything?"

This look comes over his face. I drop my hip and cross my arms over my chest. He better give me a straight answer. If I even smell a hint of a lie, I'm going to jump on the first plane out of here. My sister always comes first.

He sighs. "I'm not going to lie to you. Ally has gotten herself into something you can't get her out of. Clay is handling it. Trust me, my brother will keep her safe and make this all go away."

"Make what all go away?"

"That I truly don't know. Clay couldn't tell me in detail over the phone, but he mentioned some names that give me an idea."

"Oh, hell no. I want to go home."

"Chloe, like I said, it's nothing you can do anything about. She's a big girl and my brother has it under control."

I narrow my eyes at him. "You don't come before my sister. Send me home."

"I know I don't. I never asked to. Even now, I'm not asking to. What I'm telling you is, you're safer here with me. I send you back, I'm placing more weight on my brother's shoulders because he's the only one I trust to keep you safe, and he already has Sid and Ally."

I roll my eyes. "I've taken care of myself for thirty-two years. I don't need you or your brother."

"That might very well be true, but this is beyond the obstacles you've had thrown at you. The people who are involved in our world and in this situation aren't like the street thugs you once told me you had to fight off to keep your sister safe. She's graduated to people Clay and his friends are better off handling."

"Okay, well, it's time for me to graduate right along with her. Nobody will go to war for my sister like I will. Trust me, Brodi. You need to send me home." I pause and suck in a breath. "You know what? Why am I asking you to send me back? I can afford to do it myself. I'm out of here."

"*Cee*," he groans.

Just then my phone rings. I turn my back on Brodi and answer the call. "Hello," I bite out.

"Hey, sorry about that. What's up?"

"What the hell is going on with you, Ally? Don't give me any bullshit either."

"I'm fine. Clay and Cane have been helping me out. It will all be fine."

"What will be fine?"

"I can't get into it over the phone. We can talk when you come back, but you don't have to rush. Everything is fine."

"If everything is fine, why aren't you in Europe?"

"That wasn't for me. I didn't like it. I wanted to come home. I just didn't know how to tell you."

"Ally," I drag out.

"Stop worrying so much. Cane showed me a picture of Gregor. Why don't you focus on him? I don't think I've ever seen you date before. I'm okay. Stop being a mom for once. I'm okay, sis."

I huff and roll my eyes. I still feel like everyone is hiding something from me. Maybe I shouldn't run back because I might hurt this girl if I find out what's really going on with her.

I turn to look at Brodi. He pushes a hand through his hair as he looks down at his phone. I work my jaw and roll my eyes to keep the tears from falling.

"Ally, if something is going on and you need me, call. I'll be on the first flight home."

"Please don't," she says a little too quickly. "I'm a big girl. I have this handled."

"I love you," I sigh. "I'd never forgive myself if something ever happened to you."

"I love you too. I have to go."

She hangs up before I can even say another word. I purse my lips. There's never a dull moment with that girl.

"Are you up for that meal?"

I lift my gaze to find Brodi watching me closely through his lashes. I check myself before I hurl my anger with my sister at him. Running my hand through my hair, I release a breath and my stomach chooses that moment to growl.

"Yeah, okay. I could use a beer or a stiff drink from the bar now that I think about it."

"Come on, my treat." He gives me a weak smile.

"Give me a sec to change."

I still have on the paint-splattered T-shirt I've been wearing all day. I look a mess, if I'm honest.

"Take your time. I'll be in the common area. I need to make a call."

I don't reply. I turn for the closet to find something to throw on and head to the bathroom. A part of my thoughts is still with Ally. I know she's an adult now, but I still feel like it's my job to make sure she's a successful adult.

My mother had such big dreams for the both of us. I may have put my dreams off, but there's no reason Ally can't succeed. Other than her ability to land right in the middle of trouble. I've fought so many battles to keep her safe.

Sid and I beat down gang members to get my point across. My sister is off-limits. We had to move after that one time, we were all in danger, but for Ally, I'd do it all over again. I know Sid would too.

Gregor

"Hello," my brother answers his phone.

"Clay, we need to talk," I say into the phone as I run a hand through my hair.

"If you're calling to add one more thing to my plate, I'm hanging up."

I blow out a breath, feeling bad I'm not there to help him wade through everything that's going on. My frustration rises. It's like all this shit is snowballing.

"I don't want to add anything. I'm just trying to find out what's going on with Ally. Chloe's starting to freak out."

"I'm digging her out of one hole, but another one looks to be opening. This one looks like Cane's attached. I've got it though. Chloe doesn't have to worry about it."

"Clay, I'll give my life for that woman to be happy. If I need to wrap things up here and come back to handle this, you say the word. I'm there."

"I have this handled. It's the least of my worries. I've been keeping Sid busy and as far away from Ally as I can. I need you focused on those contracts that keep falling through."

"I'm on it. I swear this has to be coming from somewhere inside. There's no way it isn't. Still nothing on where all of this is coming from?"

"No, I'm working every angle. Still nothing, but you're right, I get the feeling this is an inside job. I'm going to look at everyone on my side. You should have Ethan dig into your teams."

"I agree. I'll get him on it."

I don't mention that I've had Ethan busy with my personal dealings and that's why he hasn't already dug into my theory.

"As soon as I connect some dots, I'll let you know. Don't worry about the Ally situation. I have that one covered for now."

"Thanks, Clay."

"Anytime."

I hang up and work my jaw. Tension builds between my eyes. I close them and pinch the bridge of my nose. Add to my list trying to keep Chloe from going home to get involved in things over her head.

I know how much she loves her sister. One more hole has been added to this ship. *It's going to sink.* And don't I know it.

CHAPTER TWENTY

Bottoms Up

Gregor

We sit in the bar downstairs in the hotel and there's so much tension between us. She looks gorgeous in the loose jumpsuit she has on. I thought it was a maxi dress when she first stepped out of the bedroom. However, from behind, I could see the legs of the outfit and her sexy ass.

I can tell she's still angry over the situation with her sister. However, sending her back now will sink all my plans and she'll only get in the way. As I said, my brother couldn't give me all the details over the phone, but I trust him to handle it.

"Wow, this lamb burger is so good. The beer isn't bad either," Chloe says, seeming to finally relax.

"It is pretty good. I had a salad from here yesterday."

"The food you ordered for lunch was from here?"

"Yeah, you can order up to the room from their kitchen. It was better than I thought it would be. A lot of times the room service sucks, and the hotel bars and restaurants aren't that much better."

She chews on a fry as she studies me. I love the puff she's pulled her hair up into. It puts her features on display and makes her freckles pop.

"You've done a lot of traveling over the last seven years. Was it hard being away from your family?"

"At first, I was so homesick, I almost gave up. I think I missed you the most. Clay and Cane would fly into wherever I was after we got things off the ground. That took some of the sting out, but no one could replace you," I reply.

I guess that was the wrong thing to say. She drops her burger and looks away. I wipe my hands on my napkin, frustrated with myself. I wave the waitress over for a refill on the beers.

"You know, at first, I hated you so much, but still hoped you'd come back. I was in denial. I didn't think you would really stay away. Then a year turned into two and two into three and by the fifth year, I gave up. My anger won out."

"Thanks," I say as the waitress places our beers on the table. I look at the side of Chloe's face as she refuses to look at me. "I wish I could turn back time. If I would have known you were willing to welcome me back, I would have returned sooner."

"Yeah, well, we are where we are." She pauses to sigh, lifting her beer to take a sip. "I have so much on my mind. Do you mind if we talk about something else?"

"Of course, anything you want. How's the painting going?"

She finally turns to me, and a genuine smile comes to her face. "It's good. I'm still a little rusty, but it feels good. I can get lost in it."

"That's a good thing, right?"

"Yeah, I think it is. I needed the escape, to be honest."

"If you make a list, I'll be happy to order you more supplies."

She tips her head at me with a larger smile. "Thanks. I'll get that to you tomorrow."

"Anytime."

We fall into a comfortable conversation as the beers keep flowing. It's like old times. I almost forget all the drama for a bit. Hours pass and all I can do is smile at her.

Chloe

I drop my eyes to the table, trying not to get caught up in his eyes. He hasn't stopped smiling at me. It's a sexy, gorgeous smile that's calling on feelings I shouldn't have.

"What are you smiling at?"

"You. This. I almost forgot how easy things used to be. I miss this."

My belly drops. He's right, this does feel nice. However, I have had a lot to drink so I don't know if I can trust my judgment at the moment. Memories surface and I find myself smiling too.

"Now why are you smiling?" he asks as his eyes crinkle around the sides.

"I remember my first beer. It was with you. At your apartment."

The blood drains from his face and he groans. I burst into laughter, knowing what he's probably thinking. I should make him suffer.

"It wasn't while I was seventeen. I used to pour those down the sink. I never drank while we hung out. Remember, I turned them down most of the time."

He frowns. "Which is reason number one hundred and one I should've figured out the truth sooner."

"My first beer was at your place when you were stressing about a fight you had with your dad. Sid wasn't into drinking, so I never tried before then. I had Ally to think about too."

He narrows his eyes. "I think I remember that. You were wasted after your third longneck. It was adorable."

"Ugh, the headache the next day wasn't worth it."

"Looks like you've gotten your tolerance up."

I wipe at my forehead. I'm not sure that's so true. In fact, I'm starting to feel that last mug.

"Ha, I might need an assist to get back to the room. This stuff packs a punch after a few. I think I was sleeping on it."

Brodi gives me a sexy smile. "Yeah, I do have a nice buzz. You ready to head up?"

"Yeah, my lids are heavy. I'm fading."

He closes out our tab and we stand to leave. I start to sway the moment I'm out of my seat. I place a hand on the table to steady myself.

"Easy, I've got you," he says as he wraps an arm around my waist.

I lean into his warmth. I can't wait to get upstairs and into bed. My brain is exhausted.

We step into the elevator and Brodi presses for our floor. I move to lean against the back wall. He steps in front of me with a wide stance. All that dominant energy rolling off him. He runs his fingers along my hairline. I look up into his eyes and forget everything as I get lost in his gaze.

That familiar comfort draws me in. I don't see the man who hurt me. I see the man who I once loved and who had been my best friend, the man who taught me the best pleasures in life.

I blink a few times to clear my thoughts as he cups the side of my face. There's this hum between us. His hand against my flesh scorches my skin. Brodi starts to lean in, and I close my eyes.

"Please don't," I breathe out.

He kisses my forehead instead of my lips. "Sorry, I got caught in the moment."

"It's okay. I think we both did," I murmur as we reach our floor and the doors open.

He moves aside to help me out and to our room. The last thing I remember is face-planting on the bed.

CHAPTER TWENTY-ONE

This I Can Do

Chloe

I eye Brodi warily as he walks out of the bathroom in just a pair of pajama pants. He moves around the room lighting candles and dimming the lights.

This isn't the first time in the last week he has set a romantic ambience and tried to seduce me into his web. I'm standing my ground. I won't fall for any of it.

"Turn onto your stomach and lie down for me," he says as he comes to stand at the side of the bed.

"Excuse me?"

"It's a massage, Cee. Stop looking at me like I'm a snake about to strike," he huffs.

"*Well*," I drag out.

"You're so damn stubborn," he mutters.

Swiftly, he grabs my ankles and flips me over. It's not forceful. It's actually playful, something he used to do all of the time.

I go to crawl away, but he brings his hand down on my ass, slapping my cheek. I gasp and turn to scowl at him. He gives me that sexy grin and lifts a brow at me.

"Did you just hit me?" I snap.

"That was a love tap, baby. You remember those, don't you?"

"I'll show you a love tap."

I hop up to stand on my feet and run across the mattress to him. Before I can lunge at him, he wraps my waist and brings us both down onto the bed with a hard bounce.

"I'm still fast for an old man," he teases as he hovers over me.

I wiggle beneath him, finding the right angle to use to flip him onto his back. I throw my arms up in victory as I look down at him with a wicked grin. He chuckles, reaching for my waist.

"And I still got it, so what are you saying?"

"I miss this." He chuckles again.

"Yeah, I—"

I cut myself off and climb from straddling him. It's days like this that have made it too easy to fall into the safety net he has offered. Yes, we used to horse around all the time. It was one of the things I loved about him. His playful side.

Brodi can go from teasing and playful to a complete dom at the drop of a hat. I don't want to remember where our harmless play used to lead. I won't let lust make my decisions for me.

"It's okay to be us," he says while watching me retreat.

"There are some parts of us I'm still not ready for."

"Are you ready for me to work those kinks out of your shoulders? You were painting all day," he says.

I turn to look at him. The candlelight dancing in his eyes takes me somewhere. As hard as I try not to remember the past, it hits me.

"Brodi." I giggled as my back hit the couch in his apartment.

He hovered over me as the light from the fireplace and candles danced in his eyes. They were full of so much love and playfulness. I reached up to cup his cheek.

"I love you," I said, causing his eyes to darken with lust.

"I love you too, baby," he said. "Do you trust me, Cee?"

"What kind of question is that?" I scoffed.

I trusted him with my life. I had no doubts that he would do everything in his power to keep me safe. This was Brodi, my Brodi. He cherished me.

I still couldn't believe he forgave me for lying to him. I knew we were meant to be together. Yes, he had my trust.

"I need all of your trust for this," he said. "If you think you're not ready, I need you to tell me."

I drew my brows in as I looked at him. We had sex already. It was amazing. Every time he touched me, I felt like I came to life.

"Ready for what?"

"The real me," he said with a sexy, dark look in his eyes.

"I'm ready," I breathed on blind faith.

"You're thinking about it. The first time we played." The sound of Brodi's voice brings me back to the present.

"What?"

"I can see it in your body," he says, his eyes training on my nipples.

Goose bumps cover my thighs as his gaze slides down my body. He has always had the power to touch me without touching me.

"Are you ready?" he says when I don't reply.

I blink as those words threaten to throw me back in time. Silently, I turn onto my stomach and take the easy way out. Or at least, I think it's the easy way until his warm oil-covered hands touch my skin.

Gregor

Ten minutes. It takes ten minutes for her body to relax under my touch. Each minute has been like a dagger to the heart. Yet, I haven't stopped.

I refuse to give up, even if this is just a simple task. I push through, showing I'm here to work for what I know is mine. It's torture to be this close, yet so far, but I endure it.

"Hold on," she says softly.

I pause, pulling my hands from under her tank top. She sits up, tugging off her shirt and returns to lying on the bed.

I close my eyes to compose myself. I'm crazy about the freckles that fan across her back on that smooth honey-brown skin. I used to spend hours tracing them with my tongue. What I'd give to have that freedom now.

"Are you okay?"

I open my eyes to find her staring back at me. I nod silently, working my jaw. Reaching for the oil on the bedside table, I pour some more into my palms.

"How is your sister?" I blurt out, searching for a distraction.

I curse under my breath as she stiffens again. I know what she's thinking. I should know how her sister is doing. Clay and I are taking care of her situation as far as Chloe is concerned.

"I mean, tell me about her. She had big dreams when you last told me about her. I want to know more about *her*. I know how much she means to you," I say.

"She's Ally. Super talented, funny, tough, loving," she replies.

"Just like her big sister." I chuckle.

"Not sure about that."

"I am. I still have that painting you did for me. As soon as I could afford it, I got it out of storage. It comes with me everywhere I go," I say as I think of the painting hanging in my office.

"What do you mean, it goes everywhere with you?"

"I move between the offices. My base changes from time to time. When I was here for a stint. It hung in my office here. When I was in London, it hung there. North Carolina, it was the same. I'll be in New York for a while so now it's there," I reply.

"Seriously?"

"Yes, I've actually been offered money for it a time or two. You're talented, baby."

"Someone offering you lunch for my painting off your wall doesn't make me talented." She laughs.

"I've never eaten a half-million-dollar lunch in my life."

She turns over, covering her breasts as she looks at me with wide eyes. I fight not to look away from her face. She searches my eyes for the truth.

"You're kidding me?" she breathes.

"I'm very serious. I think you should consider showing some pieces. I know just the people to invite. You'd clean up."

She starts to chew on her lip while she thinks. I shift to climb off the bed. I lean in to kiss her forehead. Leaving her to her thoughts, I go into the bathroom and start a bath for her.

I grin to myself. I'll call in some favors with some friends. When we get home, Cee can have her first show. It will be something for her to look forward to.

She'd love that. This, I can make happen for her. It's time she lives out her dreams.

CHAPTER TWENTY-TWO

Sorry

Chloe

It's been almost a month and I haven't been out of this hotel for much. I step out of the bedroom dressed in jeans and a T-shirt. I'm thinking about going out to explore today. I want to give myself space to think.

However, I stop in my tracks as Brodi comes into view. He looks like he might be sick as he looks up at me. He's sitting in one of the accent chairs and it looks like he's been running his hands through his hair.

"Everything okay?" I ask cautiously.

He swallows hard and runs his hand through his hair, proving my point. I move to take a seat on the sofa. Something tells me I want to be seated for whatever he's about to say.

He blows out a breath. "I know I'm about to ask for a hell of a lot. I've been trying to avoid this for as long as I can."

"What? What's going on now? Is something wrong with Ally?"

"No, no, everything back home is fine. It's... listen, my daughter is two, she has lost her mother and I'm all she has left. I'm trying here, baby. I really am, but I need to be there for her as much as I want to be here with you.

"If you move into the house, you won't even have to be on the same side of the house as her and my mom. You can take your time getting to know her, them."

I'm speechless. It's clear in his eyes how torn he is about this. I don't have it in me to keep this man from his child, no matter how big an ask this is of me. It's one thing to know his little girl exists, but to see her, to make it real is a pain I'm not sure I'm ready for.

My heart pulses with an ache I don't want to give attention to. I look into his eyes and a new wound starts to open. However, I can't be selfish.

"How long do I have?"

"My mother plans to go out today. You can move in while they're out. I'm so sorry about this."

I hold a hand up. "Don't. I'm not heartless, Brodi. I'll pack my things."

"I'll have someone take care of your art supplies. I've had a studio set up in your wing. You can paint whenever you want."

I stand and head into the room to start packing. I get to the room door when he calls my name. I turn and look into his troubled eyes.

"Thank you."

I only nod as I mentally question myself. I promised him I'd try. Trying means someday I'll have to meet his daughter. As much as that hurts, I suck it up and try to prepare myself for this.

Gregor

"Eric, what was the point of me flying you here to Dubai if you can't handle this?" I snarl into the phone. "I'm trying to move Chloe into my home today."

"I'm sorry, sir. I did all I can do. I tried not to bother you."

I sigh. "I'm on my way back in. Have all the documents ready."

"Yes, sir."

I look up as Cee rolls her suitcase out of the bedroom. My heart sinks for the thousandth time today. Watching the big fat tears in little Chloe's eyes this morning as I stopped by the house before my morning meeting almost broke me.

I know she misses her mother, and I haven't been there like I would like to be. Between work and trying to work things out with the woman I want to marry, I've been stretched thin. Even when I can make it to the house, my daughter is usually asleep or too fussy to spend time with me.

"I'm sorry, baby. I need to run into the office. Mom and Chloe should be gone by the time you arrive at the house. You'll be in the east wing. The staff will get you settled. I'll be there as soon as I put out this fire."

"Wait, I'm going to your home I've never been to before alone. The home your daughter and mother I never met are in," she says with wide eyes.

"Yes, it will be fine. They're going shopping. You can move in, and I'll be there before they arrive."

"Fine." She rolls her eyes and her shoulders sag. "I'll be fine."

I can't for the life of me catch a break. I'm not trying to ruin any chance I have at fixing things with her. However, it seems like the Universe is hell-bent on making me work for this.

"I'll make this up to you. I promise."

She doesn't reply and at this point, I honestly don't expect her to. Words aren't going to mend any of this. I have to go.

I run a hand through my hair and reach into my pocket for the ring she still hasn't placed on her finger. I move over to the seat she's flopped in and kneel before her. I purchased this ring the day after deciding to pursue this route.

"I need one more favor. I need you to wear your engagement ring. Remember, we're doing this for a reason. My father is still holding an engagement over my head."

She frowns but holds out her hand for me to place the ring on her finger. I sigh in relief and slide the ring into place. This is the easiest I've breathed in weeks. The ring looks right there.

I suddenly have new hope. Knowing my ring is on her finger gives me a new determination.

CHAPTER TWENTY-THREE

Hello

Chloe

I've called myself a million different kinds of a fool. Each one attached to a dollar. I don't know what I'm doing. I've questioned if I'm even doing it for the money.

My mind is so jumbled. Everything is happening so quickly. One minute we were in the hotel suite. The next Brodi convinced me to move into his home here in Dubai.

I know I've lost it. I should have stayed right in that suite. However, seeing the distress in his eyes. It tugged at something inside of me.

Apparently, his little girl is having a hard time without her mother or father. I'm not a bitch. I know this has to be hard on her. I was much older than she is when I lost my mom, and it was confusing for me and Ally.

Brodi looked like it was tearing him in two to have to decide who to take care of first. I would never make him choose between us. Which is the only reason I'm here.

The sound of voices heading my way reaches my ears as I try to shuffle through the house with the butler who's carrying my things. The voices are ahead of us. Brodi said I'd be in the east wing away from his mother and daughter.

The problem is, we need to get to that wing. The two were supposed to be out shopping when I arrived. From the sound of the voices, that's definitely a woman and small child.

I grind my teeth wanting to strangle Brodi. He had to run off to handle some business at the last minute. Again, he looked as if he were torn between a rock and a hard place. I told him I'd be fine. Now, I'm not so sure.

A woman and a small girl turn the corner and I lock eyes with little green ones. She's Brodi's. I have no question about that. Her sweet chubby cheeks give her a cherub look.

She runs over to me and wraps around my leg. I'm stunned. She's holding on to me so tightly; you would think she knows me.

"Chloe, honey," the woman says.

"Yes," the little girl and I say in unison.

The little girl's voice comes out in a small whisper as she looks over her shoulder, still clinging to me. I close my eyes. I forgot for just a moment that we share a name. Once again, I don't understand Brodi. Yet, I do.

"Oh, my. You're Chloe. Well, we're going to have to do something about this," the woman says as she purses her lips. She shakes her head. "That son of mine."

"You can call me Cee if that helps," I say the words without thinking.

The woman's eyes light up. She moves forward and pulls me into an embrace. I'm taken aback.

"It's very nice to meet you," she says warmly. "You're more beautiful than my son described. No wonder he's so in love."

I ignore her words as I look down at the ring on my finger. Brodi put it there this morning before he left. It feels like it weighs a ton as I stand here.

My gaze moves to the little girl still holding me tightly. With a shaky hand, I run my fingers through her curls. She looks up at me with sad eyes but gives me a beautiful smile.

"Hello," I say to her. My heart crumbles as I speak.

I have so many emotions warring inside of me. I can't believe this is happening. I'm staring at the child of the man I love. Not the one we were supposed to have together, but the one he had with someone else.

"Hi," she says softly. "Mommy's not here."

"Chloe—" his mother starts.

"It's okay," I murmur, bending to get level with the tiny sad girl.

"I know, sweetie," I say when we're eye to eye.

"No outside. I wanna stay here. Grandma, no outside. We stay here," she says.

"Oh." I nod, sitting on my butt.

She climbs right into my lap. My heart squeezes. I look up at Brodi's mom and she gives me an apologetic smile.

"I stay here with you. Pretty," she says, holding up the doll she has clenched in her tiny hand. With her other hand, she touches my face. "Pretty lady, pretty baby."

My lips part when I look at the doll. She does look like me. She has red hair, brown skin, and hazel eyes. She even has freckles. I can't help but wonder if her father gave it to her.

"She's very pretty," I say. "Like you."

Her little cheeks glow. Her tiny teeth show. My eyes mist over as I feel the boulder that blows through my chest.

"Chloe, sweetie. I think we should let Ms. Cee get settled in," her grandmother says softly to her.

"No, we stay here. We leave, she no be here," she says sadly.

I swipe quickly at my tears. My mother used to always say you don't punish a child for their parents' sins. I hear a child in need. Maybe I need her just as much as she needs me.

Perhaps time with her will fortify my heart against her father, instead of me yearning for him to soothe the pain he caused. I run my fingers through her soft locks. Her eyes bounce between me and her grandmother.

"It's okay. Maybe Chloe can help me get settled into my room. Then we can all take a trip out. I think I'd like some fresh air and to see some sights. I haven't been out much since arriving," I say to his mother.

A smile comes to her face. Those gray eyes searching mine. She's a pretty woman. I can see why her sons are so handsome.

"Fair enough. I think both Chloe and I would like that. I'm Eileen, by the way. Gregor's mother," she says.

"Nice to meet you," I reply.

"Oh no, dear. I'm very happy to finally get to meet you. You have been the source behind my son becoming the man he is, whether you two know it or not," she says.

"I don't know about that."

"Trust me. I do," she says.

Gregor

"Hello, mother. Where are you?" I say into the phone.

"We're doing a little shopping. Why on earth do you sound like the world is coming to an end?"

"Is Chloe with you?" I rush out.

"Ah, I see," she says with a smile in her voice. "Would you be talking about little Chloe or the lovely Cee?"

"Mother," I groan.

"Yes, they are both with me. Cee has taken Chloe to the restroom. I'm watching our things," she says.

"Where are you? I'm on my way," I say as I start for the door.

I couldn't help the panic that rose when I arrived at the house and Chloe was gone. It took my staff informing me that she went out with my mother and daughter to calm me down somewhat.

I've still been ready to tear my hair out. I can't believe they ran into each other. My mother and daughter were supposed to be gone by the time Cee arrived to head to her quarters.

"I don't think that's best. Give her time, Gregor. This hasn't been easy for her. I think you joining us will create more distance than you might want. I've been watching her. She's a very strong woman... but there will always be one's limits," she warns.

I stop in my tracks and crease my brows as I think over her words. What if she's right? I blow out a breath and run my hand through my hair.

"Fine." I nod as if she can see me.

"I love you, son."

"Love you too, Mom," I sigh into the phone.

Chloe

"All better," I say as I look down at Chloe.

She gives me that gorgeous smile and nods. Her curls bounce around her head. She has her father's strawberry-blonde hair.

For the millionth time, I try to breathe through staring at the resemblance. She's such a sweet little girl. As hard as this has been for me to do, she alone has made it possible.

Chloe hasn't left my side since finding me in the hallway earlier. She went from being my little helper to being my shadow. If I want to try something on, she is in the fitting room with me.

"Ice cream now? Please," she asks softly. Her little voice hopeful and so polite.

"Let's ask your grandma, sweetie," I say with a smile.

"There you two are," Eileen says as we return to her and our bags.

"There was a bit of a line. I wasn't sure if we were going to make it," I say and laugh.

Chloe danced at my side as we waited our turn. I felt bad for the poor little thing. I wondered how long she's been potty trained and if she would revert to wetting her pants. A few nice ladies noticed her dancing and allowed us to skip the line.

"I think we may have just made it," I breathe in relief.

"Oh my, I'm glad you did. How about we get that ice cream before we start back for the house?" Eileen says.

Chloe squeezes my hand and nods her head. I look down and she beams up at me as she nods. I return the smile, tickled by the joy I feel emitting from her.

Her arms go up for me to lift her and my heart tightens for the thousandth time. I scoop her up before claiming my bags. Eileen gives me a side-glance. She has warned me about spoiling Chloe more than once today.

"Something tells me you two are right on time for each other," she says as Chloe places her head on my shoulder.

"I think you're right. Thank you for allowing me to come along," I reply.

"It has been a pleasure getting to know you. It has also been a few weeks since I've had this much adult interaction. I should be thanking you."

"This must have been a shock for you," I say, drawing my brows.

I was shocked when it set in that Brodi had been hiding his daughter from everyone. His mother being here to help him says a lot about a mother's love. It makes me ache for my own.

"You have no idea. I wanted to strangle that Brodi," she huffs.

I smile. I noticed that she calls him Brodi when she seems to think more affectionately toward him. She may be annoyed with him, but it's clear she still loves her son.

"I know the feeling," I reply.

"Ah, yes, I believe you may have tried to make good on that," she says, side-glancing me.

My cheeks heat. I bow my head. I did feel bad about the bruises on Brodi's face after the fact. Tears well as I think of all the emotions I felt in that moment.

"I don't know what to do. A part of me... a part I've tried to bury away loves that man so much. Another part of me—" I cut the words off.

I probably shouldn't be having this conversation with his mother. I just need to have it with someone before it consumes me. This isn't something I want to dump on Sid from long distance over the phone.

"Love is an interesting thing. It can bind you to a soul without your permission. My husband and I went through something like what you and my son are going through.

"There was a time I didn't think I'd ever forgive him. Eventually, we both learned we're better together than without each other," she says.

"Respectfully, I don't think that's going to happen for us," I say softly.

I regret the words the moment they're out of my mouth. I'm skating a dangerously thin line. I'm supposed to make this woman believe we're getting married.

"I said the same thing. Yet here I am thirty-eight years later. Married to one of the most stubborn men in the world," she says and laughs.

I smile and look down at a sleeping Chloe.

"Oh, wow. That was fast. Can we get some of that ice cream to go?"

"I've already called ahead to the kitchen staff. I had a feeling her nap was going to win out soon," she says with a smile.

"Right."

I should have seen it too. Just like I should have noticed sooner that we should have gone to the bathroom before Chloe mentioned it. All things I would have known to think of....

"Cee, I don't think I learned to read a toddler as well as I do now until Clay turned her age. You've only been with her for a few hours," Eileen says as if she has read my mind.

I nod, still feeling the sting. I should have more experience. That's the part that hurts.

I swallow hard and follow Eileen to our ride back to the house. I get lost in my conflicting thoughts as we travel in the SUV.

Gregor

I know there was no way to keep them separated forever, but I wanted Cee to have time to adjust. My stomach is in knots. I don't know what to expect when they return.

I'm ready to wrap Cee in all the love she needs. As soon as we fix things between us, I want to try for a child of our own. It won't make up for the one we lost… the one she had to make such a difficult choice with.

"Gregor." My mother's voice pulls me from my pained thoughts.

"*Daddy*," Chloe sings with her little voice.

She rushes to me, and I lift her into my arms, raining kisses all over her cheeks. She looks happy. Happier than this morning when I dropped in before my meeting.

I look over her head to see Cee watching us. The sadness that's in her eyes tears a hole in me that threatens to cause me to bleed out. I step forward and she takes a step back, halting my advance.

"Thank you, Eileen. I had a lovely day. The retail therapy went a long way. It was nice getting to know you," she says.

"Yes, indeed it was. Thank you again for joining us," my mother replies.

"I'm going to call it a night. I'm suddenly not feeling well," Cee murmurs.

"I'll come with you," I say before thinking.

"No, thank you," she says emotionlessly.

My jaw works but I don't reply. I watch as she turns and walks away without a single glance back. Releasing a breath, I lift a hand to run through my hair.

"Daddy," Chloe coos, placing a hand on my jaw.

I look at my daughter and give her a tight smile. At least one Chloe will talk to me. I kiss my daughter's forehead.

"You ask a lot of a woman who loves you with the very depths of her soul," my mother says, pulling my attention.

"I don't know what I'm doing," I reply, swallowing hard with the admission.

"I wish I had answers for you. After spending the day with that young lady, I can see you have your work cut out for you. As a mother, I can only imagine what's going on in her head," she says, tilting her head to look at my little girl in my arms.

"Your one saving grace may be the little angel that's rubbing her raw. I can't explain it. I thought she…" She clamps her mouth shut. "Be patient, Gregor. You boys have never been patient."

I nod as I let her words sink in. I'll be as patient as six months will allow. At least I'll try.

"Come, let's get cleaned up for dinner," my mother says as she takes her granddaughter in her arms.

I watch my mother with Chloe in her hold. I knit my brows as her words play in my head. I would never try to use my child to get my woman back. Especially for the exact reason my mother mentioned.

This is going to rub her raw.

I'll find a way. I have to find a way. If I can't reconcile this relationship… that's not an option. It's a must. I'll find a way.

God, help me.

CHAPTER TWENTY-FOUR

Time to Heal

Chloe

"You look gorgeous," Brodi murmurs against my skin before kissing my temple. He runs his hand down my bare back, then pulls my chair so I can sit.

I inhale deeply and regret it. His cologne fills my head and it's like a punch to the gut. As if sensing I'm ready to fall apart right where I sit, he reaches for the back of my neck and massages it gently before he moves to take his seat across from me.

Goose bumps cover my skin. I try not to look at him until I can get my racing heart under control. I'm having a hard time keeping a lid on my emotions. This is our first date since moving into the house with little Chloe and his mom.

Old feelings have suffered as I see hints of the man I once fell in love with. I chide myself. That's the man I can't fall for again. I have zero ability to trust him.

"Did you enjoy the concert?"

I take a sip from my glass of water. It gives me a moment to compose myself, so I don't gush over the concert he surprised me with.

"It was nice," I say as calmly as I can. "I didn't know she would be performing here."

He took me to see one of my favorite artists. Ash has a sex sound that draws you into her music. I'm not going to lie, her sultry lyrics and sensual vibe didn't help much as I sat next to Brodi with all that sexual energy he always gives off without even trying. I'm going to order a vibrator as soon as we get back to the house.

Maybe that will help me keep my head. My heart and my body have two different ideas of what should be going on here. He gives me a crooked grin, proving my point.

"She wasn't. I pulled some strings. She's a friend of a friend. I was able to get her to detour and come this way for one night."

I force my mouth to remain closed, but I'm impressed. I only mentioned that I was a fan a few days ago. He's pulling out the big guns.

I see you, Brodi.

Yet I'm not going to give in that easily. It's going to take more than a concert for me to forgive this man. Still, slowly I'm starting to peek through the blinds to see who he has become.

"You seem different," I blurt out.

"I am. That's what I want you to see. I was a boy when we were together. I may have been older, but I lacked the wisdom to control my own life. I should have done a lot differently."

"Um," I say as the waiter arrives. "I want to try the saffron chicken in wine sauce. That looks good."

"I'll have the same," he says and closes the menu.

I'm surprised. I expected him to go with the seafood. I tilt my head and watch him closer. I guess people can change, but can they change enough to make you forget such a painful past?

He narrows his eyes at me. "I'll tell you something I learned," he says, breaking into my thoughts.

"What's that?"

"To get to the things you want most in life, you have to be willing to adapt."

"But you have to want it to be willing to adapt, don't you think?" I counter.

He licks his lips. "Tell me you don't remember how good we are together. Remember that one time, you couldn't even walk from my bedroom, nonetheless my apartment?"

I remember that day very well. So well, I fist my hands in the table linen. The way he made love to me made me believe in him, in us.

He paid attention to every nuance of the vibes I gave off. My breathing, the way my skin changed under his touch or lack of. All while explaining it in detail to me and why he responded in turn to each change.

I lick my own lips. "The way you made me feel back then isn't the issue here. The results of days and hours like that one are."

The sexy look in his eyes fades. He looks down at the table as if searching for his next words. When he looks back up, the determination in his gaze makes me want to stand and run.

He reaches for my hand and links his fingers with mine. While staring deep into my eyes, he makes circles in my palm with his thumb.

"A part of learning to adapt is knowing when to move forward. I'm asking you to take these steps with me. I can't mend what I've broken if you continue to point at the smoking gun in my hand."

"I'm not the one who pulled the trigger. You did, you killed me and left the body."

He swallows hard and tightens his finger against mine. "And then turned around and fell on my own sword and have been bleeding out since. Baby, I'm trying to stitch us both back together."

I blink back the tears and drop my eyes to the table. "I know," I say through trembling lips. "I know, but I need you to understand this will take time. And even then, I can't promise I'll get there."

He closes his eyes and nods. When he opens them again, he brings our joined hands to his lips. I bite down on my lip, closing my eyes as I try to breathe.

"I love you, Chloe. I'll walk through fire to get to you. I'm not giving up on us."

I say nothing, because a part of me wants him to make good on that promise, while another part of me is deathly afraid he will. One of the ribbons tied around my heart loosens and floats away, taking with it my tight hold on the resentment I have.

Gregor

I stand with one leg crossed over the other as I lean in the threshold of the living area of my Dubai home. I have a glass of brandy in my hand as I watch Cee with my daughter in her lap. Her bare back is exposed in the black dress she's wearing, I've admired the view all night, every chance I got, but that's not what has me mesmerized at the moment.

What has my attention is how Cee has opened her heart to my small human, the reminder of what we've lost. The sight both warms my heart and fills me with so much anger and sorrow. I wish I could remember that night.

If I could remember the moment I consciously decided to betray my soul, I'd take accountability for my choice and man up to step away from Chloe once and for all. However, I don't remember and that's killing me as I stand here.

It's taking everything in me not to demand Cee forgive me so we can move to the next phase of our lives. The part where I make love to her, and we create a new life to love together and cherish.

I look down into my glass. Nothing can replace the life we lost. I don't think there will be a time when I forgive myself for what Cee had to do.

"Daddy, play with us," Chloe squeals as she looks over Cee's shoulder.

When we returned from our date, Chloe was still wide awake. She ran straight for Cee and dragged her to sit and play with her and her dolls. I give a tight grin as Cee's shoulders stiffen.

Yet the dominant part of me who wants to claim what's his forces my feet to move. I took my shoes and socks off before pouring myself a drink. Now I pad barefoot over to the two loves of my life.

Cee looks up at me. So many emotions swim in her eyes. I lower to sit behind her, caging her and Chloe between my legs. I can't help myself. The pull is there.

I wrap my arms around Cee and hold her against my chest. Placing a kiss on the top of her head, I then rest my chin on the spot I kissed as I sway with her in my arms.

I close my eyes when she sinks into me, and her body relaxes. I open my eyes when I feel Chloe's tiny arms reach between us to go around Cee's neck. I release a relieved breath because this feels right. For the first time since the plane landed in Dubai, I breathe freely. I have my world in my arms.

"Trust me," I whisper.

I think that's the last straw because Cee's body starts to shake, and she breaks down sobbing. I tighten my hold and keep rocking.

"I love you, baby. I love you so much," I breathe the words like a promise to heal all I've broken.

CHAPTER TWENTY-FIVE

Small Friends

Chloe

"Cee, *Ceeee*," Chloe sings in the hallway.

I smile at the canvas I'm working on. This is the second day she's gotten away from her grandmother to come looking for me. I place my brush down and wipe my hands on a towel. I'll get back to this later.

I move to the door of the studio Brodi gave me and find Chloe sticking her head in one of the rooms up the hallway. "Ceeee," she sings.

I watch as she comes back out of the room with a pout on her little face. That is until she looks up to find me watching her. She runs forward on her little chubby legs and holds her arms up to me. I smile down at her and bend to lift her into my arms.

"Hey, you. Where's your grandma?"

"No grandma. Want you to play with me."

"Okay, we can play, but I think your grandma will be upset if she can't find you. How'd you get away again anyway?"

"Grandma nap."

I chuckle. "Oh, I see. Well, maybe we should let her rest. We can have a tea party in your playroom. She'll find us easily there."

She claps her little hands. "Party. Tea. Cee play with me."

I kiss her little cheek. "Yes, sweetheart. I'll play with you."

My heart can't help but melt as I look into her sparkling green eyes. The other night while I broke down in Brodi's arms, she fell asleep in mine. Not a care in the world.

I wish I could ignore the pain the way she can. Each day I wake and mentally check to see if this will be the day the hurt stops. That day hasn't come yet.

"Oh, thank God. There you are," Eileen says. She looks like she was in a panic before finding us.

"She's a quick one," I tease.

"Yes, she is. I only dozed off for a second. I'll take her out of your hair. I'm so sorry."

"She's not a bother. We were about to go have a tea party in the playroom. Want to join us?"

"I'd love to."

I smile and place Chloe back on her feet. She reaches for my hand right away. I still get the feeling she thinks I'm going to disappear on her. I give her little hand a gentle squeeze.

She looks up at me with a bright smile. "My Cee," she coos.

"It looks like you have a friend for life," Eileen says.

"I believe so."

"You know, when Gregor told me he wanted to bring you here, I wasn't sure it was the best idea. You're a bigger woman than I am. I still regret not being able to open my home and heart to Clooney's other son."

I stumble a little at her words. I'm speechless. What exactly do you say to something like that?

"Oh, dear. I didn't mean to dump that on you. Do you mind keeping this between us? The boys still don't know they have a brother."

"Of course, your secret is safe with me."

"It's not my secret, but my husband's. He wants to be the one to tell them. However, it's taken him all these years because of me. Clooney walks on eggshells when it comes to his son and me.

"Watching you, I see it shouldn't be that way. I guess I never had to face that the boy needed a mother figure. He had—" she cuts off. "Listen to me. I'm sure you don't want to hear this."

I want to tell her that I do. I'm nosy and this is some Maury shit, I wasn't expecting from this prim and proper woman. I get lost in my thoughts as we enter the playroom and set up for tea.

Of all the things I'm still hurt and angry about, I don't think I can place Chloe on that list. I don't know when it happened, but this little girl has stolen my heart. I want to see her happy. If I can fill a void for her, I'm here.

"I'll have them bring us some finger food. We can have lunch while we're at it," Eileen says, breaking into my musing.

"Sounds good. I've worked up an appetite."

"I'm sure you have. How's the painting coming along?"

"It's doing. The love is still there. I think that's the biggest thing I was worried about when I stood before the first canvas. I was afraid I lost the love."

"Um," Eileen hums. "Sounds familiar."

My cheeks heat but I don't want to dig into her words or go down that road. Instead, I take a seat at this little round table in the center of the playroom. My thoughts go to finding Brodi in here a few days ago, sitting with Chloe as they had their own tea party.

She was so happy to have the attention. Yeah, this little girl needs a friend more than I need to hold a grudge I shouldn't have against her. As I take a seat at the tiny table and Chloe climbs into my lap instead of sitting in her own chair, I know I'll be here for her as long as she needs.

She's not her father and his choices. She's a baby in need of love and comfort. I can relate.

"You will make a wonderful mother," Eileen says a few hours later as we wrap up our tea party. Chloe is now asleep in my arms.

Tears fill my eyes, but I hold them in. I give her a nod as words won't come. She rubs a hand up and down my arm before she takes Chloe so she can place her in her room.

I go to my studio, close the door and slide down it to the floor, landing on my butt. I pull my knees into my chest and start to sob. To be a mother, I have to have a partner I trust. Since I can't seem to allow anyone else in, I either need to find a way to forgive Brodi or give up on ever being a mom.

"Mommy, I wish you were here. I don't know what to do. I'm so scared," I cry, feeling like a lost child.

CHAPTER TWENTY-SIX

Off The List

Gregor

It's been a long day. I'm waiting on one more call before I head home. Clay needs to check in and update me on what's going on back home.

I sit in the sitting area of my office in the accent chair with a tumbler in my hand. I take a sip as I stare off into space. My thoughts go to Cee. She looked beautiful this morning. She had on one of my T-shirts that's now paint splattered. It hung off her shoulder, revealing her freckle-covered skin.

It made me think of the time she did a striptease for me. I run my tongue over my teeth and push a hand through my hair. My cock swells with the memory.

We'd watched that Fifty Shades of Grey *movie and she was all excited because we'd played a few times and she understood the difference between the movie and the life.*

Chloe turned on one of the songs from the soundtrack of the movie, "Earned It" I think it was. She then stood before me in patent leather heels and one of my shirts hanging off her shoulder. I sat in an accent chair, a glass in hand as I kept my eyes on her.

She turned her back to me and bent at the waist as she reached beneath the shirt and peeled her panties down her long legs. I slumped down in my chair and took a sip of my brandy, narrowing my eyes as her pussy lips glistened back at me.

Slowly she lifted the panties and tossed them back to me. I caught them in one hand and brought them to my nose, inhaling deeply. A grin came to my lips.

"You smell like heaven, baby. Come here."

She turned and gave me a bright smile. Before making her way to me, she reached for the hem of the T-shirt and slowly tugged it up. With a wicked smile on her lips, she peeled the shirt over her head and tossed it.

I remained in place, waiting for her to obey my command. She started for me, rolling and rocking her hips. I downed the rest of my drink and set the glass aside.

Chloe stopped and beckoned me forward with her finger. For her, I broke my rules. I slid to the floor and crawled my way to her. Once I stopped in front of her, I lifted her onto my shoulders and buried my face in her core. She cried out my name and locked her fingers in my hair.

I groaned into her as I devoured her heat. Slowly, I stood with her legs locked around my head and shoulders. A gasp left her lips.

"Brodi, oh, God, babe. Just like that," she cooed as she rode my face, her legs locked tightly around my neck.

I moved us to my bedroom and dropped her onto my bed. She tried to crawl back away from me as I wiped my mouth and looked her in her eyes.

"Don't run now. You wanted my attention. You have it, baby. I'm going to fuck you senseless then pamper you so I can do it all over again," I crooned as I stripped down.

My phone rings, pulling me from the memory. I bite my lip and squeeze my erection. The ghost of her hot, wet pussy around me feels so real in this moment. I down the glass of brandy in my hand and clear my throat to answer the call.

"Hey, Clay. What you have for me?"

"We can scratch Dad off the list. I don't think this is him. He proved he has no malice toward Sid. He's taken to her, and he shut all that legal shit down where she's concerned. That leaves Wade and Dupont."

"You still think they're working together?"

"They have to be. I don't get the connection if they're not." He sighs. "Vault is still looking into it. Some of the other Lost Souls have gotten involved."

"So we're back to owing Spider favors?"

"No, this is all going through King. Listen, I'm stretched thin. I need the help this time."

"I'm not saying anything. Only asking questions. What's going on with the Ally situation?"

He releases a heavy breath. "She and Cane are still hiding something. Once I know what, this might be easier for me to handle. Still can't give you more than that over the phone."

"Okay."

"Listen, can you have Chloe call Sid? She's worried about her."

"I'll talk to her and have her call tomorrow."

"Thanks. You sound exhausted."

"I am."

"What's up with you? When are you heading back?"

"I still have some shit I need to handle here. I'll head back once I get it all straightened out."

I still haven't told my brothers about my daughter. There are still so many questions. No one has found Addison's friend from the hospital. Against my better judgment, I'm still trying to find out what happened that night Chloe was conceived. I know I should give up, but I can't.

"I'm here if you need me. Get some rest. You think clearer with a fresh mind."

"Yeah, I know. Good night."

CHAPTER TWENTY-SEVEN

I'm Okay

Chloe

Sitting here on the bed in my room, I want to punch something. I hang up the phone, still frustrated with my little sister. She's always too busy to talk and can't give me a straight answer about anything.

With the time zone difference, it's been frustrating as hell trying to reach someone at her school to get some real answers. No one is ever available when I do sync up with their office hours. I want to go into mom mode, but Ally is a twenty-two-year-old woman.

It's hard to let go of the control and the responsibility I've had for so long, especially when I know she's lying to me. I growl and punch the bed. It does nothing to soothe the burning in my chest.

I sigh. Brodi keeps telling me to give things time. Speaking of Brodi, he mentioned Sid being worried about me. I feel like shit for not returning her calls and texts.

It's just Sid is my best friend. She knows me too well and I'm barely holding on to my emotions as it is. I'm trying to balance the feelings I think I should have versed the ones I want to have.

I know, crazy, right? My first mind keeps telling me to pack my things and go. Forget the money, forget all this drama, and save my sanity.

However, there's the other voice in my head telling me to give him a chance to fix this. I roll my eyes before the tears start and dial Sid. It's now or never.

"Hello."

I suck in a breath as I hear the panic in her voice. She doesn't deserve this. I close my eyes and wrap an arm around my middle.

"Hey. What's up, Sid?"

"Oh my God. Are you okay? Where are you? Clay said you're in Dubai. Is that true?"

"I'm fine. Yes. I've been here since the day after we went to that club."

I then mumble to myself, "Biggest mistake of my life."

"Is he treating you okay?"

Is Brodi treating me okay? He pampers me and waits on me hand and foot. He's ten times more tentative than he used to be. However, he's left once before after giving me the world. I still don't have it in me to trust it.

"Yeah, he's treating me well," I reply. "But forget about me. How are things with Clayton? I didn't miss you called him Clay."

I fall back on the bed and stare up at the ceiling. God, we've come a long way from the projects in Brooklyn. I had always dreamed of traveling to places like Dubai. When I met Brodi, I fantasized about all the places we would go. Now I'm here and it's so bittersweet.

"He's… um… things are good, I guess. As good as they can be under the circumstances."

"*Owww*," I squeal. "He's knocking the dust off that pussy, isn't he? Go, Sid."

I truly am happy for her. I want to see her with someone who treats her well. If Clay treats her half as well as Brodi treated me once and sticks to it, she deserves it and more.

"Maybe." She laughs into the phone. "Listen, I'm so happy to hear from you, but we're getting ready to board a flight. We'll be in Georgia for a bit."

"You in Georgia?" I snort.

"Yeah, I'm going to start my novel while there. I'm excited."

"That's great. Oh my God. You've dreamed of this for so long. I'm so proud of you."

"Thanks. Chloe, please stop ignoring my texts, I'm worried about you. You're sure you're fine?"

"Yeah, I'm cool. Listen, there's a lot going on here. So if I don't call, I'll text or something."

"Please."

"I'll reply even if it's an emoji. I don't have a sex blog to add to my million. I don't want to use it all on long-distance-and-roaming charges and shit," I tease.

She snorts. "Whatever. Just check in every once in a while. Love you."

"I love you too."

I hang up and continue to stare up at the ceiling. I smile. She sounds happy.

After all Sid has given up for me and Ally, I want this for her. If she knew the Hennessy men like I do, she'd know that no matter what, Clay's never going to fully be out of her system. I saw the looks he gave her.

"Good luck. I hope he stays," I whisper.

CHAPTER TWENTY-EIGHT

Chipping Armor

Chloe

We've been Jet Skiing, on a helicopter ride with the most majestic views, observed the views from Burj Khalifa, had dinner at the Burj Al Arab and dined like royalty. I could go on and on about the romantic dates Brodi has taken me on. With each one he's been needling his way in, chipping away at the icy pain surrounding my heart.

However, this date, this one might be my favorite. A cruise through the Dubai Creek. Dinner and dancing, I've loved this date because it's the core of who we used to be.

Slowly, I've allowed myself to remember how easy it used to be. For one night, I don't want to hurt. I've shut off the pain to be in the moment and I've laughed and smiled more than I have in years.

I look up into Brodi's eyes and the genuine smile on his face tugs me in. I think the fact that the music is native and neutral aids to pull us both into the moment.

"How's the painting going? Have you thought about a theme?"

"It's going well. I don't know. I'm pretty much painting my feelings."

"I want you to meet with Eric. He's going to coordinate for your showings."

"My showings? What showings?"

"I told you I have friends who love your work. When we return home, I have a friend with a gallery in Alphabet City. You can start there and then move to Soho where another friend of mine has a bigger gallery."

I look up at him with my mouth hanging open. This is the first I'm hearing of this. I don't know whether to hug him or fuss at him for not telling me sooner.

Tears fill my eyes. "Thank you."

"For what?"

I shrug. "Sid has numbers and now her writing. Ally has her flute. I've never had anything of my own to pursue. Or it least it felt that way. I almost forgot how much I love to paint. Now, I have a chance to see if I can make something of it. Thank you."

He leans in and places his lips to my temple. I close my eyes and absorb him. My entire being hums from the connection. A shiver runs through me. I might be allowing him in more than I intended to.

He's chipping at my armor, and I don't know if I have it in me to hold him back. His breath fans my lips, causing me to hold my breath in anticipation. I guide my hands up his chest and link my fingers behind his neck.

However, the kiss never comes. I knit my brows in confusion.

Gregor

I'm so close to having the one thing I long for. Her lips are so close to mine, I can almost taste her. Yet, something feels so wrong.

"Chlo," I whisper as she trembles in my hold.

It's going to kill me to do this, but I know she's not ready. I can read it in her body. She's still terrified of taking this next step. As much as I want this kiss, I want her with me when it happens.

My first thought is to kiss her into submission, but that goes against all my rules of trust and care for my woman. That's not what Chloe needs. This time I'm putting her first.

When she opens her eyes, I see a mix of fear and hurt. Just like that, I'm losing her again. We were having such a good time. I thought I would finally reach her tonight. The connection was there. Her eyes said she was open.

Yet the trembling in her body tells me all I need to know. I'll always go with what I know when it comes to her needs. However, now she's slipping right through my fingers once again. My need for control bucks up against my understanding of her fragility. I ache to the depths of my soul for the hurt I've caused.

"If I could turn back time, I'd make this all right again," I murmur.

"But that's the thing. You can't do that. You told me I could always trust you, but I couldn't. You left me. You broke my heart when you said you wouldn't."

That burns because it's the truth. When I told her that I believed we could find a way to make it work. I'd planned to take her with me.

I work my jaw, loathing myself. This wariness is my doing. I offer her the only thing I know for sure.

"I love you, Chloe. I'm so sorry. Know that I do love you."

I release her and go out to the deck to clear my head. This is starting to feel more impossible with each day. I may have lost her forever.

Never, you're no quitter.

CHAPTER TWENTY-NINE

Missed Steps

Chloe

Another night, another date. Once again, dinner was amazing, as it has been on the last few dates we've been on. I'm reluctant each time Brodi comes to sweep me off my feet, but I also know this is what I told him to do. To work for my heart if that's what he truly wants.

Yet, my emotional and mental states are as conflicted as ever about cracking open the door. Perhaps I should've placed a lock and dead bolt on it because Brodi seems to be pushing it open no matter what I think I want.

"Have I told you how beautiful you are this evening?" His velvety voice pulls me from my thoughts.

He reaches to stretch and twirl a lock of hair around his finger. I'd spent hours trying to flat iron it, but I couldn't get it anywhere near as immaculate as my girl back home. In the end, I wet it down with water and conditioner and let my curls spring back to life.

"You've said it a few times," I reply.

"I like your hair better this way. It's like you. It looks one way to the eye but reveals so much more to the touch," he says.

His words tug at something deep within. Our eyes lock and I can tell he wants to lean in for a kiss. I haven't allowed things to go that far.

I've been doing a better job of keeping my wits about me. At least, I'm trying my best to do better at keeping my wits about me. The smoldering look in his gray eyes at the moment threatens all my sanity. I force myself to turn away from him and the energy swirling between us.

"Where are you taking me?" I ask as I look out the window of the SUV.

"I thought we could take a stroll," he replies as we come to a stop.

Brodi opens his door to step out, reaching back in to help me exit the vehicle as well. The first thing to assault my senses is the ocean air. The saltiness settles on my tongue and burns my nostrils.

My wild curls whip around my face. I can't help the smile that comes to my lips as I remember our trip to Rockaway Beach— what seems like forever ago. It was a summer night, but the breeze off the ocean and bay made the night cool.

Brodi had taken off his shirt to cover me as we walked the shore. I still remember that night because it was the first time he told me he loved me. I look out at the water and wonder if he thought of that night before bringing me here. It's a night I haven't allowed myself to think about in such a long time.

"You remember, don't you?" he says, calling me out of my thoughts.

"Remember what?" I feign ignorance, not turning for him to look into my eyes.

He pinches my chin and turns my face to him, causing my gaze to lift to his. There's a softness to his eyes that I'm not expecting. It pulls at my heart. Another ribbon floats from around it up into the sky.

I'm deathly afraid that when all the fibers holding my heart together fall away, they'll reveal a bleeding heart that can't be repaired. As if reading my mind, Brodi places his free hand over my chest. I allow my lids to fall closed as his lips touch my forehead.

"I meant it then and I mean it now. I love you, Cee. My heart will forever belong to you," he says against my skin.

I nod, as it's all I can do not to fall apart right here. Seemingly sensing my need for a reprieve, Brodi starts to take his shoes off. He holds my hand to steady me so I can do the same.

Handing our shoes to Ethan, he then wraps an arm around me and leads us onto the sand. We walk along the shoreline in silence.

Even though I know his security surrounds us, I feel like we're the only ones around. I don't know when it happens, but I let my guard down. I lean into his warmth and rest my head on his chest as we walk.

More memories flood me. The memories of all of the things that led me to fall for him. The safe moments in our past.

"I've dreamed of walking out here with you a million times before. I'd come out here to think and thoughts of you would fill my head," he says into the silence.

I don't reply. I want to enjoy the moment a little longer, not think about the reasons he had to think about me instead of being with me. The breeze blows my dress around my legs as the water kisses my toes. These are the things I allow to ground me.

"I'd dream of our wedding day. Right on a beach like this. You walking toward me, taking my breath away," he continues.

"A man can dream, right?" I snort cynically.

"Yes, he can and if he's determined enough, he'll make that dream come true," he replies.

"That's some determination."

"You have no idea."

"Um."

We fall into silence once more. After a few feet, he stops, turning toward me. I look up into his eyes as he crowds my space. My heart starts to race, I know the look in his eyes.

His gaze drops to my lips. His arms band around my waist. I hold my breath.

"Cee?"

"Yes," I whisper.

"I miss you. Are you ready for me to kiss you?"

"No." The word slips out so easily.

It's the truth. I'm not there yet. These dates have been sweet, and I'll admit they're chipping away at the steel and ice, but I'm not ready.

He nods. His eyes lift to mine. His jaw works as he presses his forehead to mine.

"Then dance with me," he says gently.

"Okay."

This I can do. I close my eyes. Allowing him to dance us around the wet sand beneath our feet to whatever tune is playing in his head, I relax. It's actually just what I need.

I'm lost in the comfort of his arms. This is dangerous, but it's what I need.

Gregor

She looks so beautiful tonight. It seems like she's becoming more gorgeous by the day. I want to kiss her so badly, but I won't push her if she's not ready.

Tonight has been one of those nights where she's been more open than not. However, I still feel like I'm walking on eggshells. From moment to moment, I don't know which Chloe I'll get.

Still, right now—as I dance her in my arms—this has been the closest I've felt to her yet. It's like time and space stills. We are one as the water laps at our feet. I savor the feeling of having her so near.

I don't know how long we dance in circles before a grin takes over my face. I dip to wrap my arms around her thighs and lift her over my shoulder. In the next instant, I'm running into the water like a teenage boy.

Cee squeals and beats at my back, but her laughter rings out as I enter the water. It's a joyous sound. Nothing in the world can touch my heart the same way.

Allowing her body to slide down my front, I lock eyes with her as she stands before me. Her lips are turned up into a genuine smile. She reaches down to splash water up at me. I laugh and return the gesture.

"You're going to pay for this." She laughs.

"To hear that laughter come from you, gladly," I croon back.

She lifts a brow just before trying to take me by surprise. She would have too if I didn't know her so well. I anticipate her right before she tries to push me back into the water.

I wrap my arms around her, pulling her down with me. We both go under. When we surface at the same time, she has a scowl on her face, but the mirth in her eyes tells me she's not too angry with me.

"I can wash your hair for you when we get back," I tease.

She looks away. Once again, I've forgotten how much things have changed between us. It was something I would have done with no question in the past. Reaching to brush her hair out of her face, I look into her eyes.

"I can pamper you anytime you want without it turning sexual. I care for you. Which means I'm always here to take care of you," I say.

I see in her eyes when my words take a wrong turn. I curse myself in my head. Eggshells. I'm always walking on eggshells.

"Now... I'm always here from now on. Now until forever, baby," I say before she can hurl harsh words at me.

She wraps her arms around her middle and her teeth start to chatter. I sigh. I think we're done here for the night. One step forward, two steps back. I'm still learning this dance, but I don't intend to give up on it.

One day at a time, Gregor. One day at a time.

CHAPTER THIRTY

Patience

Gregor

"You really don't have to do this," I say as I hand Chloe over to Cee.

"It's fine. We're going to have a pajama party, watch a few movies, and play with dolls."

I look at the two dressed in pajamas and want to stay home and join them. They look adorable. Chloe wraps her arms around Cee's neck and gives her a tight squeeze.

"I could always bring someone in to stay with her. You're more than welcome to come with us to dinner."

"I think your mother is looking forward to dinner with just the two of you. We'll be fine here. I'm excited for our playdate. You enjoy yourself."

I want to tug her into my chest and kiss her, but I hold back. Cee has made my little girl so happy over the last four weeks. The two are always together when I arrive home or when I come out of my home office when I work from home.

"Okay, dear, I'm ready," my mother sings as she meets us in the foyer.

I look at Cee and Chloe one more time before turning to leave. The way Chloe beams up at her says a million words. I know the feeling, I'm in awe of this woman too.

"If you need us to come back, just give me a call. Ethan will be here with you."

"Shouldn't he be with you? We're in no danger here watching TV and playing with dolls."

"He'll be with everything I hold dear in this world, right where he needs to be. Mother and I will have enough manpower with us."

Cee's cheeks glow with color and she looks down. It's the truth. These two are my world. If anything happened to either of them, I don't know how I would move on with my life.

"Have fun, girls," my mother says as she wraps her arm around the one I offer.

I lead her out to the car feeling like I've left a part of me behind. I'm silent the entire ride to the restaurant. It's someplace my mother heard of and wanted to try.

***

"You know what's most important, Gregor?"

I look up from my plate at my mother. She's watching me closely. I wipe my mouth and give her my full attention. I've been a bit distant throughout dinner. My mind is back at the house with the two loves of my life.

"Sorry, what did you say?"

"I said, do you know what's most important?"

"No, what's that?"

"You haven't given up. When your father and I were having trouble, it was his persistence that won me over. I'd pushed him away and filed for divorce, but I still loved him.

"I made the mistake of allowing him to see that. From that moment, he fought with everything he had to make things right between us."

"It's funny. I don't remember you two ever showing that you weren't in love. Despite how harsh he was with us. You always stood by him."

"You were only a few months old when we first separated." She takes a pause and purses her lips. "You boys think your father is so hard on you. He truly does it all out of love. I think that's what made me want the divorce in the first place. Unlike you, your father had no patience for the grief I was going through.

"He saw a healthy baby boy and wanted another. I mourned the loss of having you in my womb. I saw it as betrayal of our bond to have another. Clooney didn't understand any of that and used his high hand to force me into snapping out of it."

She shakes her head. "The mistakes we made. I think you're doing the right thing being patient with Cee. Don't give up."

I snort. "I won't, but I'm starting to question my sanity. I know how determined she can be. If she doesn't want to forgive me, she won't."

Mom places her fork and knife down. "Gregor, if she didn't want to forgive you, she wouldn't be here. Trust is a fragile thing. When it's lost, it's a hell of a long road back to building it again."

"I annihilated ours."

"Yes, that you did. Stay the course, son. You'll find your way back. I don't believe all is lost."

I blow out a breath and pull a hand down my face. My thoughts race. I lift my hand to order another drink.

"And, Brodi?"

"Yes, Mother."

"Not to rush you, but you will need to fix this before you go home and your father finds out about her. He'll see right through all of this." She sighs. "I told him to leave you boys alone. I hope Clay isn't playing the same game you are. I want more grandchildren and daughters-in-law. I do believe Sidney is stalling on buying her wedding gown because you boys have concocted a way to lock horns with your father."

I look at my mother and give her a mischievous smile. She snorts and gives me a pointed look.

"You do know he always wins. You boys will learn one of these days." She eyes me as she laughs.

Somehow, I believe her. The old bastard is going to figure out a way to beat us all in this. I shake my head and grind my teeth.

Was it all for nothing?

Chloe

"Hey, your buddy bail on you?" Ethan says as I walk into the kitchen.

He sits with his phone and a bowl of cereal. I'm so used to him standing silently, I'm surprised by his words. I give him a warm smile as I pour a glass of water.

I take him in and note that while very handsome, he's not my type. My type has and will always be strawberry-blond hair, gray eyes, and six-four.

"Yeah, she fell asleep on me. Didn't even make the end of *Frozen*," I reply with a laugh.

He chuckles. "She's a sweet kid."

"That she is."

He stares at me for a moment. I feel like he's looking through me. It's as if he wants to say something more but isn't sure he should. I go to take the seat next to him at the kitchen island.

"He's trying, you know?" he finally says.

"I get that. I want to open up, but it's hard. I've forgiven him once before and he left me again."

He nods. "I was the one who told him about your age the first time around. I felt like shit after. He was totally destroyed, but I had to protect him. Things could have turned out so much worse."

"I've always had his back." He takes a pause and swallows hard. I feel an exception in there somewhere.

"Except?"

"Addison," he says.

"Chloe's mother?"

"Yeah, I wasn't there that night. You mean so much to him. He never wanted kids with anyone but you. He was so sure she was lying. I thought so too. Now, I... no one knows what to believe.

"My sister died. He let me go home. I failed him. Now seeing how much you two are hurting, I wish I had waited at least until someone I trusted could step in for me."

"This isn't your fault. Brodi is a grown man. He made his choices."

"But that's just it. I don't think he made this one. He was fooling himself, thinking he'd never come for you. I saw that. I knew it was only a matter of time. Addison did this right when he was about to break and show up on your doorstep."

"It takes two to tango."

He opens his mouth to say something and snaps it back shut. He nods and stands. I watch as a few things cross over his face.

"You have a good night, Chloe. Just think about giving him a real shot. He's not a bad guy and he's always loved you. You guys have shit timing, but I think this time you two can make it work."

"Thanks, Ethan. I'll think about it."

I do think on his words long after he's left me sitting in the kitchen. I think about it for so long, I'm lost in thought when Brodi and his mom return.

"Hey, how was the playdate?"

"The little munchkin passed out on me."

"It was probably from all of the excitement of having you all to herself."

"How was dinner with your mom?"

"Enlightening."

"That sounds interesting."

He turns and sneezes loudly. I frown. I've never seen this man get sick. Granted, I've only been around him in six-month intervals.

"Excuse me. Sorry."

"Bless you. I have some black seed oil in the refrigerator. You're welcome to take some."

He waves me off. "I'm fine."

"Says the man with the red nose. Are you sure you're okay?"

I look at him more closely and he doesn't look so well. His eyes are a little watery, his nose has turned red in the short time since he entered the kitchen.

"I'll be fine. Nothing a glass of brandy can't knock out. Want to have a drink with me?"

I get ready to say no but think of Ethan's words. If it weren't for Chloe, would I have been able to forgive Brodi by now? I don't know. That time in my life felt like I'd never get over it. I loathed myself as much as I hated him for so long.

I look down at my hands, spotting paint on my fingers. Once Ally left for college, I didn't think I'd paint again because the inspiration was gone, now I get lost in the studio for hours all because this man opened that door again.

"Okay, sure, why not?" I say, thinking I should at least try to spend time with him outside the dates designed to win me back.

We go to the sitting room and he pours us both a drink. I smile as he hands me a glass of clear liquor, not the brown drink he's having. I take a sip and find it's a smooth tequila, just what I like.

Brodi has never been into light liquor. I remember his preferences, although I marvel at how much he remembers about mine. He grabs the two decanters and moves to the sofa.

I follow and watch him as he takes a seat across from me. He looks tired and his nose is still red. I finish my drink and hold out my glass for him to refill as he goes to pour another for himself.

"You might be working too hard. You haven't taken a day off since you returned after we arrived here."

"Things are different. I oversee more. When I worked for my father, there was always a way to hand things off. Now, if I drop the ball, it falls on Clay or Cane. It causes a ripple effect."

"I guess I can see that. Do you miss the freedom?"

He snorts. "Working for my father wasn't freedom. It's why we can't be forced back into that life. I've lost too much to be forced back into his palms," he says bitterly while staring into his glass.

"Help me understand. You were never forthcoming with information on your family. What's so bad about your dad?"

"Clooney Hennessy thinks he can force everyone around him to do as he wants. Forget your dreams, your desires, your thoughts. It's his way or no way.

"He thinks money can change everything. He gives it and takes it to get what he wants. I didn't want to go into politics at twenty. I was looking into doing something in tech. He threatened to cut me off and I ended up following the path he wanted.

"I was willing to walk at first, but he made it clear he'd make my life hell. Any door I tried would be closed to me." He pauses to work his jaw. "I was accepted to the college I wanted to go to and suddenly my acceptance was revoked. I could go on and on about all the ways he made his point.

"That's the reason I knew I couldn't let him find out about you. It's why I had the apartment, but—"

"But now we're engaged, and I'll be right in the line of fire?" I cut him off and pull a sarcastic face.

"My father is evil, not crazy," he deadpans. "I don't play when it comes to you. Fuck him and all this money. I'm never fucking things with you up again and anyone who gets in the way of that will find out how serious I am about that shit."

I nod, starting to feel the tequila. "Okay. So, your dad isn't an issue. Got it."

He smiles. "You don't have to worry about anything, Cee. My father, your job back home, I have you covered. You have my word."

I look into his eyes and search them. Another ribbon floats from around my heart, yet I remain silent. The room is charged with the energy he always gives off. I'm almost consumed by it.

"Remember that one time—" His words are cut off as he sneezes again.

"Bless you."

"Excuse me," he says and sniffles.

"That's it. Off to bed with you."

He gives a cute pout. "But I'm not ready for bed. I miss our talks."

"Go sleep whatever this is off, and I promise I'll hang out with you to talk tomorrow."

"Promise?" he says with his red nose, flushed cheeks, and a drop-dead gorgeous smile.

I don't know what makes me say it, but I reply. "Promise."

CHAPTER THIRTY-ONE

Helpless

Chloe

"That was delicious," Brodi says after finishing the soup I brought up for him.

I smile as I watch him settle beneath the sheets and pull the covers up over him.

"It should help," I reply, gathering the tray and setting it aside.

It's been two months since we made that deal. I'm eight weeks closer to leaving this man behind. Sixteen weeks away from owning two million and my freedom.

So why do I feel like I'm in quicksand and I'll never be free?

"Do you want to play cards again?" he asks hopefully.

I give a warm smile. We had fun this afternoon. He was able to play for a bit before passing out and sleeping for a few hours.

I actually feel bad for him. Not just him but Eileen as well. It's been two days since they went out for dinner. They both returned with some type of stomach bug and a cold. I've been nursing the two since while trying to help keep little Chloe busy as well.

"Sure, why not?" I shrug and kick off my shoes.

Grabbing the cards from the nightstand, I climb onto the bed to get comfortable beside him. He pulls himself up weakly, resting against the headboard. I pause long enough to watch him, wondering if he should rest instead.

"I'm fine. Come on, deal," he says.

I narrow my eyes. "What are we playing?"

"Need you ask?" he says hoarsely.

I shake my head but start to deal the hand. He grins over his cards when I'm done. Even under the weather, his eyes work magic I need to steer clear of.

"Do you have an Ace?"

"Go fish," he says with a smile.

I stick my tongue out at him and pluck a card. I can't believe we're playing this game again. I feel like a little kid.

"It's your turn. What are you staring at?" I say as I look over my cards to find his intense gaze fixed on me.

"You're gorgeous when your eyes sparkle like that," he replies.

I tilt my head at him. I look into those gray eyes and my heart squeezes. I turn my gaze away to focus on my hand.

"Do you remember when we went to that vineyard?" he asks instead of taking his turn.

I drop my hands into my lap. My shoulders sag. These trips down memory lane are bittersweet. They were some of the best times in my life, but they also led to my biggest heartache.

"Yeah, I remember," I say quietly.

"My favorite moment from that day was sitting out on that blanket while playing cards and sipping wine. You were adorable when you got tipsy, and I had to carry you back." He chuckles.

I bite my lip as I remember that day for a different reason. It was the heated lovemaking after he carried me back to the bed-and-breakfast on the vineyard that flashes in my head. My nipples harden with my thoughts.

"Yeah, that was a fun trip," I say breathlessly.

He lifts a brow at me. I lift my cards back up, placing my focus on them. I don't think we should continue this trip he has started.

"Do you have a five?" he asks instead of pushing me.

I appreciate that and will admit he hasn't forced me into conversations I don't want to have. I take a shaky breath.

"Go fish," I reply.

We continue to play round after round. He's able to get me to laugh a bit during our game. I try not to let my guard down, but I feel it slipping the longer I remain in this room with him.

I reach for a card, but he covers my hand with his and my breathing stops. I don't want to feel. I don't want this connection that's been building.

Yet the spark hums up my arm, sending warmth throughout my body that can't be ignored. My eyes lift to his face. His forehead is covered in sweat. I think we've overdone it.

"Thank you," he says after swallowing hard.

"For?"

"All of this and… just being here, being you," he says.

"You're welcome," I say as I drop my eyes to stare at his hand over mine.

"Tell me something that I can do for you. I feel like I should be taking care of you, but here you are taking care of me and my family," he says.

"I told you it's fine. I didn't like that woman who came to babysit for Chloe." I frown. "I can help out. It's not like I'm doing much else."

"You haven't been painting," he states, it's not a question.

"A certain little angel likes to call for my attention. I haven't had time to." I grin, thinking of Chloe singing through the halls as she peeks her head in doors looking for me.

She's gotten away from her grandmother and father a few times in search of me. I've come to listen out for her calling Cee through the house. It's a big place but she finds my corridor every time.

"I'm sorry," he starts before having a coughing fit.

I wave him off, handing over a glass of water as he leans forward. I shift on the bed, fixing the covers around him for something to do with my hands. He places the glass on the nightstand and turns his attention back to me.

"I'll make sure you get some time to yourself," he says after clearing his throat.

"Actually, I've been enjoying my time with Chloe," I say, surprising myself.

It's the truth. I laugh so much during our little tea parties with Eileen. We play in the yard, and I've been teaching her new words and singing the alphabet with her. I've read her a story the last two nights before she's gone to bed. She's such an adorable little girl.

She still asks after her mommy and that's heartbreaking. In those moments, I just want to hold her tight and make it all better for her. I hope with time it will get better.

"You, I… I'm in awe of you," he says, shaking his head.

I tilt my head at him. "Why? Because I've grown to love an innocent child. She didn't break my heart, you did," I say to remind myself as much as him.

He closes his eyes. I watch as his face tightens with his own emotions. I look down into my lap. Once again, I realize I don't know if I should still be this hard on him. He has been trying.

Walking on the beach, the extravagant dates, and flowers are just the tip of the iceberg. Brodi has spent time allowing me to get to know him again. The problem is, I'm falling for this man. He isn't the man I used to know.

He has changed. I still see pieces of the one who stole my heart so long ago, but this more mature Brodi is chipping away at my armor every day.

"Gregor, I need to check on Chloe," I say.

Yes, this is a different man which is why I've started to call him by his given name. When I think about it, my source of conflict comes from seeing two sides of him. In my mind, I believe I've started to separate the two.

That's dangerous in so many ways. I stand and go to collect the tray I brought in with his dinner on it. One of the staff members could have done this, but I choose to.

"Yes, I'm in awe of you because you've fallen in love with a child that isn't yours. I'm in awe of you because you hate me and care about me at the same time.

"As much as you may want to deny it. You don't see me as the monster you once did. Knowing the pain I've caused you… I…

you're amazing to sit here and care for not just me, but my mother and my child. You're only reminding me of all the reasons why I love you," he says.

I lift the tray, looking away from him. That's the other thing that threatens to break me down. He doesn't go a day without telling me he loves me.

We both stay in the east wing of the house. However, when I asked for space, he took a room across the hall from mine. Every night when I go to my room for bed, he walks me to my door and tells me he loves me before planting a lingering kiss on my forehead.

I keep telling myself I can't trust his words, but they bring a sense of peace to the disarray of feelings I have for him. Like now, when I don't know whether to be annoyed with him for his assumption or to cling to his words of praise.

"I'll check back in on you after I feed Chloe and put her down for the night," I say.

Gregor

I don't say another word. I watch as she leaves the room, allowing the anger I feel inside to simmer. It's not anger toward her. It's anger for the time we're still losing.

I'm frustrated with Cee, not angry. I see her walls slowly crumbling, but then she throws daggers at me to keep me at bay. I want to have hope, but I don't know if I'll ever get around her self-preservation.

"God help me," I huff through my sore throat.

I still can't believe both my mother and I have fallen ill. I think the stomach bug has passed. That soup was the first thing I've kept down in two days.

My phone rings, drawing me from my thoughts. My brows furrow when I see it's a number I don't know. With all the shit going on back home, my lips tighten in anticipation of more bullshit.

"Hello," I say tightly into the phone.

"H-hello. This is Emma. Addison's friend."

My jaw starts to tic. My stomach sinks. Addison's name still sparks such anger inside of me. I also want to know why this woman ran off the day her friend died in the hospital.

"Yes, I remember you," I say, my voice coming out hoarse. "You have somehow managed to stay off my team's radar. My men have been looking for you."

"I…I…" She pauses and huffs. "I thought I was going to return home. I was going to, but something has kept me here. I've been with an acquaintance of Addison's. That's probably why you couldn't find me."

"Um, I see. Why are you calling now? How can I help you?"

"I think… I… I want to help you. Or at least… I think you should know something. It's about Chloe," she says.

I sit up in my bed. A chill runs through me. I toss the cover back and throw my weak legs over the edge. When I go to stand, my body protests. It's not ready to leave this bed.

"You have the address to the house?" I ask in frustration.

"Yes," she says in a soft whisper.

"Be here tomorrow morning. You can tell me what you have to say then," I snap and hang up without another word.

I glare at the wall. I've known from the beginning Addison was playing some type of game. My jaw works as I think of all the things this Emma may tell me.

My mind turns to Cee. I think she would be just as devastated as I would be to find out my daughter indeed isn't mine. My teeth grind at the thought of putting her through all this unnecessary pain.

I stop. My head hammers as I think of my daughter. She has no one else. If I'm not her father, I'm still the only one she has. I don't think I would be able to walk away from the little angel I've only ever known as mine.

"What the fuck did you do, Addison?" I breathe out.

CHAPTER THIRTY-TWO

So Sorry

Chloe

Gregor has a tight grasp on my hand as the woman before us fidgets in her seat. Her nose and eyes are red from the tears that have been rolling down her cheeks. I can feel Gregor's patience is running thin right along with mine.

"You've come to tell me something, but you've yet to spill a word," Gregor says, his voice still raspy from his cold.

I never did make it back to his room last night. I was exhausted from caring for everyone and warring with my own emotions and thoughts. I found him showered and slowly getting dressed this morning.

When he told me of the call and this woman coming to see him, something within told me to be here for him. He looked as if he were going to come unglued. I hate to think the worst, but I know it will rip him apart to find out that little girl isn't his.

It hurts to say it, but he's an amazing father. He's patient and so attentive when it comes to Chloe, and she adores her father as much as he does her. I think I'll fly at this woman if she says the wrong words this morning.

"I never wanted to be in the middle of this. Addison thought you would get here in time for her to tell you. She was going to come clean," she sniffles.

"Come clean?" Gregor growls. "What the hell does that mean?"

"When Addison first asked for my help, I begged her to tell you. She told me everything. None of it was right. I... I couldn't believe she would do something so... so." She shakes her head.

"I'm going to need you to spit this out," I snap.

Gregor squeezes my hand. I clamp my mouth shut and frown. I'm growing annoyed by the minute.

"Chloe isn't mine?" Gregor asks in a strained voice that has nothing to do with his physical health.

The amount of pain I hear in his voice tugs at my heart. Another large chunk of my armor falls off and floats away. I turn to look at him and his gray eyes look so... afraid.

"No, no. She's yours," the woman says as her cheeks turn red. "Do you remember donating...do you remember giving. This is so personal."

She looks between me and Gregor, licking her lips. She reaches to wipe the sweat from her upper lip. I swear I'm about to take my shoe off and throw it at her.

"You were a sperm donor at a clinic. Do you remember that?" she continues.

"Yes," Gregor says, moving forward in his seat. "My samples were destroyed."

Emma—the woman who calls herself Addison's friend—shakes her head. She looks Gregor in the eyes as she drops a bomb on us both.

"Addison overheard your call to the clinic. She got in touch with them and made arrangements to intercept your instructions. She'd been plotting all along. When you tried to pull away from her, she played her final hand. Karma had the last laugh. She only found out about the cancer because of the pregnancy.

"They advised her to terminate the baby to undergo treatment. I think… I think she was going to try to use the baby to blackmail you into marrying her, but the illness progressed faster than she expected.

"Trying to trap you became less important. I… I just thought you needed to know the truth. She knew you were on to her. You knew something wasn't right. She feared you would figure it out on your own.

"You never slept with Addison that night to make Chloe. She drugged you in the bar and took you up to your room where you passed out." She finishes looking back and forth between the two of us. "Even your decision to take her on the trip was orchestrated by her. She manipulated it all."

"And you came to tell him this now. Over two months later," I say.

My face is burning with anger. I don't know who I'm angrier with. Addison for her scheming, Emma for waiting until now to come clean, or Gregor for putting himself in this position to begin with.

"I don't know why. I just couldn't return home without telling you this. It didn't seem right. It's been weighing on me heavily. She should have told you, but I just couldn't... I stood outside that hospital room door praying she would tell you before she took her last breath," she says.

"I want you to go," Gregor says, the word barely escaping his lips.

His head drops into his palms. I can feel his pain rolling off him. Emma stands, looking like a lost little mess. I nod for the butler to see her out.

"I'm so sorry," she murmurs before she leaves.

My attention turns to Gregor. When I see his shoulders start to shake, I feel for him. He's the victim in all of this.

I can't even wrap my head around someone stealing your sperm to blackmail you. It's the sickest thing I've ever heard, and I've heard a lot. Here this man thought his donation was destroyed, but she manipulated a truly vulnerable situation.

I place a hand on his back and start to rub. He lifts his head to look at me. His eyes are red. I reach to thumb away the tears that start to escape.

"In the beginning, I felt so guilty for not wanting to believe Chloe was mine. I knew what the facts said, but something was still off. It took me so long to get involved and start to build that bond." He gives a bitter-sounding snort.

"Do you know how she really ended up with your name?"

My brows crease and I nod for him to continue. He reaches to brush a hand over my hair, palming my face as he looks into my eyes. He's searching, but I just don't know for what.

"When I first saw her, I thought of you. Your name slipped from my lips as the pain of you not holding my child seared

through me. Addison thought I was naming our little girl. Now…
as I think of the sinister grin on her lips, I think she knew.

"I went along with naming her after you, because for the first
time—since walking away from you—as I looked down at that
little girl, I felt like I had… hope.

"But in the back of my mind… something always felt so…
wrong about the situation. I think that's why I never told my
family. I just knew." His words come out brokenly.

"I… I don't even know what to say. This is… it's." I can't even
find the words.

"It's what I deserve," he says and stands. "Thank you for
sitting through this with me. I…."

He shakes his head and leaves. He stumbles forward like a
drunken man. I sit staring after him with my mouth open and my
heart breaking.

I don't want to hurt for him, but I can't help being human—
because what that woman did… it wasn't human at all. Karma
was truly swift with dealing out her punishment.

"I overheard." I turn to face Eileen as her voice fills the silence
Gregor left behind.

I blink and realize my lashes are wet. Eileen comes and takes
the seat next to me. She looks as if her legs barely carry her to the
seat. She reaches for my hand and squeezes it.

I see the tears in her eyes as her lips purse. Her cheeks are red
as her nose starts to turn as well. I can see the deep hurt of a
mother for her son.

"I don't know what to say." I shake my head.

"Cee, can I ask you something?"

"Sure."

I've grown fond of Eileen. She and Chloe have made my time here more enjoyable than I thought it would be. Although, I have seen that Eileen watches me and Gregor when we're around each other.

"How does all of this make you feel?"

"I… I feel for him," I say, looking down into my lap. "I just don't understand how you do something like that to someone."

"I've seen many things in my life you wouldn't believe. When money and fame get involved, it can cause people to do some unthinkable things," she says.

"I'm angry for Gregor. No one has a right to just take a piece of you. Especially not with the intention to blackmail you or to use your own flesh and blood as a weapon against you. It's so wrong on so many levels," I say, vibrating with anger.

"Can I be honest with you?"

"Yes," I say, looking back up at her.

"My heart aches for my son. I've been quiet up until this point, but I've been watching the two of you. You're holding so much against him." She holds her hand up when I go to cut her off. "Let me finish."

I nod and roll my lips.

"I understand you're hurting. I'm not saying you don't have a right to your hurt and anger. I've told you this before.

"I also know that my son has left out pieces. Something more is going on between you two, but I won't pry. I'll say this.

"Sometimes the timing of happily ever after isn't perfect. However, when it comes back around—if we fight it, we may lose it. You both are scarred deeply. But I can also see that you both love each other. I think you need each other." She points in the direction Gregor just walked in.

"That's a broken man, dear. A broken man who could use the woman he loves. Maybe—and I know it's a lot to ask—but maybe you can find it in your heart to forgive him for now. Just for now," she says when I frown.

My gaze drops to my lap. Tears fall without my permission. I have so many emotions and feelings. I feel robbed, cheated, betrayed. I also feel torn. My heart is broken for Gregor and for that innocent little girl.

"I'll think about it," I reply.

"Please do."

CHAPTER THIRTY-THREE

Drunk

Gregor

"You might want to slow down. You're still recovering," Ethan says as he sits beside me in this bar.

I needed to get away from the house to think. I have so much going through my head. I feel violated, lost, enraged. I can't even imagine how Addison pulled all of this off. I want jobs, licenses, lives. That bank will be lucky to keep its doors open when I'm done.

I snort. "Slow down, I haven't even started."

"I thought I'd be able to breathe easier once we got the truth," he says.

"You and me both," I say bitterly. "Now, I wish I didn't know. I was starving. I had no fucking money. It was the lowest point in my life. I already felt like shit for what I had to do. It was only a couple of bucks. Man, that was the most expensive hot dog and soda of my life."

"I wish you would have reached out sooner. I would have helped out any way I could."

"I had nothing. I couldn't involve anyone in the shit I went through."

"Bro, you're my best friend. I'm here now. I would have been there then before you could offer me a salary and cushy setup."

I toss back my drink and wipe my mouth. "It's all water under the bridge."

"What do you plan to do now?"

"I have no fucking idea," I breathe and signal for another drink. "I might have to let Cee go. This is all too much. It's going to kill me, but for once I'm choosing not to be selfish when it comes to her."

"Um. Maybe you should sleep this off before making any decisions. You may think differently in the morning."

"Whatever," I scoff and down the drink placed in front of me. "Hey, can you just bring me the bottle?"

Ethan sighs and settles back in his seat.

"Hey, I've been meaning to ask you for something," I say.

"What's up?"

"I don't think Addison pulled this off on her own. I'm wondering if the person who helped her is one and the same, whoever's been feeding information for these deals falling through."

"You want me to look into your staff?"

"Yeah, everyone."

"You got it. I'm on it. I was thinking the same thing. It shouldn't have been so hard to find the friend or connect the dots on all Addison did, but we were met with roadblocks as if someone knew we were digging."

I grunt and toss another drink back. "Send my brother everything we know."

"Everything?"

"Leave out Chloe, that should come from me, but send everything else. He thinks Wade and some asshole are behind this. I need to know if either of them links to Addison in some way."

He nods and we remain silent for the rest of the night while I drown myself in my sorrows. I get shit-faced wondering how I got here.

CHAPTER THIRTY-FOUR

Just Be

Chloe

I've paced my bedroom for hours waiting for Gregor to return. He took off not long after I spoke with his mother. I've been concerned.

He still wasn't a hundred-percent well. Eileen looked better but even she needed to take a nap as she's still recovering. Noise in the hallway grabs my attention.

I rush to the door and pull it open. Gregor is leaning against the wall, looking disheveled.

His eyes roll to me and lock on mine. Sighing, I move to his side and wiggle underneath his arm. He dips his head to kiss my temple and a wave of alcohol comes from his breath, nearly knocking me over.

"Come on, big guy, let's get you cleaned up," I huff.

"My Cee," he says against my skin, a bit slurred. "Beautiful."

My lips purse as I lead him into his room. I manage to get him to the bed where he flops down and groans. I lower to my knees to get his shoes off.

Then, I work on his pants as he mutters to himself. Once his pants are off, he rolls and climbs up the bed, flinging himself onto his back. Shaking my head, I follow him to work on his shirt.

I rest on my knees beside him, reaching for the buttons. He shoots his arm out, tugging me onto his chest. The air is knocked out of me as I land on top of him.

"I just need to hold you," he says.

So much hurt laces his words. I relent, placing my hand over his heart. We're both silent for a long time. In fact, I think he has dozed off. That is until his hand goes into my hair.

"I had planned to take you with me. Before that week. Before you told me about everything going on in your life. I was going to board that plane with you by my side.

"One of my biggest regrets was not looking deeper into your life before I reentered it back then. I would've known it wasn't the right time. I should've waited a year or two…" His words trail off and he releases a heavy sigh.

I remain silent. I don't want to go back there. All the different choices we both could have made won't get us anywhere. For me to even consider what Eileen asked of me, I need to stay in the here and now. His words are only unsettling old wounds.

"I'm trying. Some days you're with me. Others… it's like we're oceans apart all over again. How can I reach you if… you won't open up? I just… I… I love you," he murmurs.

Silence fills the room again, and this time I know he's fallen asleep. If I gave a dollar for every time he has said those words in the last few months, he wouldn't owe me a dime. I don't know how I feel anymore.

He's right. I haven't opened up completely. Self-preservation won't allow it.

"I just don't know what to do, Gregor. I don't know if I can survive you again," I speak aloud my feelings.

Yet, like a glutton for punishment, I want to be near him. I want to get lost in his warmth. I want to feel his body next to mine.

I take advantage of the moment. I can have what I need for just a little while. No one will be the wiser.

I curl into his side and wrap an arm around him. There was a time where I wished he could know my pain. Now, I just wish I could make this all go away for him. For us both.

Gregor

I wake up to a dry mouth and something heavy on my chest. Prying my eyes open, I look down to find a crown of red hair lying on me. I reach to run a hand through it.

I must have died and gone to heaven.

I groan as my throat demands lubrication. I need to find a glass of water quickly. Reluctantly, I gently move from beneath Cee's body. She clings to me at first, bringing a smile to my face.

I can't help watching her for a few moments before I stumble to my feet. Dragging my body to the bathroom, I get a glass of water to chug down. After two more glasses, I brush my teeth to get the rank taste out of my mouth. I turn and look at the shower longingly.

I strip the rest of the way out of my clothes and push my way toward the waiting stall. As the water beats against my skin, I welcome the warmth that begins to release my muscles. I wish I could wash away my problems.

The tension in my body isn't all that's released. Tears begin to fall. My desire was to be my own man. I've done that. I made it happen.

But at what cost?

I feel more like I've lost my soul along the way. I would give away every dime if it meant I could have back all that I've lost. I spent hours drinking and trying to figure out where I went wrong, which moments I could have changed to get it all right.

I ball my fist and pound it against the tiles. I've never felt more helpless in my life. Not even when I was starving and trying to get my foot into the right doors.

"It's okay," Cee's soft voice coos.

I look down at her small hands that glide up my chest. I close my eyes. I must be dreaming. That or the alcohol in my system has taken me for a trip.

"Gregor," she calls, causing me to turn in her arms.

I open my eyes to look into hers as they search mine. She brings her hand up to cup my stubbled jaw. I close my eyes again as I turn to kiss her palm.

"If this isn't a dream and you don't want me to touch you, you should leave," I say tightly.

"It doesn't have to be a dream. Instead, let's be in the moment. You said I won't open up. This is me trying. You need me and I need you. Let's just be," she replies.

I open my eyes and we lock gazes. Uncertainty radiates from her orbs. I hate seeing it there. Knowing as much as I value my word as a man, I've let her down and she has reason to be wary of me, cuts deep.

"But you know that's not enough for me," I warn. "You can't give me a taste and tear it away."

"Let's be honest. You never intended on letting me go," she scoffs. "You've only been trying to see what pieces you can salvage and put back together."

I dip my head to place my forehead to hers. It doesn't go unnoticed that she's allowing her hair to get wet. It's already starting to curl into those tight red ringlets I love so much. I put my arms around her waist, tugging her closer to me. I inhale her as if I can suck her into my own being.

"I don't exist without you. I barely breathe. Say the word, Cee. Tell me that you'll open up and let me in, not for only one night. Drop the shield and allow me to mend what I've broken. I'm here and I'm trying.

"Say yes and I'll take care of the rest. I'll make it all right again piece by piece. Say it."

I lift my head to look into her gaze. There's so much turmoil there. I know I'm asking for a lot, but it's time. I've tried the more patient approach and it didn't work.

"I'm asking you to trust me, Chlo. I'll take the lead if you trust me. I only want to make you happy. Trust me."

Her lips tremble and tears spill over. I move my hands up and down her back, not in a sensual way, but to comfort her. She places her hands on my chest and nods.

"Okay," she whispers.

"That's not what I asked for. I need to hear you say it," I reply.

She narrows her eyes at me and for a split second, I think I've pushed too far. She tilts her head, moving her body closer to mine.

She glides her fingers up my chest, over my shoulders, locking them into the hairs at my nape. Tugging my face closer to hers, she allows her breath to fan my lips.

"Yes," she breathes.

I take her lips the moment the word is out of her mouth. It's like air to a man that's been freed after being buried alive. I devour her in one deep gulp. The groan I release comes from my toes.

I feel our connection with every cell in my body. My scalp tingles. I sip from her lips and savor her handing herself over to me. Reaching behind me, I wave my hand over the panel to shut the water off.

Bending my knees, I dip and wrap my arms around her thighs to lift her onto my waist. I don't break the kiss. Inhaling her is giving me the strength to not just surge into her body.

I've been waiting too long for this not to cherish her in my bed. I need to reacquaint her with why we crave each other. We used to spend entire days in bed, while I gave to her body, and she took from mine.

She locks her fingers into my hair as she clings to me and whimpers into my mouth as I climb onto the bed and gently place her on her back. I break the kiss and look down into those big eyes.

Fear radiates from her glance. It's my mission to erase that look. With my eyes still on hers, I lower my head and kiss between her breasts.

"I love you."

I palm her large mounds and drop another kiss on her soft skin. Her lids close as tears slip free. My heart tightens, but I remain determined.

"I love you," I say the words again.

She gasps in a breath as her body shudders. Moving back up her body, I take her lips. Our tongues meet and dance against each other's as our connection deepens. I breathe her in.

"I love you," I repeat.

I nip her lip, causing her eyes to open. Her hazel eyes meet my gray ones. Her love for me is there. It's just covered in the wake of our past. I cup her face as I continue to feast from her mouth.

"I love you," I say as if releasing a prayer. "I always have, always will."

Our eyes lock and I silently ask for permission to continue. She gives a small nod and I start to descend her body. I kiss my way down her curvy, toned, lush body.

When I get to her stomach, I pause. My child was once here. I grasp her waist and bury my face there, silently making a promise to right my wrongs.

My seed will live here again.

I swallow thickly. It's a promise I make to both Chloe and myself. I'm determined as ever to make this right. To place a wrinkle in time that will allow me to mend all that I've broken.

"I love you," I say into her belly as my own tears drop to wet her skin.

I start to kiss and lick my way down her body again. It's not lost on me that she's tight with tension. It's never been like this with us, but I know this time I have to push through. The atmosphere is there for me to remind her of us.

Settling between her toned thighs, I run my nose through her slick folds. My tongue darts out for my first taste. Her fingers go into my hair and her back bows off the mattress as her legs lock around my head, bringing a smile to my lips.

"Gregor," she breathes.

I close my eyes. I love the sound of my name on her lips. Not Brodi, but Gregor. A man worthy of her body and her love. I know I'm a better version of me.

"I love you," I groan into her pussy.

Her legs tremble and her body begins to quiver. I push her legs back to release their lock so I can go deeper. Sucking her lips into my mouth, I savor the juices that drip and cling to them. Her nectar is the elixir of life. I've needed this more than I ever knew.

I part her open for me and dive in deeper. If she only knew. I haven't eaten another pussy since first tasting hers.

"This mouth has only belonged to you since the first time you gave yourself to me." I lift my head to say, placing a kiss on the top of her mound before diving back in.

"Gregor," she cries out breathlessly as I bring her to her first orgasm.

My wet lips turn up. That's one, at least six more to go. One for every year we've been apart and that's just for starters.

Chloe

I must have lost my mind. How could I forget the pleasure this man puts my body through? I'm clinging to the sheets, wondering if I'm clinging to my last breath.

I've lost count of the orgasms he has given me with his mouth and fingers alone. His words are still ringing in my head, chipping at my shell as I wonder if they're true. They can't be.

This mouth has only belonged to you since the first time you gave yourself to me.

Gregor eats pussy like it's a passion. I can't believe he hasn't gone down on anyone else in over seven years. To prove my point, he smacks his lips and licks them as he finally relents and starts a slow crawl back up my body.

My lids are drooping as if I'm getting ready to fall asleep. I feel drunk with pleasure. I haven't had this sated feeling since the last time we were together. I quickly shove that thought behind me.

"I love you," he says the words again.

Yet, this time—as he hovers over me, looking deeply into my eyes—something deep within cracks open. It's the box that I've been hiding my heart away in. His words are like a thunderbolt right through the center of the sealed-shut lid.

It's not hearing it. No, it's more like seeing it. His eyes are revealing his feelings for me. If I know nothing else about this man, I know when his eyes are revealing the truth.

I let it sink in as I root myself to this moment. The here and now are a safe place. I'm safe to give myself to him for now. That's a start for me. It's where I have to begin.

He takes my lips in a hard, all-consuming kiss. I can taste my essence, toothpaste, and a hint of the brandy he must have been drinking earlier. I'm so lost in his kiss, I barely notice when he pins my arms above my head with one of his hands.

His other hand rests on my thigh, caressing my skin gently. Teasing me just the way he knows I like. I melt into the sheets, whimpering when he releases my lips.

"I love you," he says again.

My lids slide closed, and I nod my acceptance of his words. I hear them. I know. I don't know how much that changes anything, but they've gotten through my wall.

When I hear him shift, followed by the opening of a drawer and the rustle of a foil packet, I bite back a sob. We've never used condoms after we talked about it, and I told him I was on the pill. Hearing that sound both rubs me raw and gives me a new level of respect for him.

He understands.

I'm just not ready for that level of connection between us. I know him well enough to know this is a decision he's making for me.

"Cee, look at me," he says huskily.

I look into his eyes. He slides into my body for the first time in over seven years as he holds the connection. A sob does leave my lips as he slides in. It's mindboggling how I open for him without question.

My walls yield to him as if it's his home. My legs wrap around his waist as if they have a mind of their own. Like the perfect puzzle pieces, we fit together as if made for each other and never meant to be apart.

He leans into my ear as his slow strokes stir so many emotions. "I love you so much. I knew you were mine the first time I laid eyes on you. I don't have it in me not to be yours. If you asked me to die for you, I would."

Releasing my wrists, he covers both my hands and laces our fingers together. Again, I use his eyes as my guide as our gazes connect. They say all the things my ears and mind won't allow me to hear.

His eyes speak right to my heart. They tell me all the things I need to know. He leans in and our lips connect.

Our tongues dance together as my orgasm begins to build. His hips pick up the pace to chase it down. He breaks the kiss, his lips part and his cheeks turn red.

That power that has always put me in awe of this man surges to the forefront. It drives into my body, speaking of the possessive protector I can't help falling in love with. Yes, I've fallen in love with him again.

It hits me fast and hard. I can't deny it, but I still won't admit it out loud. I can't for fear the acknowledgment will burn me again. I cling to his fingers like they're a lifeline as my heart starts to pound.

When my peak hits, it's like an explosion within. I'm breathless and shattered. Yet, Gregor doesn't stop. He pushes through my pleasure as I tighten around him.

"Fuck," he groans. "This pussy is better than I remember. Are you ready for me to take you there, baby? Say the words and I'll beckon your soul out of your body."

I give him a lazy smile. I know just what he's asking me. It's the reason my body has only ever been his.

"Do it," I challenge, relishing in what I've just unleashed.

No sooner than the words are out of my mouth, he pulls out and flips me onto all fours. He thrusts back into my body from behind. Lifting one leg to plant his foot in the mattress, he begins to pound down into me.

When that's not enough, he plants his other foot, grasps my hips, and rides me hard. I bury my face into the pillow and start to scream. His grunts and groans fill the air as he works my body.

"Shit, this pussy drives me insane. I'm just getting started, baby. Hold on," he says through his teeth.

Oh, he plans to go there.

Gregor

That was beyond amazing. Hours of learning my woman's body all over again. I've taken her in every way I know how.

I trace my fingers lazily over her skin. My thoughts are running all over the place, but I know this much... this feels right. It's the most whole I've felt in years. If it were up to me, I'd spend the rest of the day making love to her while we forget about the world.

Reaching to twist one of her curls around my finger, I smile at her still-damp hair. Cee's palm has her heat searing through to my heart, scorching my skin, but I wouldn't have it any other way. Her heavy breasts against my side, her long legs intertwined with mine—heaven.

"I'm hungry," she murmurs.

I chuckle. "I bet. We can go down for something to eat or go out. Your choice."

"I want you to make me scrambled eggs. I haven't had those in forever," she says.

"I can do that. I'll clear my day."

"Just to make eggs?" She snorts.

"No, I want to spend it with you. It's just a few meetings. I can have the contracts I need to sign brought here."

She laughs, bringing a smile to my face. Lifting my head, I brush her hair from her face to look down at her. Her eyes sparkle as they meet mine.

"What's so funny?"

"You. I don't remember you being such a workaholic when.... You never used to work this much. I know you told me why, but I still find it funny to see," she says.

"A lot about me has changed, I guess. Work is all I've had over the years," I reply.

I intend to change that.

I let my thoughts wander a bit. I've had one thought pushing its way to the surface for the last hour. I search her eyes, but she looks away from my probing and rests her head back on my chest.

No matter how much she opened up to me last night, it's clear we still have a long way to go. It stings to wonder if she will ever love me the way she once did. However, like always, I'm a man of action.

I know what I want. I've never had a question about that. I never will.

I begin to trace her soft skin again, my fingers taking a lazy trip. "Marry me," I say without hesitation.

Chlo pops up, turning to look back at me. I lock eyes with her and hold her gaze. I keep my face impassive as I wait her out. Her face, on the other hand, speaks of her shock and confusion.

"What?" she says when I say nothing more.

"Marry me," I repeat.

"Have you lost your mind?"

"No. Your biggest worry is that I'll leave you again. Marry me. If you're my wife, you will know for sure I'm not leaving. You will never have to question whether I plan to stay or not," I reply.

"Bullsh—"

"*Chloe*," I warn. "Watch your mouth."

She narrows her eyes at me. I love that fire I see as she stares back at me, but she knows where I stand when it comes to that mouth. I sit up and palm her beautiful face.

"I love you. Marry me. If you still feel you can't bear to be with me in a year." I pause as I work my jaw. "In a year, you can walk away, and I'll let you live your life without a worry about me."

She takes a shaky breath. "Gregor... you said piece by piece. What the—" She pauses and takes another breath. "I opened up. Isn't that enough?"

"No. I want you as my wife. We've... I've wasted so much time without you. I know what I want and it's you, baby. Marry me," I repeat the words.

"So you want to go through with a real engagement when we go back?" she asks with furrowed brows.

"No," I say, shaking my head.

Her lips pout and her shoulders sag. As I see the hurt and disappointment, I don't think she realizes what I'm saying. Leaning in, I peck her lips.

"Marry me today," I say against her lips. "We'll go through the engagement party and wedding for the sake of my family, but I want you to marry me today. Here, now, me and you. I want you to be my forever, Cee. Or at least..."

"For a year?" she says softly. "I can go in a year?"

My heart squeezes. I never want to let her go, but if I haven't convinced her how much I love her in a year, I will finally set her free. It will kill me, but I'll do it.

I nod. Not able to say the words. I don't even want to breathe life into them because I plan to do everything in my power to show her we belong together. We'll be celebrating a year of marriage and making our way into many more if I have anything to do with it.

Somehow, I will find a way to break through to her heart again.

She brings her hands up to cover her face. I tense as I think she's going to burst into tears. Instead, she releases a long groan.

"You make me crazy. I know I should get up and walk out of this room, but I'm considering this insanity," she says.

I wrap my arms around her and pull her into my chest, kissing the top of her head. Breathing her in, I try to find the right words. This is right, now how do I make her see that?

"You, as my wife, makes all the sense in the world to me. I'll place the world at your feet, baby. Marry me, Chloe. My heart needs your heart," I reply.

"I'm terrified," she breathes.

"So am I. I'm terrified of losing you. I love you, Chloe. Will you marry me?"

"Yes," she says it so low I barely hear her.

I tilt her head back to look into her eyes. I ask again with my gaze, and she nods as tears spill. I take her full trembling lips and pour all my love into the kiss.

Finally. I'll make everything work from here.

CHAPTER THIRTY-FIVE

All My Desire

Chloe

"I didn't think she'd be so mad at us," I say as we walk the hall hand in hand toward our bedrooms.

Our private wedding ceremony was so beautiful, not what I was expecting, but stunning. It was on the beach with just the two of us, but the location and the gorgeous little setup Gregor arranged was amazing. However, Eileen was more than miffed when we returned, and she saw the wedding bands.

"She's not angry with *us*, she's furious with me."

"Now that I think about it, I think I'd be livid with Ally if she married someone without telling me first."

Gregor shrugs. "It will blow over. It's not like we're not going to go through with the wedding and engagement party she has planned."

"No, but I get it. She was right here. She could have been there. I see why she's upset."

I go to release his hand and head to my room. He tightens his hold and pauses in the middle of the hall. I look up into his eyes.

"Where do you think you're going?"

"To my room. My things are there."

He shakes his head. "No, Mrs. Hennessy, they aren't. Your things are all in your husband's room, where you will be staying for the rest of this trip."

"Oh, I didn't think about that," I say as he wraps me in his arms and tugs me into his chest.

He pecks my lips and begins to sway, then places his lips against my forehead. My skin hums with that undeniable connection. A smile comes to my lips when he starts to sing the lyrics to "If You Don't Know Me by Now."

He reaches into his pocket and pulls out his phone. "Come on, I want to dance with my wife," he says and nods his head toward his bedroom.

My heart stutters every time he calls me his wife. I'm still trying to figure out what made me marry him. At this point, I'm taking it a moment at a time. It's how I'm breathing.

I lace my fingers with his and allow him to take me into the room. The song begins to float through the room, and he pulls me into his arms again. I stare into his eyes and latch on to the love I see there.

The song he's chosen isn't lost on me. I used to think I knew this man better than I know anyone. Now, I'm learning I've only begun to know him. I think I love this version more than the one I fell for so many years ago.

He cups my face and kisses me tenderly. Tears start to fall. It's as if he's kissing away the last of the past and the pain it holds. I open to him and allow him in.

"I love you," he says before he deepens the kiss.

I ground myself to the here and now, allowing him to back me up toward the foot of the bed. He turns me so swiftly, I gasp. Wrapping me in his arms from behind, he starts a slow trail of kisses against my skin. I bite down on my lip and close my eyes.

Each kiss is scorching but holds so much promise. When he releases the zipper on the white dress I'm wearing, a chill runs through me. The dress floats to the floor and I shiver.

"Trust me, Chloe. I'm going to cherish you with every breath I have."

My reply is caught in my throat as he cups my breasts and begins to knead them as he sucks on the flesh between my neck and shoulder. A moan slips from my mouth as he starts to slowly slide his palm down my center.

"Gregor," I cry out as he pinches my nipple while slipping two fingers inside me with his other hand.

"I love you more than life itself. You're so wet. I want you so much."

I turn in his hold and place my hands on his waist. He pulls his hand from between my legs and places both his palms on my ass. Kneading, massaging, and caressing my skin before spreading my cheeks to slip his fingers in from behind.

I bite my lip as I look into his eyes and start on the buttons of his shirt. Neither of us is in a rush. I take my time pushing his shirt from his shoulders once I have the buttons free.

I take my time to take in the raw power that comes from this man. His body is still as powerful and impeccable as I remember from the first time I ever gave myself to him.

I lift on my toes as my body tightens. I gasp as the song changes to "I Wanna Be Closer" by Switch. I'll give him this, when it comes to his taste in music. It always meets the occasion.

Seeming to mirror my feelings, Gregor takes my lips and kisses me passionately. I lock my fingers in his hair and hold him to me. I release his belt and pants and push them down his legs.

"I love you," he groans as he lifts me onto his waist and climbs on the bed.

I writhe beneath him as he kisses his way down my body. My fingers are still locked in his hair. I look down my body into his eyes as he starts to feast on me.

It doesn't take long for me to come all over his face. He crawls back up my body and retrieves a condom to put on. I hold his face as he looks down at me.

"I love you," he says as he slides inside me.

I gasp and buck off the bed. My flavor is on his lips and tongue as our mouths connect. He feels amazing. His strokes aren't too slow or too fast. There just right for the moment. He's stirring my soul and calling it back to him.

Those words are on the tip of my tongue. I try to tell myself it's safe to release them, but caution wins out. However, his groans in my ear make me question everything.

Gregor

My heart feels like it's going to come out of my chest. She's so tight and wet, but I think it's the fact that she's mine, my wife. That's making this feel like heaven on earth.

I reach to palm her thighs and push her legs back as I slide my thigh beneath her ass and pump deeper into her heat. Her body quakes and she starts to cry out.

"Yes," I hiss between my teeth.

"Gregor, please."

"I've got you, baby. Let go, I'm here, I'll catch you."

She looks up into my eyes and I'm blown away as I see trust there. I'm getting through. The hope that fills me almost consumes me. I start to thrust deeper, trying to chase down what I know we both need.

"Yes, yes," she cries.

I know I'm hitting her spot, but it's not enough. I want her crazy with pleasure. Pleasure only I know how to give her. I grab the top of the mattress and dig my toes into the bed as I work my body into hers.

She wraps her legs around me as if trying to anchor herself. I grind my teeth and piston into her.

"I love you so much. You belong to me, Chloe. Always have, always will," I roar.

She doesn't have to say a word. I see our truth in her eyes. We're going to make it. As long as we can stay on this path, I know I can make this right.

CHAPTER THIRTY-SIX

Newlyweds

Gregor

I wanted to make our honeymoon week special. The look in Cee's eyes says it all. This has been an amazing day. I woke her with breakfast in bed and then we took a ride for this.

A hot-air balloon ride. I watch her face as it beams with joy. I had no idea she would enjoy this so much.

"This is beautiful. I can't wait to get back to the studio. This has sparked so much inspiration," she gushes.

"I wish I had the talent to capture you in this moment."

She laughs. "That's what cameras are for."

I chuckle and move to stand behind her to wrap her in my arms. I lift my phone and hold it out in front of us as she snuggles into my embrace. I take a picture, then kiss the top of her head as I take another. Closing my eyes, I breathe in the moment.

She takes my phone from my hand as I remain in the moment. My net worth could never match the wealth I feel in this moment. I'm at peace. Life is starting to make sense again.

"You know, I would never do something like this back home. Sid is terrified of heights."

I open my eyes. "I wonder if Clay knows. He loves skydiving and bungee jumping."

"She would totally shit her pants. This one time in high school, we went on a trip and had to walk over this overpass. The fit she threw."

"Clay will eat that knowledge up. A reason for him to protect her," I scoff.

"That is if she'll allow him to protect her. Sid has always been so independent. She deserves someone who will allow her to relax. You know, someone she can trust to give control to."

"And you, what do you deserve?"

She turns in my arms and places her palms on my chest. I peck her lips before she replies.

While keeping her gaze on her hands, she says, "I deserve the same. I used to have that. I deserve to have it again and to trust it won't change on me."

"It won't. I promise it won't. Nothing will ever force me to hurt you again, Cee."

She wrinkles her brows and lifts her gaze. "Is it crazy that I want to believe you, but I don't know how?"

"No, it's not. All I can do is show you. I know one day it will sink in. Consistency. That's my goal."

"Letting go. That's mine. Letting go of the past and letting go to trust. That's where I'm trying to get to. I am trying, Gregor."

I take her lips in a deep kiss. The sound of the flame coming to life above our heads is the only thing to break us apart. I place my forehead to hers.

"We can be anything we want. Our marriage marks a new beginning. Walk this journey with me, baby. Trust me with our future and I'll lead the way."

"Consistency. I need to see it consistently."

"I know."

I've got this from here. She'll see.

CHAPTER THIRTY-SEVEN

Dreams of Us

Gregor

"Cee," Chloe squeals in my arms as we walk into the art studio.

Cee looks up with a bright smile on her lips. I love that smile. I see it more often these days and it makes my heart feel lighter.

"Hey, you two," she sings.

"You haven't eaten. We thought we'd come to get you for lunch. Have a picnic with us."

She turns to look out the window and pulls a face. "It's so hot out there. Are you sure? Chloe will burn, your butt will be next. I'll be nursing sunburns for the rest of the day."

I laugh. "I have ice coming in to drop in the pool. We can take a swim when it arrives. For now, we'll have shade under the pergola."

"Please, Cee, come play," Chloe pleads, showing off her little teeth as she smiles.

"See, we want you to spend time with us. We'll leave you alone after we feed you."

"All right, all right. I can finish this later."

"It looks great, by the way."

I look the painting over. It's a play on the hot-air balloons. The colors are so vibrant and happy. It evokes joy as I look at it. If that's what she was going for, she nailed it.

"I wanted to capture the joy of that moment. You know?"

"You hit it right on the head, baby. I love it."

Her face lights up as she stands and wipes her hands off. She reaches for her rings from the cup she keeps them in while she works.

When she has them on, she moves into my side. I wrap an arm around her as I hold Chloe at my side. This feels so right to me. I've wanted to broach the subject of having another child, but it never feels like the right moment.

For now, I settle on being satisfied with having my wife and daughter in my arms. These are the moments I live for. Cee's happiness fuels my determination each day.

This is what I've dreamed of.

Chloe

I feel like I'm living in a dream. The sun is beaming down on me as I sit by the side of the pool in a bikini. Chloe's squeals ring out as Gregor swims her around the pool on his back.

I turn to look at them, covering my eyes with my hand and pull my shades down. A smile comes to my lips. They make the cutest sight.

My phone rings beside me, pulling my attention. I pick it up and answer. "Hello."

"Hello, Mrs. Hennessy, this is Eric. I'm calling with a few questions from the gallery curator."

I'm thrown for a second as he calls me Mrs. Hennessy. It still hasn't sunk in that it's my new last name. Especially since we haven't told anyone other than Eileen we're married.

"Hi, Eric. How can I help you?"

"Michelle would like to know if you have an idea of how many pieces you'll be showing?"

"Oh, I haven't nailed that down yet. Can I get back to you on that by the end of the week?"

"Sure, she sent over a few display options. I'll forward those to you and maybe that will help you decide. It's a much smaller gallery than the Soho show will be in. I love your work, by the way. I'm excited, I hope I can snag a piece for my new loft in New York."

I can't help smiling from ear to ear. I still can't believe this is happening. I'm going to show my work at not one but two real galleries in Manhattan.

"Oh, by the way, I have your resignation letter for Steinway & Schwartz. Would you like me to send you a copy to go over before I send it off?"

"My what?"

"Your resignation letter. Mr. Hennessy had me contact them about your leave. Your time is up. I was informed to draft a resignation letter."

"By who?"

"Mr. Hennessy."

"Eric, I'll call you back."

I hang up and glare at my husband. He comes over and places Chloe next to me. Eileen comes out right at that moment and takes Chloe to sit with her in the shade.

"Have you lost your mind?" I hiss low.

He looks at me with a puzzled expression. Lifting out of the pool, he sits on the edge and places a hand on my thigh. I glare at him as my anger rises.

"What did I do now?"

"You decided I'm quitting my job without my knowledge. How dare you?"

He has the nerve to give me a smile. "You hated that place. You told me so. I want you to be able to focus on what you love. I'm worth enough for you not to have to work. I'd prefer if you didn't. However, if you want to paint full-time, that's better than working in the district. Come on, Chlo."

"Gregor, I understand you have money, but you should have run this by me."

The man is worth trillions. He's being very modest. However, I don't plan to sit on my ass for the rest of my life.

He cups my face and kisses my lips. "I'll keep that in mind for next time, but your resignation goes in this week," he says against my lips.

"There he is. The man I know."

"And love. The man you know and love, baby. I'll always do what's best for you. Focus on your art. I'll handle the rest."

I sigh, what's the point? "We should talk."

"About?"

"You want me to know what life will be like with you. We should talk about what that means."

"It means we live the dream. The life we talked about having together."

I clamp my mouth shut. That dream included children, a home in the burbs, and me being a stay-at-home mom. It was a dream all right. A dream I don't know if I still want and honestly never thought I would have. I'm not that same twenty-five-year-old.

"Trust me."

I sigh and rub my forehead. "Okay."

CHAPTER THIRTY-EIGHT

Really Happening

Chloe

I sit in the living room on the phone with Eric as we nail down details for the wedding and showing. Gregor sits next to me going over some work documents. He looks so handsome as he focuses on his work.

This seems so normal. Like we do this all the time. We were having some family time until Eileen took Chloe to put her down for a nap.

"Thanks so much, Eric."

"No problem, ma'am."

"Lord, can you stop calling me ma'am? My husband is old. I'm not."

Eric chuckles as Gregor looks up from the docs in front of him to glare at me. I stick my tongue out at him and wiggle my toes under his thigh. He wraps his hand around my ankle and gives it a gentle squeeze.

"Mrs. Hennessy," Eric chuckles over the phone.

"No, Chloe or Cee is fine."

"Chloe, I have the approved invitation for the showing. I'll send that to Michelle now. You'll let me know about the wedding invitation after you show Mr. Hennessy and make a decision. I just sent you the menus for the showing and the wedding reception. I have you booked for a tasting for both once you return to New York.

"Give me a day to get you those paint samples and designs for little Miss Chloe's room in New York. Will there be anything else?"

"No, that's a lot. I know my husband is already working you to death."

Eric laughs in my ear. "I'm here if you need me. Call me if you need anything else. No matter the time."

"Thanks, hon."

"No problem. Have a good evening."

"You too."

Gregor looks at me as I hang up. "You love teasing me. Are you sure you're ready for the results?"

I bite my lip, getting ready to give him a naughty reply. However, his phone rings, drawing his attention. He looks at the device and frowns.

"I need to take this," he murmurs and stands to leave the room.

I watch after him, wondering what that's about. My mind goes to Ally. I dial her number and wait for her to pick up.

"Hello?"

"Why the heck do you always sound like you're fucking or running a marathon when I call?"

"I'm twenty-two. Have you ever thought I might be fucking?"

"*Ally*," I drag out.

She laughs, still sounding breathless. "I'm messing with you. You can always dish it out, but you can't take it. What's up?"

"I'm checking in. How are you?"

"I'm fine. Your timing sucks though. I'm heading out the door. Can I call you later?"

"Fine," I huff.

"Love you, Chlo."

"Yeah, I love you too, big head."

I hang up and roll my eyes. I can't wait to get home and find out what's been going on with her.

Gregor

"What's up?" I say into the phone.

"That deal in Vegas, it's about to fall through," Cane grumbles. "The investor group wants to pull out."

"You tell Clay about this?"

"He did," Clay says, letting me know he's on the line too. "I say fuck them. Gutter has a contact who would be interested."

"More Lost Souls?" I lift a brow as if he can see me.

"No, Stormy and Ramon are civilians. Just as dangerous and loyal though. Their pockets are deep enough. We'll still have the desired effect."

I have nothing against the Lost Souls. However, they have had trouble in the past that I'm not interested in tying my money to.

Clay, on the other hand, has a deep loyalty to King and the rest of the Lost Souls. I get it. He got his start with their help.

"I want to know why these deals are falling through," I mutter.

"The moment it got out we might start running for a few offices, this shit started."

"Yeah, but my gut says it's deeper than that." I sigh. "Make the deal happen with your people. I'll take over once they commit. Call me if something else comes up," I say and hang up.

"Fuck, can't I catch a break?"

We need these new deals for some bigger moves we plan to make. It's like someone is picking away at our plans. I can't wait to get back so I can look at things with Clay and see if I can pull the needle out of the haystack. I'm almost done wrapping up all affairs here. I won't need to return for a while.

The sale of the house will be done in two weeks, and we can leave then. I'm saying goodbye to my past. It's time to shut the door on Addison and the mess she created in my life. I've purchased an apartment at Burj Khalifa. That's where my family will stay when I need to come in for business.

"Everything okay?"

I turn to find Cee with her eyes on me. I give her a smile and beckon her to come to me with my arms open. She comes into the room, and I wrap her in my embrace.

"I love you," I murmur into her neck.

CHAPTER THIRTY-NINE

Promises & Vows

Chloe

"Oh my God, that was fun," I sing as I step out of the SUV. I fan at my face as the heat blasts me. It's hot as hell but it's been so worth it.

I fix the scarf on my head and look at Gregor in his. His hair is covered, but his skin has taken on a golden-brown hue, and his cheeks are red.

He gives me a broad smile. "I couldn't allow you to go home without this experience. Dune bashing is thrilling, but I think you're going to love the quad ride. The day is just getting started though, wait until tonight."

"I can't wait, the camel ride was awesome. I'm excited about the henna painting too."

"You're going to love the food. The entertainment is always fun."

"*Oh*," I sing and move to bump Gregor with my hip. "Check Ethan out. That chick has been all over him since we got here."

Gregor looks over at his head of security and smiles. "She's not his type, but he's too polite to say something," he murmurs for my ears only.

"Is that right? What's his type?"

He turns and winks at me. "Watch his eyes. It's her friend."

I look at the friend of the woman trying to get Ethan's attention. My mouth falls open as I catch the hungry look on Ethan's face as he looks at the thick ebony friend with the cute top and short shorts.

"Okay," I say and pull a face. "I see you, Ethan."

He looks up as if hearing me and gives a small smile. Just as quick, he moves to catch the curvy friend as she trips. The way she looks up at him and he looks down at her is straight out of a romance novel—as if she's seeing him for the first time and he's ready to devour her whole. Sid would love this.

"Baby, come on. You can ride with me," Gregor calls as he straddles one of the quads waiting for everyone. He holds out a pair of goggles for me to put on, his are already on his face.

After getting my goggles on, I climb on behind him and wrap my arms around his waist. I place my cheek against his warm back. This has been such a fun day. I get a pang in my heart as I think of the fact that we're getting ready to go back home.

I'm afraid of this bubble bursting and the real world coming in. I hope this feeling can survive what awaits us back home.

Gregor

The night has turned out amazing. I look around at the vibrant-colored covered tables, pillows, and rugs for seating. The tables are sectioned off into little areas for groups to sit in.

In the center of all the tables is a square carpeted area that acts as a stage before everyone. I can't wipe the smile off my face as I turn to watch Cee. She's looking at the flamethrower with awe in her eyes. I think she may have found more inspiration for her paintings.

Today has been awesome. The heat was the only thing I can complain about. Cee has laughed, she's gotten to know a few of the other women on the tour. I've watched her light up all day.

"You look happy," I say as I watch her.

She turns to me and cups my face. "Right now, I am."

I take her lips in a searing kiss. It's so easy to get lost in her. Everything else falls away. I go to deepen the kiss, but she pulls away.

"This place is magical. I wish we could stay. I have this sinking feeling like everything will change when we get back."

"I wish we could stay here too, but I know how much Ally means to you. We need to head back for the engagement party as well. My mother has been busy planning while she's been here.

"I walked in on one of her calls. I had no idea she was so far into the planning. I thought she wanted to return home back to her life when she kept asking when I'd be heading back."

Cee laughs. "It all makes sense now."

"What?" I give her a questioning look.

"She's been asking me questions and I think Chloe gets away when she's planning, if not napping."

I start to laugh. "I can see that. Mom has been paying the party planner extra to work on her time. I'm sure it's going to be quite the affair."

I look around us, then turn back to face her with a smile on my lips. Reaching up, I run my hand down her cheek.

"As beautiful as this night is, you outshine it all. I love you. If you want to come back, we'll make a trip as soon as all the events back home are over."

"Events, ugh. Don't remind me. Your mom has taken over planning our wedding. Sid is lucky Eileen's here with me. Did you know she's been having Sid FaceTime her for dress shopping?"

I chuckle. "I may have heard something about that."

Chloe frowns and a puzzled look crosses her face. "Sid and Clay are planning a real wedding too. Do you think they'll go through with it? I think your mother will be heartbroken if they don't, she really likes Sid."

"We don't talk about it when I get a chance to talk to him. I can't say either way."

"He better not hurt my friend. She sounds happy."

"Cee, Sid and Clay are both adults. He's not going to intentionally hurt her. Neither of us knows what's going on in his or Sid's heads. When we get back, we'll learn what's going on. Until then, let's enjoy our life."

I don't tell her I plan to call Clay to tell him we're heading back. I don't want to be placed in the middle of Clayton's situation. He's obsessed with Sidney. I can't say he won't go through with the wedding.

This is Clay. He's always a step ahead. I wouldn't be surprised to find out he's already married Sidney. Whatever's going on with them, I don't get the feeling Clay would allow Sidney to get hurt in any of this.

Chloe snorts, but she moves to come sit between my legs. The richly colored rugs are so cool beneath us. The night has cooled down and is much more bearable.

I can see why Cee wants to stay. There is a magic here, but I'm determined to find our stride back home.

CHAPTER FORTY

Going Home

Chloe

It's time to return home and I'm not too sure how I feel about that. Here in Dubai, Gregor has become someone else in my mind entirely. I fear going back home to the reminders of my real life and remembering that he's still Brodi.

Like I told Gregor the other night, the last few weeks have been magical—I've remained in the moment. Eileen has been talking about the huge plans she has for the ceremony when we return home, but I don't think that will compare to our intimate wedding.

Standing before just Gregor and the officiant while draped in white—after being pampered and given a twenty-four-karat facial—I felt like a princess or something. My greatest fear is that

I've been carried away into a fairy tale and when it all comes crumbling down, it will explode in my face.

I mean, we've been living like a king and queen since the wedding. When we're not off on some adventure, we're home with Chloe playing the role of a perfect family. Looking from the outside in, you'd never know the festering pain that lies within our relationship.

Honestly, my heart is still rattling around in my chest. Yet, the time we spend together—whether with Chloe or not—just feels right. Which totally confounds me.

From time to time, I find myself looking at her with thoughts of what if, but those moments are becoming less painful as Chloe clings to me as if I were her mother.

"Are you all right?" Gregor asks, pulling me from my thoughts.

I look up from the suitcase I should be packing and give him a weak smile. He puts down the stack of shirts in his hands and rounds the bed to me. The first thing to engulf me is his scent.

"I'm just thinking," I say as he wraps his arms around me from behind.

"Nothing is going to change. We will go home and move forward with our lives as man and wife. Clayton and I will figure out who's behind all of this drama and then we'll focus on what we want to do next," he says as if reading my mind.

"Meanwhile, we'll be attending our engagement party and planning a wedding," I say as I turn to face him.

"Yes," he says cautiously. "Humor my mother, you saw how pissed she was with me for taking you off to marry you. I'm sure my father is going to have something to say as well. They need to keep up their appearances, after all."

"Don't you think this is all... a lot? You're taking a wife and child home with you. A child you were hiding and a wife you secretly married. It's bound to cause some type of drama," I say.

His brows are drawn as he looks at me. I can see the wheels turning. Those gray eyes pierce me in a way that stops me from breathing.

"What drama, Cee?" he says gently. "You and my daughter belong to me. As far as everyone back home knows, you and I were already engaged anyway. No one has to be the wiser there. I will tell my brothers and father whatever I feel like sharing.

"These last four weeks haven't been some fantasy we've created within our own bubble. My feelings for you are real. Everything I've done has been genuine. I will continue to pamper you, shower you with gifts and love, and do my best to restore your love for me.

"That's my only focus when we return home. You and Chloe are all that matter to me," he says.

I look away, not wanting him to see how his words affect me. He reaches for my face to turn it back to him. Our gazes meet and I see so much vulnerability staring back at me.

"Learn to trust me again, baby. I've done nothing but show you that you can."

I pull away and turn back to my packing. He's right. He's done everything to reassure me that he cares for me, including marrying me.

Still, in the back of my mind, I just can't reconcile the way I still feel with the man standing before me. I've tried, but there are moments when I look at him and think of all the pain I've been through.

Which is why you shouldn't have married him. What were you thinking?

I honestly don't know what made me say yes. As much as I hate to admit it, there is a part of me that needs him. I hate it, but it's a truth I bear.

He's still at my back as I place more items into my suitcase. He sighs heavily but kisses my shoulder before going back to packing his things. Silence fills the room as I get lost in my thoughts again.

"This will always be your choice," he says quietly.

I look up to find his eyes on me. He pushes a hand through his hair. I crease my brows.

"If we return home and you feel a year is too long. Whenever you want out… it's your choice. Say the words," he says, before turning and leaving the room.

I stare after him. Relief runs through me with the false security of his offer. He may be offering me an out, but I know it's not real. Or it could be that some part of me doesn't want it to be real.

I sit on the bed and place my head in my hands. I don't know why my brain can't separate the difference between the old Brodi and this man I've fallen in love with. I freeze.

That's not the first time I've allowed myself to admit that truth. I've fallen in love with him, and I think that's what scares me most. He has crept his way around my wall and defenses.

"What the hell do I do now?" I blow out.

CHAPTER FORTY-ONE

Not Welcome

Chloe

I don't know what I was expecting when I arrived in New York. What I wasn't expecting was for my sister to be besties with this arrogant asshole who's also my brother-in-law. His twitchy ass is about to make me break my foot off in his behind.

"What I don't get is why you're living here with him when you could have stayed in Gregor's apartment and had it all to yourself," I seethe as Ally and Cane sit on his sofa, looking like they're hiding a million secrets.

"I felt more comfortable here with him," Ally says.

"How? You don't even know him. I need you to start making shit make sense around here. I'm not buying any of the bull you've been selling me since I walked in that door."

"I'm not telling you anything until you calm down. I'm not a child, Chloe. Stop talking to me like one."

I turn to look at Gregor to make sure I'm not being punked. She must have lost her damn mind. I turn back to my sister with my mouth hanging open.

So many emotions war on the inside of me. We've only been home for a few hours, but I'm ready to knock some sense into my sister because clearly, she has lost what good sense she once had.

I look at Cane and glare at him. While he looks like he could be related to Gregor, he looks more like a younger version of Clayton. I don't miss how my sister could have lost her mind, but I'm questioning the job I've done for her to arrive at this point in her life.

"I'm your sister. I've always had your back. If you have a problem, you need to talk to me. I don't understand what's going on with you. Why can't you come stay with us now that I'm back?"

"Because I don't want to. I'm fine here with Cane. We understand each other."

"Hello, this is my apartment, and I'm still in the room."

"So, what's your point? I'll break my foot off in your ass right after I'm done with her if that's what you want. Sit tight, I've got you."

"Chloe," Gregor speaks up.

I spin to face him. At some point he moved from standing to take a seat in the accent chair behind me. I'm too pissed to sit.

I only came here to get my sister so we could talk about her situation. I wasn't expecting for her to tell me she'd prefer not to talk, and she wants to stay here.

"Don't Chloe me. This is your little brother. You better get him. I don't play when it comes to my sister.

"You're about to meet another side of me, Gregor, and trust me, I don't think you're going to like it"—I point to Cane—"I don't like him. Look at him, he moves like a damn junkie. You may not know about that life, but I know one when I see one."

"You don't know what you're talking about," Ally stands and shouts.

"Girl, who you talking to? I bet he has a stash of white powder right here in this apartment."

"Enough, Chloe," Gregor bites out. "She said she wants to stay here. We're right down the hall. If she needs you, she can come to you. Cane means her no harm and his demons are his own to deal with. Let's go. We need to get settled into our own place."

I scoff and fold my arms over my chest. "You want me to leave my sister with him? You've lost your mind too."

"Chloe, let this go. I'm not asking you a bunch of questions. Give me the same courtesy. When I can give you answers, I will. Tonight isn't that time," Ally says.

I work my jaw. My mouth tastes like I have ash in it. I don't like this, and I have a ton more I want to say.

"At least tell me when you plan to go back to school. Doesn't your new semester start in a week or so?"

Ally rolls her eyes as if holding back tears. My heart stops and so does my breathing. I'm going to kill this girl.

"I… I'm not going back. I'm dropping out," she whispers.

"What the fuck did she just say?" I bark as I kick my heels off.

I'm going to bust her ass. All of the sacrifices I've made, and she's going to sit here and tell me she's dropping out. Sid and I could have been killed fighting those gang members to keep her safe.

I've eaten so many cans of beans so she could have full meals or school supplies or a new flute or so she could go on some school trip.

Gregor catches me around the waist before I can fully lunge at her. I struggle in his hold. Tears spill down my cheeks. It hits me like a ton of bricks. I've failed my mother.

All she wanted was for me to get Ally through college. I thought having my baby would keep me from doing that, but Ally has fucked her life up all on her own and I don't know where to begin to fix the mess she's making.

"Brodi, put me down and mind your business," I hiss.

He drops me like I'm on fire. I pause and close my eyes. I haven't called him Brodi in weeks. This is bursting the fragile bubble we've created.

I open my eyes as the tears flow and lift a hand. "Ally, I don't know what's going on, but you better pull the brakes on this train wreck before I find out. I'm not your enemy, don't make me one. I'm here to help you and take care of you when you need. I'm not the villain."

With that, I turn and follow after my husband who has stormed from the apartment. My head hurts. I'm torn between my sister and my husband. Ally always comes first, but this time it doesn't feel like she should. She's hiding things from me.

Gregor

I don't know why I thought I'd catch a break coming back home. The plane didn't touch down before my father requested my presence.

I was thrown back in time to that call that made my decision final. It was right when Chloe and I first went away, when I'd planned to tell her I wanted her to come with me.

I'll never forget the rage I felt after that call. It was then I realized I either had to take Chloe with me or let her go for good, because he knew about her. If I kept in touch, he could get to her while I wasn't around to protect her.

I chose to make it seem like she meant nothing to me, by leaving her behind and not showing any interest until I could keep an eye on her life. It was risky but I had hoped it would work.

Now here I am. On the verge of having all I want, but my father is lurking with his plans and Cee is slipping through my fingers because my little brother and her sister have somehow tied themselves together.

She's right, Cane has had a problem in the past. However, I want to give him the benefit of the doubt. Old habits die hard, Cane may move like a junkie, but those are tics that have stayed with him. I know them for what they are. It doesn't mean he's using now.

I look down at a sleeping Chloe. She's the only one in my life who I seem to be able to keep happy.

Just wait until she's a teenager.

I snort at the thought. I can't even blame Cee for her anger. She's done so much to see Ally be successful in life. I remember the way she talked about doing whatever she could to honor the promise she made to her mother. Those words were the ones that made me leave and allow her to care for her sister.

Movement by the door causes me to turn my gaze to it. Cee stands in the threshold of little Chloe's room. She has her arms around her waist. Her eyes are sad as she looks back at me.

"I'm sorry. I didn't mean for you to get in the middle of that," she says softly.

I turn to kiss Chloe's head and then stand to leave the room. I lace my fingers with Cee's. She looks up at me pleadingly. I'm not angry with her.

Yes, it stung for her to call me Brodi. I thought we were beyond that. However, like I said, I understand.

"This isn't about me and I'm not going to make it about me. Give her time, you should cool off and then talk to her. You're right, my brother has had a troubled past, but he's not going to hurt her.

"I can see it in his eyes. I know Cane better than anyone. It was me he came to when he needed to sort his shit out.

"He's not that person. Not the one you see and want to paint him as. Cane is deeper than what meets the eye."

I stop us in the bedroom and turn to her as I finish my words. She purses her lips as she searches my eyes. It's clear she's thinking my words over.

"She's all I have, Gregor. I've spent my entire life looking after her. And what? I'm just supposed to forget that role now? What about my promise?"

"No one's telling you to forget. She's an adult. Give her space to figure out what she wants. I'm sure your mother will forgive you for not keeping your promise.

"You've done a great job trying. I can promise you this. I'll protect her with my life. Allow her to make mistakes and learn.

Clayton, Cane, and I are all here watching out for her. She's in good hands."

"Yeah, but I want her to tell me the truth. What's really going on?"

"Give her time."

She releases a heavy breath. "Fine."

"Come on, take a bath with me. It was a long flight. It's been a long day. Tomorrow I'm introducing Chloe to my family. I could use some time to relax with my wife."

This gets me a small smile. I'll take it.

CHAPTER FORTY-TWO

Meet My Father

Chloe

"I was hoping to get to talk to you alone," Clooney, Gregor's father, says as he joins me out on the veranda.

I turn to look into his blue eyes. Clooney Sr. is a handsome man, however stern he may be. Although, he's been kind to us all this evening. He seems to be fond of Sid and to my surprise he has a bond with Ally too.

I haven't gotten to know him much. Gregor has been running interference whenever the man looks like he's going to get too close. I turn to look at the house to see if Gregor will come running out this time.

"He's putting Chloe down for a nap," Clooney says as if reading my thoughts. He sighs. "So he's already poisoned you against me."

I look back at him. He looks truly concerned. "No, he hasn't. Gregor has never been too forthcoming about his family. I know at one point you two were at odds."

He nods. "I've interfered a time or two when it came to the two of you. I wasn't sure of your intentions and in the beginning, I didn't know what Clooney was thinking. You were so young. I had to make sure the truth came to light."

My lips part and I narrow my eyes. "I've only ever loved your son. I didn't even know who he was to want anything from him. I never cared about his money," I seethe.

"I understand that now. You're nothing like that Addison woman. If not for my anger with Clooney, I would have seen her coming and… I don't regret my granddaughter. Only not being able to protect my son from the hurt caused by her conception."

I'm getting the feeling that Gregor and his brothers may be underestimating this man standing before me. I look at him more closely.

"What do you know about me?" I say cautiously.

"I know you're a bright young woman. You truly love my son. Your care for your sister is honorable. I know your sacrifices.

"I know I owe you an apology. My ambitions got in the way of your and my son's happiness. I wish I'd gotten to you before the choice you made. I would have taken care of you both until Clooney came to his senses and returned. I know a lot, my dear."

I nod as tears come to my eyes. I never thought about finding and going to Brodi's family. He made his father sound like a monster, I would have been too afraid to come to him.

"Please, no tears, my dear. I've caused enough of those. I thought I was doing the right thing.

"It took me some time to learn life is too short not to spend it with those you love. Everything I do, I do to protect my sons. However, I've learned many times they need protection from me most.

"I'm happy to see you and Clooney have found each other again. I look forward to getting to know you more. I hope you can find it in your heart to forgive me for my role in pulling my son away from you."

"I... I don't know what to say to that. I mean, you made sure he found out about my age. I can't blame you for that, but he made the decision to leave the second time. That's not on you."

"Oh, yes, it is. I told him to end things. Clooney decided to start over because I found out about you. I was the catalyst to him taking off."

"Can I be honest with you?"

"Please."

"I think the Gregor I know now is the right one for me. I've loved your son for years, but I've fallen in love with the man he is today in a way I didn't know I could."

"And yet, I can see the tension between the two of you. I have eyes, Chloe. You don't have to spare my feelings.

"I know the damage I've done. Rest assured, I plan to make up for all the things my actions have caused. Starting with paying for the wedding of your dreams. Anything you want, don't hesitate to get it.

"You don't have to do that. Eileen has already done so much."

"Nonsense, I know there's no monetary number for the pain I've caused, but... money is the one thing I have to share. The one thing I'll leave behind when I'm gone."

I look into his sad eyes, feeling like this conversation means something much deeper than the words spoken. I wipe at my tears and give him a tear-filled smile.

"Your son is teaching me to forgive. I'm not going to lie and say I've learned the lesson in its entirety, but I'm getting there. Thank you for coming to me. I appreciate your words."

"Maybe now you can cut Gregor some slack. He's a man of action and his actions were driven by me. Judge him not on his past, Chloe. Love him for the future he wants to share with you."

I place a hand over his. "I'm trying, Mr. Hennessy."

He gives me a smile. "That's all I ask and please call me Clooney."

"Cee," Gregor barks as he steps out of the house.

I turn to him, and he gestures with his head for me to come to him. I look to his father once more. He gives me a sad smile.

"One day, I'll prove to him I meant no harm. Today's just not that day. I hope you'll start to join Sid for our lunches."

"I'll think about that. Thank you."

Gregor

I'm still stewing about my father cornering Cee while I put Chloe down for a nap. I'll never forgive him if he tries to get between us. I'm not the young man he once controlled.

I take a sip of my drink and stop glaring at my father. Dinner was civil but I don't trust my father. He's up to something.

I turn my attention to my brothers having what seems to be a heated conversation. I'm reminded that I've yet to get a chance to talk to Clay to find out what's been going on with Ally or anything else. I start for Cane and Clay just as Cane storms off.

"What's all that about?" I ask as I stop at Clay's side. We watch Cane rush out of the house.

"He's using," Clay bites out.

I jerk my head back. I have a hard time believing that. I would know if Cane were using again. I think he's hiding something, but I don't think he's snorting blow.

"You're fucking bullshitting me, right?"

My words come out with as much disbelief as I feel. Cane may have tics from his past, but he's not still using. He has a gambling problem. That's his vice, not drugs.

"Nope, he owes, and he owes big. Those two think everyone around them to be idiots. She's into some shit that's taking a shitload of favors to try to get her out of," Clay says and nods his head toward Ally.

I pull a hand down my face. "How much time do we have to fix this one?"

"Ally's out of time. I've been keeping her hidden. I'll tell you about that later. As for Cane, I think it's time we fall back and let him figure shit out."

I scowl at my brother and turn my glare on him. He sounds like my father. I'd never abandon Cane or Clay. I can't believe Clay is even suggesting we abandon our baby brother.

"You sound like Dad," I snarl. "I didn't leave you to figure it out."

"I wasn't stuffing white powder up my nose either. He has a problem, gambling debts and crazy-ass girlfriends, fine. We can get him out of that shit any time. This other bullshit will have us digging a grave for him, not keeping him from one. It has to stop."

I work my jaw. He has a point, but I'm not going to leave Cane out to dry. This is just one more thing I don't need on my plate. If Cane is using, Chloe is going to kill me. I hope he's not putting me in this fucked-up position.

"Fuck," I blow out. "This is the last thing I need."

"Tell me about it. I'm still trying to wrap my head around all of this shit you brought to our door." He shakes his head.

"You?" I snort.

Telling my brothers out loud about how I've returned with a two-year-old was a lot for me. I can only imagine how they felt, especially Clay. He thinks it's his job to fix and control everything. This he can't fix and I'm the one who needs to be in control.

He pats me on the shoulder. "I'm here. Whatever you need. You did the right thing. She loves you." He squeezes my shoulder.

I'm beginning to believe he might be right. I hadn't planned for any of this, but it feels right. I love my wife and my daughter. I'll spend the rest of my life making sure they're both safe and happy.

"She's mine. I didn't plan any of this, but they're both mine," I affirm.

"Clay." David rushes toward us, and I know this night is about to take another turn. The look on David's face says it all.

"What now?" Clay grunts.

"You're going to want to see this, boss," David says, handing over a printed email.

Clayton takes the page and scans it. I move to read it over his shoulder. My eyes nearly bulge out of my head. I'm going to kill Cane and Ally before Cee gets a chance to. My head starts to ache.

"Un-fucking-believable," I mutter.

CHAPTER FORTY-THREE

CHAPTER FORTY-THREE

Lost Your Mind

Chloe

I'm trying my best to enjoy this shopping trip. However, it's hard with my husband keeping things from me that I know have something to do with my sister. Gregor has been acting strange since dinner at his parents' the other night.

I saw him, Clay, and David huddle up with a piece of paper. The next thing I knew they were ushering Ally into Clooney's study. I had gone to follow but Clooney and Eileen intercepted me.

It's been two days and Gregor hasn't given a single explanation for what happened. However, I don't think it's his place to tell me. It's Ally's and she's playing with me like I won't hurt her.

"You guys are so lucky. Back home you can't find guys like you have. I mean, come on. They send their personal security to shop with you," Marnita sings.

"Trust me, it's not as romantic as it seems. It's just another form of control," I say dryly.

I love her, but I nearly roll my eyes. Gregor didn't send Ethan to protect me. This is his way of having control, something he's been establishing more and more since we've been back.

Gregor's dominant side hasn't gone anywhere. I just want to know what he's trying to control this time. Whatever it is, it has my sister's name all over it.

Her jumpy behind isn't helping my mood in the least, with her X-Men-looking ass. I've been tempted to snatch that damn wig right off her head.

Whatever Ally has ever wanted, I've made it happen no matter the cost of what I had to sacrifice, just like my mother did for me. I didn't want her to miss out on having that type of love and care. I tried to give her the mother's love I got to have.

In a way, she soothed the pain of me not raising my own child. I've bent over backward for Ally and now I don't know who I'm looking at. What has she gotten into that she feels she can't talk to me about?

I blame Cane. She's always up his junkie-acting ass. I swear, when his brothers aren't shielding him from me, I'm going to go upside his head. The thing is, I don't even know if the two are fucking or what. His weird ass treats her like she's his possession, but Ally swears he's just a friend.

"Can we go in this store?" Marnita asks, pulling me out of my thoughts. I look at the store she's pointing to. On any other day,

I'd want to go in. Not today, especially not with Miss Storm and her long-ass gray wig.

"Please," Ally groans, fanning her face.

I turn to her and narrow my eyes. If she didn't have on that dumbass wig, she wouldn't be fanning herself. Granted it is hot for September. One of those New York Indian summer days as people call them.

"You wouldn't be so hot if you didn't have on that ridiculous wig," I mutter, no longer able to hold my tongue, the wig is down to her butt, she doesn't even look like herself, and what's with the fucking shades?

I swear she wasn't this weird in high school or junior high— the times when I would have ignored behavior like this. When she takes the shades off, I bare my teeth. I've had enough.

Gray contacts? Ally is so pretty. I don't get this identity crisis. If she's doing this for some guy... I thought I did better than this. Is this the example I'm showing with Gregor?

"Okay, what's with the X-Men-convention look?" Sid teases, speaking my thoughts.

"I wanted to try something new. It's not like you guys haven't changed your hair or something in the past. Why is everything I do a problem?"

"Because you're making a bunch of poor choices and I don't like it," I hiss.

"Right, says the sister who runs off to Dubai for what? Four months and comes back engaged. Setting awesome examples, sis," Ally retorts.

I freaking snap. I lunge for my sister to choke her lights out, but Ethan catches me around the waist.

"Thanks," Sid says as she gets between me and Ally.

Tears fill my eyes. This girl has no idea all I've given up for her. I always choose her over myself or anything else. I chose her over my unborn child. How dare she?

"You have no idea the things I've sacrificed for you. No idea," I choke out.

"I didn't ask you to," she tosses back and pouts like a big fucking baby and she wants to be treated like an adult.

"Gah, you're so fucking ungrateful. I've never put a man before you, Ally. I'm only asking for the same respect. Talk to me. Tell me what's going on. Because if I have to beat that shit out of you, I promise we're going to have a long trip back to being sisters."

I don't want to take my pent-up anger out on her, but she's pushing me. I know if I beat her ass, she's not going to forgive me easily, but I don't know what to do. Something is wrong, I need her to talk to me. I plead with my eyes, *let me fix it.*

"Maybe we should all take a step back," Sid says as everyone in the store stares at us. Fuck them. This is my sister and I need to get through to her.

I roll my eyes as tears fall and I work my jaw. I didn't want to work in the financial district forever, it was what I needed to do for Ally. I could have kept my child, but I had to care for her. Yet, I'll never complain or tell her about those sacrifices because they were done out of love.

"Not everything is about you, Chloe," Ally tosses at me, sending a knife through my heart.

I lunge for her again. This time Ethan has to carry me out of the store. I start to sob. I feel so helpless and angry.

All my mother asked was that I make sure Ally had a good life and made it through college. She asked me not to allow her to go into the system, not that I would ever.

My heart is on fire because in all I've done, no matter how hard I fought, I'm losing the one person I've given my all for.

Gregor

"Have you lost your mind?" I bellow at Cane as I storm into his bedroom to find him lying under the covers with the blackout blinds drawn in the middle of the day.

"What have I done now?"

"What have you done? What have you done?" I tear the covers off him. He's lying here naked like he's some fucking king.

"Clay is digging for the truth to clean up your shit and here you lie like you haven't a care in the world. I'm not asking anyone but *you*, you owe me the truth," I seethe.

"I told Clay I had this under control. Why is he still digging?"

"Because he knows my wife's sister is involved and I'll fucking kill your ass if something happens to her."

"Your wife?"

"Yes, Chloe and I are married. I love that woman with everything I am, Cane, stop putting me in a position to have to choose. She's the one person in this world you will never come before. What have you done?"

He runs a hand through his hair. "I've come to care about Ally too. At first, I saw an opportunity and I jumped on it. We weren't in New York. How was I supposed to know she was Chloe's sister? I didn't even know who Chloe was or what she meant to you.

"I fucked up. I should have dug more into her life, but she needed my help in that moment. The situation was a gamble, and I needed the high. Dad had just served us with those bullshit terms, and I needed to gain control back.

"So you married my wife's sister," I grind out. "You know Chloe is going to cut your balls off?"

He blows out a breath. "She sure as fuck is because I'm not ready to walk away. *If* Clay figures out a way to get us out of this, I don't think I want a divorce."

"Do you love her?"

"She gets me, I need that."

"That's not what I asked you."

"I just need time to make all this other shit go away. I know I can't keep her but I want to keep my promise to her." I don't miss that he continues to ignore my question. Chloe is going to lose her shit. He better love this girl. "I'll keep paying those bastards off if it means she's safe."

"You've been paying?" I say and furrow my brows.

"Yeah, I've paid a million already. I've been moving the next million around to make the next payment. I couldn't make it obvious to Clay."

"We need to talk to him. That email threatened Ally because you failed to pay."

"What? What email?"

"The other night, David intercepted an email. I've been waiting to get you alone to confront you about it. That's how I knew you guys were married."

"Fuck," he roars and stands to jump from the bed to wrap the sheet around his waist as he grabs his phone.

"Who are you calling?"

"Royce. There's more to this. I need to get her out of here for a while."

"Cane," I growl.

"Gregor, I've got this, and I know she's too good for me."

I snort. I never said that. Cane is a good man. He's just yet to realize it.

"This needs to be handled. Ally can't cover for her friend a second more, I mean it."

This gets my attention. I narrow my eyes because it's clear my brother still isn't coughing all the details up. However, now I know Ally's problem is my problem and I'm going to fix it.

CHAPTER FORTY-FOUR

Let Me Show You

Gregor

Cane may not want to admit he's in love, but I know that look. He's totally in love with Ally. He wasted no time packing to take her somewhere safe for a bit.

However, they can't stay away long with the engagement party at the end of the week and all the other events coming up. I asked Ethan to team up with Royce to make sure Ally is safe. I agree with Clay, for now, we need to keep her hidden until we get to the bottom of all this.

Those wigs she's been wearing go a long way to change her appearance. That was a great idea on Cane's behalf. They even fooled me.

"This place is nice," Cee says, grabbing my attention.

I look up from my plate as she sits across from me. Her hair is pin straight tonight. She went to see her usual stylist and now her hair frames her gorgeous face like fine red silk. I wanted to take her on a date to get her mind off things. We've been fighting about Ally a lot.

I didn't want to get in the middle of this but now that I know the truth, I need to do all I can to protect my wife and all she holds dear as well as my brother who's truly trying to do the right thing.

However, I'm not telling this woman about the danger her sister has found herself in. Chloe will try to throw herself in the middle of things. I won't have that.

"How's the wedding planning coming along?"

"I have one more fitting coming up. The invitations will be arriving this week, if all goes well and they look good, your mom has been talking about a tea party with the girls to get them sent out. It's going…"

"But?"

"I might be distracted with the show's details. It's all so overwhelming."

"Eric hasn't been carrying his weight with the planning?"

"No, no, he has, and your mom has planned so much of the wedding, I haven't had to do much, but it's all happening so fast."

I take a sip of my brandy. "It is a lot all at once. Maybe I should take some time off to help."

"You know you don't have time for that but thank you for offering."

"I'd make time if you need me."

Her cheeks start to glow. This is the type of night I was hoping for. We need to focus more on us. She gives me a coy smile.

"There is something you can do for me," she says.

"Name it."

She tips her head to the side. "What's going on with Ally? Where did she and Cane go?"

I groan and roll my eyes. She knows I won't lie to her, so she's been trying to corner me with questions which always end up in an argument. Something I wanted to avoid tonight.

I hold my hand up. "Don't. Tonight is about us. I don't want to fight. We're going to steer clear of all Ally and Cane talk."

She purses her lips. I can see the defiance in her eyes, but she nods and starts back on her food. Maybe my surprise tonight will bring us back to neutral ground.

What Chloe doesn't get is that I'm always going to cover her and anything or anyone connected to her. I have this under control.

"Did you pick a dress for the engagement party?"

"I'm going with the gold one," she says.

I smile. That was the one I was hoping she'd pick. She looked so sexy when she tried it on. I look forward to Saturday evening. We may already be married, but I look forward to showing her off as my fiancée.

I feel for my brother. I couldn't imagine being married as long as he has been and holding it in as a secret. I blame my father, he placed all our backs to the wall and forced our decisions. I still don't understand his endgame.

"What are you thinking about? You're grinding your teeth."

"Nothing."

"It doesn't look like nothing."

"It's a conversation with my father I've yet to have. Again. None of that matters tonight."

Chloe

"A few more steps and we're there," Gregor whispers in my ear.

I step forward carefully. Anticipation is building in my tummy. I have no idea where he's taking me. This date has been nice so far. I don't know what he can do to top the restaurant, but I'm expecting something amazing from the excitement that's been coming off him during the ride here.

I wanted to be angry with him for not answering my earlier question, but after sneaking off to the bathroom to text my sister and her snarky ass reply, I decided to allow her to be grown and bump her damn head. At least, I'm trying to.

Honestly, I've been toying with the idea of seeing a therapist. I have so much pinned-up anger. I can't get the bubble back from Dubai, so I need to figure out how to deal with what I'm facing now.

"Okay, we're here," Gregor breathes, breaking into my thoughts.

He removes the blindfold from around my eyes and a gasp leaves my lips. We're in a gallery and the place is lit up by lights strung up all over the place. Music is playing from somewhere as well.

I spin around and take in the space. Clenching my hands to my chest, I look up at Gregor. My lips are trembling.

"Is this?"

He nods his head as he bites down on his lower lip. I swipe at the tears that run free and stand in awe.

"I wanted you to see the space in person. This is where you're going to debut your work to the world, my little artist."

"Oh my God," I breathe and throw myself into his arms. "This place is amazing. I'm so excited."

In this moment, I forget everything else. I've never taken a moment to be selfish. However, for now, I give myself a chance to enjoy this.

He kisses the top of my head. "I'm so proud of you. I know you're going to crush it."

I pull away and cup his face in my hands. His eyes sparkle back at me. Here and now, I dare to believe this is my life. Those three words are right on the tip of my tongue, but fear keeps them right where they are.

I never dreamed I'd be standing in a gallery in Manhattan preparing for my very first show. I have so many nerves and an entire five months before it all comes together.

"This place is amazing. I can't wait until opening night," I gush with excitement.

"This is what I want for you."

I furrow my brows. "What is?"

"When you talked about moving up in the financial world, you were excited, but not like this. This is your thing. This is what makes you happy. All I want is for you to live true happiness. I want you to do what Chloe wants. You deserve this."

I look down and think on his words. They pierce my heart and meet their mark. I gave up what I wanted for myself a long time ago. My decisions haven't been about me in a very long time.

My thoughts turn to Ally. What if this isn't the time for me to think about me? I'll never forgive myself if something happens to her. The girl knows how to sniff out trouble like Toucan Sam. I've been the buffer in her life for as long as I can remember.

Gregor purses his lips and narrows his eyes at me. "Baby, stop it. You deserve this. Allow yourself to have this." He pauses and sighs. "Would it ease your mind if I told you I think my little brother is as crazy about your sister as I am about you, and he has every intention of making sure she's happy and safe?"

"No, not really. I want to know what's going on."

"It's being handled, Chlo. Please, let it go. Enjoy the moment."

I narrow my eyes at him. Clayton pulled me aside and asked me to trust him and his brothers. He did tell me he had it handled. I hate to admit it, but I took his word a little faster than I did my own husband.

I'm working on that. Like I said, it might be time to talk to someone. I know I'm pushing Gregor away, but I don't know how to stop myself. I'm too afraid of being hurt again. We're back in the real world. Real things happen here.

He smiles and holds out his hand. "We created the magic we had in Dubai, Chlo. You and me. Give me some time with my wife, time to show her I love her and want all her dreams to come true," he says as if reading my mind.

"I truly am trying, Gregor. I wish I could let it go, but I have this sinking feeling in the pit of my stomach. Something bad is coming and I'd rather not be blindsided," I say.

He closes his eyes. I'm trying so hard to be in the moment and not be my worst enemy, but it's been a week since I had that fight with Ally in the store.

Every time I think about it, I get pissed all over again. It doesn't help that Cane was in the lobby with suitcases when we returned home from shopping that evening. I haven't seen either of them since.

"I thought this would bring a smile to your face and take your mind off things for a bit," Gregor says as he opens his eyes.

I instantly feel bad. Ally wants nothing to do with me, but here my husband is trying. I'll be honest, as long as I have Ally to think about, I can avoid all my true feelings. Gregor does all the right things. However, I'm allowing caution to win out.

Yet, tonight, I decide to let my guard down. "I'm sorry. I'll let it go for tonight."

"Good, come dance with me."

A smile comes to my face as he pulls his phone out to change the song. This man and his old music. I hold my hand out.

"Give me that phone."

He smirks back at me and hands it over. I may have a wall up, but I'm not ready for him to give up on me. The perfect song comes to mind to say all the things I'm not ready to.

Blackstreet's "Don't Leave Me" beings to play, causing Gregor to lift a brow and his smile to broaden. I know a secret about this man. He has a mean two-step, like Chi-Town mean. I take the hand he offers and allow him to lead.

He spins me out and then back in until my back is to his front, crossing our arms over my body. Guiding me into his two-step, he looks down into my eyes.

I'm lost in his gaze as he lifts his hand to brush my cheek. Placing his forehead to mine, he starts to sing along with the music. I cup his jaw and allow my feelings to flow through our connection.

This song couldn't be more perfect. I want this, but I have to find a way to allow us to have it. I'm trying. I really am. However, it's seeing him fight for it that's pushing me to find the way back to the peace we once had in each other's arms.

I've learned it's possible to love someone while being too hurt to let that love show. As if knowing this is a moment where I need him to show me, and not tell me of his love—he crushes my lips with a searing kiss.

Lifting me onto his waist, he moves us through the gallery. I have no idea where he's taking me until the heavy-sounding door of the coatroom closes, causing me to jump in his arms. I look around and laugh.

"I need you now," he breathes into my mouth.

Panic rises and I widen my eyes. I'm not ready for unprotected sex. Always a step ahead of my concerns, he pulls a condom from his pocket as he backs me into a wall, my legs still around his waist.

He works to free himself from his belt and slacks. Biting into the condom wrapper, he then rolls it on. I lock my fingers in his hair as he drags his hands up my thighs to push my dress up.

He deepens the kiss, causing my body to heat all over. His body heat sears me through my clothes. I moan into his mouth, savoring his flavor.

Pushing my panties aside, he sinks into me. My lips part on a gasp. Dropping my head back, I look up at the ceiling and roll my eyes in my head.

"Chloe," he growls through clenched teeth.

I lower my gaze to his. My mouth falls open as I lock eyes with him. He covers my lips with his.

"Now you're with me," he breathes into my mouth as he links our fingers and moves to hold our hands above our heads.

"Yes," I pant.

"I love you," he says as he works his hips into me slowly.

I should say the words back. I feel them as he grinds into me. Yet, that lock is still in place. I try reaching for the freedom he's offering. Freedom, I want and need, but am too afraid to grab hold of.

The music can still be heard where we are. I close my eyes and feel. It's all I can do. I feel him in my heart, in my body, in my soul, in my mind. It's all him.

"Stay with me, Chlo. I'm going to get us there."

Why do I feel like he's talking about more than our climaxes? *Because he is.*

CHAPTER FORTY-FIVE

The Past Appears

Chloe

A grin comes to my face as I watch Gregor's Uncle Devin dance with his wife. They're showing off with a beautiful two-step routine. The way his wife rolls her body as he steps and shows off in front of her is awe inspiring.

I was a little taken aback when Gregor introduced me to his stern-looking uncle and his fun-looking mocha-skinned wife. She oozes joy. Her tight black dress speaks of her lack of care for others' opinions.

"They're amazing, aren't they?" Gregor murmurs in my ear as he comes up behind me.

"Yes, did your uncle teach you?"

"No, Raven did." He nods his head toward his uncle's wife. "It was her way of distracting me from drinking myself to death."

"I'll have to thank her. She saved you and she taught you well. You're almost as good as your uncle," I tease.

He snorts. "You think so?" He holds his hand out as Ed Sheeran's "Shiver" comes on. "Let me show you how it's really done."

He winks at me, bringing a laugh to my lips. I take his hand and follow him out to the dance floor. It's our engagement party after all. We should be showing off for our guests.

Gregor pulls me in close and slides his hand down my back. I've seen how he's looked at me in this gold dress. I know it was the one he preferred out of the three I bought.

The gold heels are my favorite. They make my legs look long and my calves toned. Gregor's black suit and gold tie complement my dress while giving him a regal look.

I can't stop smiling as we give his aunt and uncle a run for their money. This man is so smooth as he rolls our bodies together before spinning me out to twist and turn with slow fancy footwork, then switching up to faster steps.

I slip under his arm, and he tugs me back to him as he dances us in a small circle. He stops and leans me forward as if he's going to drop me but pulls me back up quickly. I burst into laughter as he does a half split.

His uncle cuts in and does a few fancy steps with me as Raven and Gregor cut up.

"Oh my God, she's so good," I say in awe.

Gregor even seems to step it up a notch. That's when Uncle Devin gets my attention and I follow his lead as he dips, twists, and guides me around. I surprise myself as I keep up with him.

I'm breathless as Gregor switches off to come back to me. The crowd stands around the dance floor, clapping to the music as we dance. I look into Gregor's eyes as I smile up at him.

All my worries and concerns are forgotten. I'm in the moment, enjoying myself. I haven't had this much fun in so long.

This night has been so much more than I thought it would be. I thought it would be stuffy and boring. It has been anything but.

"You're enjoying yourself. Good. I love that smile," Gregor says.

"Where's Chloe?"

"With mom, she passed out. I was thinking we'd leave soon, but I don't want to miss out on this moment."

I place my head on his shoulder. "One more dance. This is fun."

"Anything you want."

"I Can't Help Falling In Love with You" by UB40 comes on and it's the perfect last dance. I gasp.

"Do you remember—" we say in unison.

My cheeks heat. His lids become hooded, and his eyes drop to my lips. "The first time we made love on the balcony."

"Yes, I remember," I whisper.

Of course, he guides us into a slow two-step. Pulling all my weight onto his right side, he steps back and dips with me resting against him.

His moves are competitionworthy, as is his aunt and uncle's performance a few steps over from us. However, I tune everyone else out as my husband guides me around the dance floor in a sensual dance that makes me want to rush home.

"I love you, Chlo," he whispers in my ear.

I look up into his eyes and close mine as I try to say the words. I'm close, but not there yet. Still my heart says the words I can't.

***

The engagement party was above and beyond what I was expecting. It was opulence at its finest. There were more people than I thought possible.

I've never smiled so much in my life. I don't remember half of the people who we greeted. The craziest part, I do believe Eileen has invited twice as many people to the wedding.

However, I did enjoy myself, even as Ally worked my last nerve. Clooney seemed to be so proud to introduce me and Sid to everyone. I wasn't expecting that at all.

"Did you enjoy yourself?" Gregor asks, causing me to turn from the window I've been staring out while musing as we ride in the back of the Bentley, headed home.

"I enjoyed your Uncle Devin," I say with a smile.

"You would," he snorts.

"His sarcasm is perfection."

"He has a way with words for sure."

I reach to run my hand through a sleeping Chloe's hair as Gregor holds her in his lap. She looks like a little angel in her pink dress.

"She was the star of the night," I murmur.

"No, I believe that was you. Between that dress, mom singing your praises, and your stellar dance moves, you had everyone's attention tonight."

I smile. "You know I was offered commissions to do pieces by several guests."

"You know your show is going to be packed if my mother has anything to do with it. She's going to make sure Sid's book is a bestseller as well. Mark my words."

I laugh. "She's awesome."

"My family loves you and Sid."

"What's the story with the taunting way Uncle Devin calls you Brodi?"

He gives a laugh. "You caught that?"

"Yes."

"He thinks it's childish and hated the fact that everyone called me by the name well into my thirties. He uses it to mock me till this day."

"He's your mother's brother, right?"

"Yes, Aunt Evelyn is Dad's sister and his only sibling. Uncle Devin is mom's only as well."

"Aunt Evelyn, that's Wade's mom."

"Yeah."

I don't miss that he rolls his eyes. I picked up on some tension between Wade and Clay as well as Gregor. I've met Wade once at the firm. He had douchebag written all over him.

My questions are cut short as we arrive in front of our building. I glance out the window and something catches my eye immediately. I squint to try to make sure I'm not seeing things.

She looks a bit different, but I think it's her. Lita, one of the girls from the old neighborhood. She's one of the girls I wanted to get Ally away from. This chick has always been nothing but trouble.

I climb out of the car after Gregor steps out. I start for Lita, wondering what the hell she's doing here. However, she turns and locks eyes with me before taking off.

"Hey," I call out.

It's too late, she's sprinting to get away and turns the corner quickly. I'm not dressed to run after her. I ball my fist and purse my lips.

"You know her?" Gregor asks at my side.

"I think that was one of Ally's old friends, but why the hell is she hanging around here?"

Clay's Phantom and Cane's SUV pull up right as the words fall out of my mouth. I scowl hard as Ally steps from the car. Gregor places a hand on the small of my back and kisses my forehead.

"Come on. Everyone's tired and it's chilly out."

I look up at him, then at Chloe. She starts to snuggle into her father as if she's cold. I tighten my fists but remind myself I'm going to allow Ally to bump her head. I'm too old to run around beating up gang members, especially if Ally insists on being involved with them.

At least that's what I try to tell myself.

CHAPTER FORTY-SIX

Brotherly Love

Gregor

Five months later…

This night has been so far beyond a success. I couldn't be more proud of Chlo. I'm watching her live her dream.

I look down at her. Her face is glowing. The tight black dress she has on is showing off her tight body and gives her a classy, sexy look. She's commanding the room tonight.

"You did your thing," Sid says and pulls Cee into a hug as she and Clayton come over to the painting we're standing in front of.

This is the one I purchased for my home office. It's one of the ones inspired by the hot-air balloon ride. This painting fills my chest with so much joy and peace. I had to have it.

"This is all so amazing," Marnita says as she rushes over and wraps her arms around Sid and Chlo.

She rocks the other two women in her arms. I don't miss the rosy tint to her cheeks. I've come to learn how much Marnita is another part of this close-knit friendship. Something I couldn't understand from a distance.

"God, I'm so proud of you," Sid gushes.

"I am too," Marnita adds.

"This was a great turnout," Clay says, placing a hand on Sid's back as the three women separate.

I don't miss my brother isn't giving Sid more than a few inches of space. I can't say I blame him. It's only been a month since she was attacked.

A lot has changed within four weeks. With Dupont and Fran out of the way, deals haven't been falling through as much and I've been able to focus more on helping with the Cane and Ally situation.

I look across the room and my gaze lands on Cane. Yeah, I'm going to have to address that before we leave for the night. Ally has been giving Chloe a wide berth all evening and I don't think it's out of respect for how important the night is.

"Congratulations," my friend Stew, the gallery owner, says to Cee as he joins us. "This has been the best turnout I've ever seen for a debut artist. You're officially sold out. Every piece has gone and for nothing less than half a million. Thanks to Mr. Claremont driving the pieces into bidding wars."

"Are you serious?" Chlo breathes.

"It was my pleasure to do my part," Wade says as he joins our little group.

"You're good for something," I say as I look my brother in his blue eyes.

I'm still working out how I feel about him being my younger brother and not the cousin I've thought him to be all my life. Wade has been a pain in my ass for years. However, I never knew my father's secret.

The old man is full of them, I'm learning. We've yet to have a conversation about all he's been hiding. I haven't been in a forgiving mood when it comes to him. Let him stew in the mess he has made.

"Where's the love?" Wade croons.

Sid shakes her head. "I'm still getting used to the fact that you're their brother."

"I know, it's hard to believe you missed out on being my woman and now you're my sister-in-law," he teases.

Clay's nostrils flare. "You keep playing with me, Wade."

Wade holds his hands up in the air. "I'm just joking. Damn, that temper is nasty."

Clay frowns and waves a hand at Wade. "You're going to learn when to stop joking with me. I don't play when it comes to my wife."

The ladies giggle behind their hands. I even have to grin a little. That is until Cane comes over and leans into my ear.

"I need to talk to you."

Turning, I then lean in to kiss Chlo's lips as she glares up at Cane. She turns, I'm sure to look for Ally as she places her hands on her hips. I move my lips to her ear.

"Not tonight," I whisper. "This is your night. Let it go."

She purses her lips. I peck them and rub a hand up and down her arm. Stew grabs her attention with more talk of the showing and the sales. I get the feeling he's going to offer her another show very soon.

The Soho show will be another hit, I'm sure. I push all of those thoughts to the back of my mind as I lead Cane to Stew's office for some privacy. We step inside and I close the door behind us.

"What's going on?"

I narrow my eyes at him as he pulls a hand down his face and blows out a breath. He looks like he's holding on to his cool by a thread.

"She's pregnant. I need this to be over. Whatever I need to pay, I need it to be done."

"Shit."

"Exactly. The games end now."

"What games, Cane? You need to talk to me."

"Ally doesn't get into this shit on her own. She's covering for an ungrateful-ass friend.

"A friend I want out of her life. I was just giving her the rope to hang herself. I think she's finally done it. This is over. I'm taking the lead. Ally has no say anymore, not with our baby involved."

"I don't like this."

A knock comes at the door. I turn to it as it opens, and Clay sticks his head in. I nod for him to enter. I'm not sure if I'm surprised to see Wade enter with him.

"What are you doing here?" Cane says to Wade.

"I know more about your life than you do. Trust me, you want me here."

"What's that supposed to mean?"

"Your father wouldn't have started this if he didn't think we could fix it."

Suddenly, I freeze as his words hit me. "What do you mean Dad wouldn't have started this?"

"Oh, come on, man. You guys haven't figured it out yet?"

"Figured what out?" Clay bites out.

Wade rolls his eyes. "He wants you all happy, he's trying to make things up to you and your mother. You think he wants control, but he's trying to right his wrongs.

"He knew about Clay's obsession"—he points to me—"your lost devotion"—he turns and looks at Cane—"and Cane's secrets. You all fell into his trap, and I helped him set it. It was my way of doing something for my brothers."

I bare my teeth and run a hand through my hair. That man has to control everything. He just can't help himself.

"Listen, you guys can't be angry with him forever. He loves you all. What you all see as control is his way of keeping each of you on the path to a good life and happiness. No, he hasn't always gone about it in the right way—trust me, I know that better than anyone, but he means well."

"But why?" Cane says. "Why all this... this meddling?"

"That you're going to have to ask him about yourself."

"Wait, hold on. Are you telling me this whole time he was doing this to get me back with Chloe?"

Wade shrugs and gives me a mischievous smile. "Among some other things. He'd hoped you would have addressed the Addison thing sooner. We didn't see the Sid situation coming, that delayed his plans a bit."

Cane blows out a breath as he runs his hand through his hair. "Wait, but I met Ally after the terms were served."

"Ah, yes, he intended to give you time to find someone and fall in love, but you stepped right into the plan as if he'd planned that part himself. When he figured out who she was... I've never seen the old man look so triumphant."

"He played us all."

I scoff. This all tastes bitter on my tongue. I rub at my chest. I want to be angry, but my feelings are so conflicted.

"I wouldn't have gone through all this if it weren't for him. I wanted to be my own man. He almost ripped that from me again," I say bitterly as I think aloud.

"No, he didn't. In time, you will see. He's trying to get something to all of you."

"And where does that leave you?" Clay asks.

Wade shrugs, his smile falling. "I don't think it leaves me anywhere. I'm doing what's asked of me as a son."

I don't miss the sad look that comes to Wade's face. I note it and shove it back for later. Right now, I need to figure out how to keep my wife from taking Cane's head off and murdering her own sister.

"I'd watch that if I were you," Clay warns. Then as if reading my thoughts, he turns to Cane. "So are you ready to talk to me about this? I know you're not using, but you're involved with someone you have no business being around. Why?" Clay demands.

Cane groans. He releases a deep breath. "I'm guessing you already know she's my wife." He's stating a fact, not asking a question. This is Clay. You have to work hard to hide things from him.

Clayton nods. "Yes, I'm aware. Which is why you have the entire Lost Souls brotherhood at your back. Now that I'm sure you're not using, I need to know why I'm racking up such a high debt."

"Where do you want me to start?"

"The beginning," Clay, Wade, and I grunt in unison.

Chloe

This should be one of the greatest nights of my life, but I can't help watching my sister and knowing something is totally off with her.

"Hey, did you hear what I said?" Sid says from beside me.

"No, I'm sorry. Is it me, or is Ally acting stranger than usual?"

"Nope, I picked up on it too. Cane isn't any better."

"Yeah, I saw that. With his feign-acting ass."

"Oh shit. That's it. I couldn't put my finger on it. The jittery tics and the way he moves. It's just like a junkie."

"Sure is, but they swear he's not using."

"You know, those habits do stick. Remember Joseph, freshman year in college? He had a bad coke habit. He kicked it junior year, but he still moved like he was an addict through to graduation."

"Yeah, I do remember him. He'd look all tweaked out when we had a test or something, especially a pop quiz. So what the fuck is Cane so nervous about?"

"I have no idea. Those two are like little kids trying to steal a snack before bedtime."

I narrow my eyes and glare at Ally as she stares out of the window. "You know, she's too smart for her own good." I look past my sister and catch the person staring at her through the window. "Or maybe she's not."

I signal for Ethan and rush for the front door of the gallery. Sidney is right on my heels, grabbing David's attention. Both men are at my back as I pull up short. My chest heaves as I stand with my fists balled at my sides.

"Fuck," I hiss.

"What? What just happened?"

I turn to look at Sid. "It's that Lita chick. It's the second time I've seen her lurking around."

"You mean West's sister?"

I wrinkle my brows. "She was West's sister?"

"Yeah, that's how Ally met him. I thought you knew that."

"No, I didn't."

I turn to head back inside to find Ally. However, she's standing in the doorway of the gallery with Royce at her back, holding her from stepping out of the door.

"Why the hell is Lita snooping around you? Tell me you're not involved with her."

The color drains from her face. My stomach twists in knots. I don't have a good feeling about this.

CHAPTER FORTY-SEVEN

Lost & Found

Gregor

I step into Club Dream with Clay and Cane and take a deep breath. It's early afternoon so the place isn't open for business yet. The space is wide open and looks vacant except for the bikers waiting for us.

I'm a bit taken aback by how many Lost Souls are here. They're taking up three side-by-side booths. If I were a lesser man, they would make an intimidating sight.

I look to Cane as he pulls a hand down his face. I think reality has finally set in. He's stepped his ass in shit and it's starting to reek.

His actions were honorable but stupid. Ally is a smart girl, she would have wiggled and maneuvered her way out of this. I think Cane stepping in caused more of an issue than a solution.

However, I get it. At his age, I probably would have done the same thing.

Yet now my wife is pissed and demanding answers. This has gotten out of hand. I shouldn't be keeping any of this from her, but it's better I handle things before I reveal the mess that's been created.

Once this is over, we can focus on us again. Maybe even try for a baby, but first I need to help Ally so she can sit and talk to her sister. Ally needs to own up to her actions.

The three of us take a seat at the table where King and Brick are seated. "Thanks for meeting with me," I say to King.

"No problem. Clay is family, he always has my ear."

"Still, you guys didn't have to come all this way."

King nods. "You may need our muscle for this. Not to mention, I have business here in New York. It was on my way. Besides, I'm interested in the outcome here. Diggs, go on and tell him what Gutter found out."

I sit back and listen to the information Diggs gives, the entire time I have my eyes on Cane. He either didn't know some of this information or he chose to hide it. Either way, my blood is boiling. Chloe is going to strangle Ally. We've all been in danger because of these two.

Clay's connection to the Lost Souls has had its benefits this time around. Ally's problem has been stalled because of it.

"What do you want to do?" Brick asks.

"If they want war, you have my army behind you," King offers.

"They're bringing this to my door. Ally is family. I think you already know what I want to do," Clay says.

"Burn all their shit down," Brick grunts.

"You're damn motherfucking right," my brother replies.

I sit forward in my seat. "I'm not disagreeing with you. Hear me out," I say and lift a hand as Clay goes to cut me off. "It's clear Dad knew about all of this. Yet he allowed it. I want to talk to the old man. What's his connection? What's his motive?"

Clay grunts and tightens his lips. I've been avoiding this conversation long enough. We're all supposed to be at the house for dinner tonight. I plan to get answers while we're there.

"You have a point," Clay mutters. "King, how long do you all plan to be around?"

"I go back in two weeks. You can hold on to a few of the Squad for another week or two if you need. New York will help where they can. Spider has his orders."

"I only need one night," I say.

"Put someone on the girl and make sure those other motherfuckers don't move," Clay says. "They want attention, I'll give them a standing ovation."

"That's what I'm talking about. They can all get clapped up," Reap sings with a sadistic smile.

King looks at her and shakes his head. I don't miss the smile on Clay's face. However, it's the white-as-a-sheet look on Cane's face that pulls my full attention.

I place a hand on his shoulder. "This is how you protect her. We don't give money to anyone who threatens our family."

Chloe

I look around at the calming grays and blues of this office. I had to make this appointment. The fight we had after the showing was enough to break up my marriage.

After sitting in the tub and calming my temper, I realized if I don't talk to someone, I'm going to lose more than my husband. So here I am.

"Chloe, what I'm hearing you say is that you were willing to let go of the past—not forget—but move past it while you were in Dubai. However, now that you're back in New York all that rage has returned, and you can't move forward. Am I right?"

"Yes."

I look up into Dr. Keller's deep-brown eyes. She's a pretty woman, maybe in her late thirties or early forties. Black don't crack so I'm not sure. It's her presence that makes me feel she might be older. Her office and her demeanor are calming and welcoming. I think I chose the right person.

"Tell me why you think that is. What's stopping you?" she coaxes.

"My husband says he wants to stay out of things with my sister, but I know he's in the middle and neither of them will tell me what's going on.

"I've been there for Ally for as long as I can remember. I've given up so much for her and she's... she's treating me like a stranger and people I've threatened and physically harmed are lurking around her life."

"I see. Have you ever thought that maybe Ally became the child you and Gregor lost? You're having trouble letting go because she represents the opportunity you lost as a mother. You did say she's twenty-two. Don't you think it's time to allow her to be an adult?"

I sit with my hands fisted tightly in the hem of my shirt. Tears start to fall. This is the truth I believe I've been avoiding.

"If you release your sister then you have no choice but to face your husband and your true feelings. Letting go will allow you to heal."

"What if it's not time to let go? She's gotten herself into something. I can't just ignore that."

"Letting go doesn't mean walking out of her life, but the hold you have now seems to be suffocating all members involved from what I'm hearing you say."

"So what are you saying?"

"Allow your sister to come to you. Cut your husband some slack and let the balance he's trying to create set in. It sounds like you have a good one."

"I know I do."

CHAPTER FORTY-EIGHT

Trust

Chloe

I'm standing next to the fire, staring at the flames as I think of my session this afternoon. Dr. Keller made some good points. I'm not trying to ignore her advice, but Gregor's insistence on keeping me in the dark drives me crazy.

"You're too hard on him," my father-in-law says as he walks up beside me.

I sigh and turn to him. He and Sid have grown a tighter bond. I'm still wary of getting attached to anyone else. Eileen and Chloe have crawled their way into my heart as it is.

"I think he should listen to my concerns," I reply.

He narrows his eyes on me. I always get the feeling he's a step ahead of us all. Gregor's father has been watching us closely since I first met him almost five months ago.

If I'm honest, so much has been going on and it's been hard to establish a relationship with this man. Between Gregor having to dive in to help Clay with the business and all the other things going on. Oh God, and that nut who tried to hurt Sid—I never liked his ass.

He was shady from the get-go. Still, even I never saw all that shit coming. In truth, I've watched my husband show another side of himself yet again.

The fierce protector of his brothers. You wouldn't think that would be the cause of the tension in our relationship, but it is when his little brother seems to be dragging my baby sister into his shit.

Gregor wants me to have patience with the two, but I want to knock some sense into Ally and pull them apart. I don't get or understand what's going on between them. Let's just say, I don't get or understand my sister anymore either.

"You've hardened your heart, but I think you should know that my son will always protect your happiness. That includes those around you who you're concerned about," he says.

I turn away to look at Ally and Cane locked in a heated conversation. I want to interfere, but I've been restraining myself as I try to remember she's not a little girl anymore. As Dr. Keller said, it's time for me to let go. I grind my teeth.

"She's my little sister. I've cared for her as if she were my own child. Gregor is asking me to ignore that. I don't think he would be so quick to ignore things if it were Chloe," I bite out more harshly than I intend.

I'm still struggling with all of this. I've yet to fully wrap my head around what I should do. What's the best thing to do.

"Cane is my unique child. Whatever you see is never what you get. Your perception of him may be clouded by your love for your sister. The thing about a shield… you can't see past it to know who's wielding the weapon," he says.

"What?" I turn to look him in the eyes.

"Sit back and watch, my dear. You will see what I see. For now, you should make up with your husband. Your wedding is in a few months. I'd hate to have to call off such a big event with so many guests," he says with a wink before he turns to walk away.

I look around to see that Sid and Clayton haven't returned. Gregor heads in my direction with a sleeping Chloe in his arms. His face is still tight from the argument we had earlier.

"Hey." I turn as Ally's voice pulls my attention.

"Hey," I say and frown.

"I'm going to leave. I just wanted to say good night," she says.

"Are we still having breakfast together in the morning?" I ask.

"Yeah, sure. I'll be there." She nods.

"Okay," I say, looking toward a jittery Cane. "Ally—"

"Have a good night, Ally. See you later," Gregor cuts me off.

I turn and glare at him. Unfortunately, my sister takes it as a cue to dart off. My shoulders tighten. I'm going to light into Gregor as soon as we get to the apartment. Enough is enough.

We say our goodbyes and make our way to the car. I keep my focus on the window as we ride in the back of the SUV. I can feel Gregor's stare on me.

"When will you learn to trust me?" he asks, breaking the silence.

"This has nothing to do with my trusting you," I turn to him and snap.

"Yes, it does. I told you I'd handle the situation with Ally. I've told you that I have it under control. Yet, you still want to get involved," he seethes.

"She's my sister. I'm always going to be involved when it comes to my sister," I toss back.

He nearly comes out of his seat as he turns to me. I can see the frustration in his face. I go to turn away, but he catches my chin and turns me back to him.

"This is one time you have to let go. Please. Let me handle this. Ally isn't a little girl anymore.

"She's made her own decisions whether right or wrong. This ship has sailed. She's in the thick of her choices and I'm doing everything I can to keep her and you safe. Trust me," he says.

"What's going on?"

"Your sister is brilliant. She just needs to pick better friends," he says, releasing me and shifting in his seat. "And before you go there. I'm not talking about Cane. My brother has his issues, but he cares about Ally's well-being more than you think."

I fold my arms across my chest and start to mutter to myself. I hate having my questions answered with riddles. Ally has been acting strange for months. Her dropping out of school almost made me lay hands on her.

I should have seen it coming. At first, I thought it was just me while I was in Dubai. She was always so short and… I don't know—something was off whenever we spoke. It's been more of the same thing, if not worse, since I've returned.

I continue to fuss under my breath until we reach home. Gregor remains silent, but I can feel the tension rolling off him. He has nerve.

He knew Ally dropped out way before I did—something I found out during one of our fights. Her tuition was cleared. If I were here instead of off with him, I would have made sure she took her butt back to school right away.

Why are my little sister and husband trying to make me break my foot off in their asses?

When we come to a stop in front of the apartment building, I'm out of the car before anyone can come to open my door. I don't wait for him to get out or to get the sleeping baby from her car seat.

I march straight for the lobby and the elevator. I roll my eyes when I hear Gregor and Ethan's heavy footfalls behind me before the doors open. Stepping onto the elevator, I ignore them both. Too bad Gregor doesn't take a hint.

He steps behind me, splaying a hand across my belly. I chide my body for melting into him. I'm still too pissed off for words.

Usually, I'd help get Chloe ready for bed, not tonight. I need some space to think. It seems everyone around me knows what's going on with my sister except for me.

I pace the living room, mumbling to myself, trying to figure out what I'm missing. Ally has always been a bit of a handful when she wants to be, but she's so talented. I've done everything I can to keep her focused on her talent.

"What am I missing?" I huff.

I make my way for the kitchen in search of my chocolate-covered strawberries and dulce de leche ice cream. I've been stress eating whenever it comes to Ally. She better get her shit together before my hips start to spread.

"Where the hell…" I say as I rummage through the refrigerator. I open the freezer and come up empty there as well.

Someone is trying to make me commit murder. Why?

I slam the door shut and place my palms on the cool surface. I scowl when suddenly my hands are covered by white ones, and I'm caged in by strong arms. If he knows what's good for him, he'll run. I'm about to snap.

"That's why the two of you ran out of this kitchen this afternoon," I say. "You ate my ice cream and strawberries and made that little baby an accomplice."

He doesn't reply, causing me to tug my hands free to turn and look at him. I try to take a step back, knowing that look on his face. I had wondered if I'd ever fully see it again.

Gregor is an alpha to the core. I've known since Dubai that he has been restraining that impulse because of the circumstances. It looks like that restraint has snapped.

"I've done this dance with you because I owed it to you. But it ends now," he says firmly. "I'm telling you to trust me because it's best for everyone. *Trust.* It used to be so simple between us. I take responsibility for my part in its loss, but I've done everything in my power to gain it back—"

"Except for telling me what's going on," I snap back.

"Because you don't need to know!"

"Fuc—"

"Don't. We're beyond that now. Don't disrespect me. You know how I feel." He moves in closer, crowding my space. Then licks his lips. "Maybe we've been doing this wrong. I think I know what we both need."

"I'm not going there with you," I whisper.

"Why?" he asks, tilting his head. "Are you afraid that it will feel right to let go? We've both been thinking too much. In our feelings about the past. It's time I free us both, baby."

"That's not going to solve anything," I say and frown.

"I beg to differ. We're having a problem with trust. I know just how to fix that," he croons.

"Gregor—"

He shakes his head to silence me. "You have too many excuses for not letting me in. I was willing to let that go before…now. You're using Ally to shut me out. No. I won't allow it."

"So what, you plan to tie me to your bed until I give in?"

"No, it just so happens your wedding gift is complete. We can go downstairs so I can show you," he says.

"We're not leaving the baby up here while—"

"Ethan is here. He'll stay within earshot of Chloe. Any more excuses?"

I glare at him but don't respond. I know he plans to push us both until our minds are numb. I'm just not sure I want to go there.

He leans into me until we are nose to nose. Power and energy rolling off him. I have no doubt Gregor would have made an amazing governor if he wanted.

"What are you afraid of, baby? You have all the power. You know this. This is about you trusting me and me trusting you. It's what we need," he says.

I swallow and look away. He might just be right. Dr. Keller hit it on the head.

While I am worried about my sister, I have been using her to place another wall between us. My real issue is my fear to trust. It all comes back to that fear.

Truth is, I'm in love with my husband. Remove Ally from the equation and I'll be honest to say that Gregor is an amazing husband and father. I love our daughter as well.

Our daughter.

Somehow these two have crept into my heart and I don't know what to do with that or how to feel. Ally has provided the perfect distraction since we arrived back here to New York.

Has Ally become the child I lost? She may have, but I have a family of my own now. I don't need to hold on so tight.

When I don't reply, Gregor dips and tosses me over his shoulder. I gasp and hold on. My jumbled feelings rush to the forefront.

I remain silent as he walks to the stairs that lead down to the next level. We go down a level before he heads for a room in the back of the apartment. I haven't been down here because he said it was under renovation.

He opens a door and moves into the room. When he places me on my feet, I keep my eyes on him. Trust, that's what he's asking for. Something that should be so simple for a couple, but it feels like giving blood to me.

"We could take on the world together. This is our time, but we have to do it as a team. You complete me. Let me complete us," he says.

Not able to say the words, I close my eyes and nod.

He cups my face and kisses my forehead. "Are you ready?"

Gregor

She doesn't say a word. A simple nod is her response, causing me to take pause. I look around the room and realize that I may have been wrong. We truly have changed so much.

This is more about her fears than her trust. I don't need to take control of things. I need to restore her control. I should have seen it sooner. Yet, now that I have, I know just what we both need from her.

"Open your eyes," I say. "We're going to switch. I'm handing you the control. You pick what we need. Show me where we're broken and how you'd fix us."

Her brows crease as she stares me in the eyes. "What?"

"Show me. If we're going to work, I can't keep guessing. I've done all I know. Now, it's your turn. Show me," I reply.

"How?"

I wave a hand around the custom-made playroom. I had it designed with all her favorite kinks in mind. All the things she allowed me to open her mind to so long ago.

"You remember the next level of connection we have when we play. You guide us. Reveal to me what you feel we need."

She gazes at me in awe for a few moments before the lights come on in her eyes. It's not lust I see but determination. I've revealed to her the keys that she's always owned.

She moves her fingers to my shirt buttons. One by one, she releases each one until she's able to push the fabric from my shoulders to the floor.

Her hands go to my belt buckle to free me of my pants and boxers at once. All the while her eyes never leave mine. I watch her remove her own clothes, letting the black dress fall to the floor along with my things.

She peels off her panties and kicks them aside. Reaching for my fingers, she clasps them and starts moving toward the shelves and drawers. I watch her curiously, but I don't open my mouth to offer help.

I want to see where she's going to take us on her own. The silence weighs the room down, causing me to take note of my own breathing. This woman before me is the only one who can get this kind of reaction out of me.

I still can't comprehend how I thought I'd be able to live without her. She opens the glass case with the stereo system and turns it on. I watch the smile that spreads across her face as she finds the settings with her name on them. Music fills the room and vibrates through me as it sets the mood.

Cee takes my hand again and moves forward to explore more. I grin and squeeze her fingers when she pulls a pair of cuffs from a glass bowl on one of the displays.

She turns her gaze toward me, but she gives nothing away. Turning back to the drawers, she pulls open a few before reaching in one and pulling a blindfold. I lift a brow but show no other reaction.

Cee leads me over to the king-size bed in the center of the room. Once my back is to the side of the bed, she gives me a gentle shove to sit. I comply and watch as she retrieves a condom from the bowl on the bedside table, handing it to me.

I nod, opening the pack and sliding the condom on. As much as I want to feel my wife's tight sheath around me bare, I know we're not there yet.

She reaches for my wrist and snaps the cuff into place. However, I'm surprised when she straddles my hips and clicks the other half to her own wrist. Our eyes connect and something shifts in the air. I find my answers right on the surface. I swallow hard against my emotions.

I'm not going anywhere, baby.

I tell her with my eyes. She nods, lifting the blindfold. Yet again, she surprises me. She places the fabric over her own eyes, not mine.

I get this too. Her need to find blind faith in us again. I place my free hand on the small of her back to hold her to me. It's my silent reassurance that I'm not going anywhere. I'm here for as long as I live.

Cee moves her face to mine, and I capture her lips. We communicate through the passion of our kiss. I swallow her whimpers and she inhales my groans. Reaching between the two of us, she finds my erection and starts to stroke me.

Her hips start to grind in my lap as the song playing sings of telling where love lies. I know where mine lies and it's with this woman in my arms. Cee lifts and sinks down on me.

I still completely. She tugs our joined hands up and places my palm over her heart, linking our fingers together—her small hand over mine. I may not be able to see her eyes, but I can see the war within her face. The need for me to meet her in all of this.

She starts to move up and down slowly, placing her free hand on my shoulder. My mouth falls open and I flex my fingers over her heart. The connection is so intense my skin prickles and my spine has already started to tingle.

When she starts to roll her hips in between bouncing up and down, it's nearly my undoing. I still don't take over. This is about her teaching us both. It's my lesson to bear if I want to secure our future.

My body quakes as she picks up the pace, but I demand my own restraint. With my free hand, I caress her neck, moving up to her face. She nuzzles her cheek into my palm.

I watch in awe as her features begin to transform. I can see the battle reaching its peak. As if a decision is to be made and I have the deciding factor resting in my grasp.

"I love you," I say as the words rise within me. "I will always love you."

Chloe

He says it just when I need to hear it. My lips part but I don't have the words to speak. I want to tell him I'm there with him and that I love him, but it's still not that easy.

Yet, I'm trying to show him. This is a huge step for me. Somewhere deep within, I've made a decision. I'm taking a risk no matter if I'm willing to say it or not. I'm placing my bets on my husband.

I lean toward him, and he seizes my lips. I allow him to devour me as I continue to build our connection with my movements. I break the connection, using my nose to guide me to his ear.

When I reach my destination, I pause before I whisper to him. "I need *you* to show me. Show my heart, not my eyes," I say.

I don't want to trust what I see when I look into his eyes. His eyes are one of my weaknesses. I want to feel him and his love, not see it. Everyone is different, for me this is what I need.

I need to feel because I no longer trust what I see. Nothing seems to be right when I do. If he can give me this, I think I can get us both to where we need to be.

He cups the back of my neck, bringing my lips back to his. He moves his other palm down from the center of my chest, covering my stomach. His fingers splay my belly and I swear it feels like he's pushing healing powers into my womb.

Tears start to fall behind the blindfold. He breaks the kiss this time. His tongue flicking against my skin to trap the tears that have fallen.

"I love you," he whispers.

I've been hearing those words for months, but tonight I let them fully sink in. Brodi would have brought me in here, tied me to the St. Andrew's Cross I noticed and put my body through the wringer until my mind numbed to it all. He would have freed me of the internal war, but it would have been all him.

Gregor, my husband—the love he has for me doesn't allow him to leave me behind. With him, I'm a part of the team, which is what I needed all along. It's what we needed.

I open my mouth to say the words. "Gregor" comes out instead.

I come down and he thrusts up just when I need it. I explode around him. He lifts, repositioning us on the bed.

I push my head back into the pillow as he drives into me with deliberate strokes. I feel him, just the way I need to and wrap my legs around him to cradle him tightly.

"Yes, baby," he groans. "Take all my love. Take everything I have to give."

"Gregor." My cry echoes through the room over the music.

"I'd do anything for you. You're my family, Chlo. You're the beginning of everything I am. Know that I'll protect my family with my life. I'll be here for whatever you need, whenever you need it," he says huskily.

"Yes, yes," I whimper.

I reach for the blindfold and pull it off. Reaching for my hands, he locks the fingers of our joined hands together. Turning my head, I then stare at our locked palms.

It's like something clicks into place. Before I can dive into the feeling too deeply, he moves his fingers under my chin and turns my face to his. His gaze scorches into me.

"This is forever. I'll love you always. I'm never letting you go," he says just before we both climax together.

He drops his forehead to mine as he hisses through his teeth. We absorb each other and the moment. His last words play in my head. I don't think I ever believed he was going to let me go. Truth is, I never wanted him to.

"I know," I breathe when my heart slows.

He rolls onto his back but keeps a hold of my hand that's cuffed to his. Reaching for my body, he drags it into his. I snuggle closer, my thoughts spinning.

Time ticks by as we lie together in a sated bliss. I start to form the words to say them out loud, but my stomach speaks up instead. Gregor chuckles and lifts his head.

"You didn't eat much at dinner. I'll go out and replace your ice cream," he says.

"You don't have to do that." I yawn and bury deeper into his warmth.

"Already done," he says as he reaches into the drawer and retrieves a key.

"It's late. Ethan is probably knocked out."

"I'm a grown man. I know how to take myself to the store for my woman. I think I even know a place where I can get you some strawberries." He winks. "Besides, I think you're going to need your energy for the second half of the night."

"Is that right?"

He leans in to lay a bone-melting kiss on me. I sink into the bed as I cling to his shoulders. A whimper leaves me when he backs away.

"I'll be right back," he promises, kissing the tip of my nose.

I can't help watching after him with a goofy grin on my face. Too soon he's wrapped in one of the silk robes hanging by the door and then he's gone. I'm left with my thoughts and feelings once again.

CHAPTER FORTY-NINE

Father to Son

Gregor

"I didn't think you would come," my father says as I step into his office.

"It's late and I wasn't going to," I grumble. "Why am I here?"

I wasn't going to respond to his text, but I never got to address the things I wanted to talk to him about earlier. After finding out he's dying, I needed to pull my thoughts together.

I'll be honest. I'm angrier with him than I've ever been. I love my father despite all the shit between us. I was devastated to overhear him and Sid earlier this evening.

I could forgive the situation with Wade, I might be able to get over his meddling once I understand what he's been thinking, but to hide the fact he's been unwell. That's something I'm going to struggle with.

"You're my oldest. I wanted to talk to you first. I've wronged you the most."

"Why would you keep this from us?"

"I don't plan to allow this to take me away from the family I love. I still have work to do here," he says firmly.

"You said the new treatment is working, but what if it hadn't?"

"That was never an option. The moment I found out, I knew I would fight. I have too much to live for. I wanted to see all my boys happy. I wanted to hold my grandchildren, but most of all, I wanted to erase the monster you boys seem to see me as."

Addison thought she could fight for Chloe and look how that turned out. I grind my teeth. This was so selfish of him, of her. I wonder did either of them think of their children they'd leave behind.

I furrow my brows and look down into my palms. If anyone could cheat death it would be the man before me. I think over his words and frown.

"I never saw you as a monster."

"Sure, you did. You don't have to lie to spare my feelings. I know I come off as a bastard. However, as a father yourself, I believe you may now understand the things I've done."

"You've known about Cane's marriage," I say.

"Yes, I didn't expect him to find someone so soon, but when I found out, I was pleased. Her troubles concerned me, but I've kept an eye on things. Cane has become the man I knew he could be in order to protect her. In the end, I'll have two birds crushed with one stone."

"I figured as much. Old deal gone bad?"

"You have no idea. You boys thought I didn't want you to become men. That's not it at all.

"I didn't want the world out there to eat my children alive. I tried to guide you all, but when you boys wanted to do it on your own, I watched proudly as you all rose from the ashes of my tight grip.

"However, I couldn't watch without interference. When my enemies decided to make themselves yours, I've blocked any harm I thought would destroy your success. No matter the cost.

"A lot has been Clay, but I've boxed with the bigger threats on all of your behalf. I have regrets and a failure or two."

"What failure?" I ask and lift a brow.

"Addison and Cee."

I ball my fists at my side as I start to fume. He has to be out of his damn mind if he thought Addison was right for me. He holds a hand up as he begins to cough.

In the past, this cough hadn't concerned me much. Now, knowing what I know, my chest tightens. I rush to pour him a glass of water from the pitcher on his bar.

"Thank you," he says as he takes the glass and drains it. "You have the wrong idea."

He pauses to take a seat behind his desk. I watch him, noticing this isn't the vibrant man I once feared standing up to. Time has passed and so much has changed.

"I wanted to protect you from Addison. I saw that woman for the demon she was. I hadn't known how far she would take her treachery, but I knew she would be an issue.

"I didn't know I was too late when I set things in motion for you to find your way back to Chloe. Although I'm well aware that I failed the two of you well before Addison entered the picture. I'm truly sorry, Gregor.

"I wish I could do it all over. I was so wrong. I deserved my losses, you did not."

"And Clay, you knew about Sidney?"

His eyes light up. "I did. He was going to lose her with that contract foolishness. It was my hope a marriage would force him to see what was in front of his eyes. Everything else just happened to work in my favor. Wade has done well looking after you all.

"I never kept the truth about him from you boys to hurt you. Your mother wasn't ready to accept him into our family. I did the best I could to respect her wishes and take care of my boy.

"Evelyn had no children of her own. She was close enough, yet far enough to help me make things work. You are lucky to have Cee. Her love for Chloe is rare."

I stumble to a chair and flop down. I want to hold on to my anger, but my mind turns to Cee. I know the things I'd do to keep her safe and happy. I don't know if I can hold a grudge against my father.

I narrow my eyes at him. "But why are you insisting we all run the company?"

"It was how I planned to reveal Wade. I want the four of you to do this as brothers. Oh, and don't worry. I still have one more son to push to the alter."

I lift a brow and grin. "Payback is a bitch. You let me know how I can help with that." I chuckle.

"I'm proud of you, son."

"I love you, Dad."

"I love you too. Now go home to your wife and make me another grandchild."

My chest burns. No matter how much I think Chlo and I have moved forward tonight, I don't think we're there yet. However, I get up to get those strawberries and her ice cream so I can get back home to her.

#

CHAPTER FIFTY

Clayton

I tighten my arms around Sid's waist as I rest my cheek against the top of her head. I needed this. Some time to think about what all happened tonight.

My father refused to talk about his prognosis. After having a drink, he dismissed us from his office without any further discussion of his condition. I needed to get out of there. I grabbed Sid and left. It was her idea to come here.

This view of the Hudson and the city has gone a long way to calm me. Along with having my wife in my arms. Correction, my wife and our growing child.

I lean back against the grill of the SUV and look down at her. She peers up at me with so much concern in her eyes. I love this woman so much.

"I think he's done it all out of love. Even keeping his secret," she says.

I close my eyes and nod. Guilt consumes me. It was my idea to break away and go out on our own. Would things be different if I didn't?

"Hey, I don't think your father wanted you to be anyone other than who you are. He's proud of you all. Don't beat yourself up. Cherish the time you still have and support him through this."

I lean in and capture her lips. I deepen the kiss as she wraps her arms around my neck. Breaking the kiss, I then place my forehead to hers.

"All of his bullshit led me to you and this one," I say, placing my hand over her belly. "I'll think about forgiving him. In time."

"Time is the one thing none of us are guaranteed."

I peck her lips. "Which is why I don't want to waste another minute not making love to my wife. Come on, let's go home."

"Can we stop for some ice cream and fruit?"

"I'll run to the store by the house once we're there. You can go upstairs."

Cane

"Just when I thought things couldn't get any worse," I grunt into my hands.

Ally places her palm on my back beneath my suit jacket and starts to rub soothing circles. I turn to look into her eyes. They're blue from the contacts she has in. I hate it.

She's still gorgeous, but it's not her. Just like the dark curly wig isn't her. My wife shouldn't have to hide. I thought I had this handled, but I'm so far in over my head, I feel like I'm drowning.

The only thing I know for sure is that I'm going to fix this. I'm going to burn down every motherfucker I have to until she's safe and I'm going to be a father to the child of the woman I love.

"He's going to be okay. Your dad is strong. He's a fighter. I know he's going to be okay."

I cup the side of her face. "Are you going to be okay? Are you ready to tell Chloe the truth about us?"

She drops her eyes away from me and frowns. Right, because I'm not good enough. I hate the day I first lifted that white powder to my nose. It has fucked up everything in my life since.

"Never mind," I scoff and move to climb out of the SUV.

After stopping with Ally for smoothies, I asked the driver to park a block away from the penthouse, not ready to go inside. I needed a moment to think.

"Cane, wait," Ally calls out as she gets out to follow me.

I spin on her. "Why? It's clear I don't matter to you. I'm not good enough, I get it. You can't bear to bring yourself to tell your sister you married a fuckup like me."

"Really, Cane? Really?"

She storms past me, bumping my arm as she goes. Royce steps out of the car to follow her. I hold my hand up to stop him and turn to glare after her.

My heart tightens, I love her little ass so much it hurts. I've worked so hard to be everything she needs. She's seen me when no one else has.

"Fuck," I roar. "Ally, wait."

She flips me the bird. I start to jog after her, my long legs eating the distance up quickly. I catch her arm to halt her.

"I'm sorry. Please talk to me."

"Why can't you see what I see, Cane? Why don't you understand this hasn't been about you? My sister is insane, and Sid is just as crazy. They have beaten the shit out of gang members for me. Lita was one of them. They put them in the hospital to keep me safe. I fucked up. I opened a door I shouldn't have and now my sister is in danger because of me.

"Chlo isn't going to fall back and allow this. She's going to go to war for me. I can't let that happen. That's why she doesn't know. Telling her about you comes with the whole truth. She's not stupid."

She rolls her tear-filled eyes and pulls her earbuds out to push them into her ears before she storms off again. I run my hands through my hair.

Chloe isn't the only one willing to go to war for her, and I need her to see that. I'm here, I'm going to make it so she can talk to her sister the way she wants. I've got her.

I just need her trust. Lost in thought, I start to follow after her. I'm dragging my feet because I don't know where to start to fix this.

I look up at the sound of Clay bellowing Ally's name. It all happens in slow motion. My heart starts to race.

"Ally," I roar.

CHAPTER FIFTY-ONE

A Team

Chloe

My phone buzzes on the countertop as I return to the kitchen for a glass of water. I tighten the silk robe around me as a chill runs through me. When I check the phone it's a text from Sid.

Sid: *Are you still up?*

Me: *Yeah, what's up?*

Sid: *I have something to tell you. Can you come down to the lobby? I'm waiting for Clay.*

Me: *Sure. Give me a sec.*

My curiosity is piqued. I can hear Ethan snoring in the room beside Chloe's, and I'm sure he has the baby monitor turned on. I take my sore body into the bedroom and change into a pair of leggings and a T-shirt.

I'm lost in my thoughts as I ride down to the lobby. I was so close to telling Gregor I love him. I don't know what's holding me back anymore.

It may just boil down to my stubbornness. I could put us both out of our misery, but I've been holding on to the past so tightly. It's a very real past for me. Yet, I know he gets that.

I sigh as the elevator doors open. Sid has the widest smile on her face as I come into view. I pick up the pace to reach her.

"You guys left before I could talk to you. I've been keeping this to myself. I couldn't wait to tell you," she gushes.

"What? You're killing me?"

"I'm pregnant," she squeals.

I stumble back a bit. It's not the reaction I mean to have. However, her words are like a punch to the gut. Sid and Clay are so happy. They've overcome their differences. Gregor and I are at an impasse that I don't know how to cross.

"Chloe?" Sid says, reaching out for me.

"I'm so happy for you," I push out.

"You know I know you better than that. What just happened?"

"It was Gregor. The guy who broke my heart, it was him," I gasp.

"Yeah, I sort of got that." She nods.

"But what I never told you was that I was pregnant. I... I terminated the pregnancy. He left to start his life over, to get out from under his father. I... I didn't know what else to do," I say.

"Oh, Chloe. I'm so sorry. I didn't know. I wouldn't hav—"

"No, please don't think you can't share this with me. I want to be here for you every step of the way," I cut her off. "I think... I think it just hit me that that's what..."

I trail off as I see my sister walking toward the lobby doors, but it's not the sight of her that grabs my attention. It's the car speeding toward her. It's like everything moves in slow motion.

Clay appears and starts to shout, grabbing Cane's attention as he walks a distance away from Ally. Cane starts to run toward Ally and Gregor's red Jag comes out of nowhere. It flies in front of the speeding car, taking the force of the impact.

I watch as my husband's car shields my sister's life by placing his own in danger. The red car flips into the air and I swear I don't breathe until it lands on its top, upside down.

"*Gregor*," I scream, my voice sounding above the ringing in my ears.

David, Cane, and Clay run for the car that smashed into Gregor's. Sid, Ally, and I run for my husband. Smoke comes from the car, and I freak out.

"Sid, Ally, get back," I demand.

I drop to my knees and look inside the car. Gregor's head is bleeding, and he looks dazed. I have to get him out.

"Baby, can you hear me?" I sob.

"Cee," he whispers.

"I'm going to get you out of here. Can you move?"

"Get back, baby… not safe," he replies.

"I'm not leaving you here."

Ignoring the broken glass, I crawl closer to get my body inside. With a shaky hand, I reach for the seat belt. It doesn't open on the first try but I don't give up.

"Get back, Chloe," he groans.

"No, you said we need to be a team. It starts here. We're in this shit together, Gregor. I love you. You're not leaving me again," I cry.

The belt finally releases as I pull and push at it frantically. I survey his body and see his right arm looks limp at his side. I'm going to need help to get him out.

"Get back, Chloe," Clay commands. "I'll get him out."

Reluctantly, I back out of the window. Clay has a better chance of pulling his brother out than I do. Still, I don't go far. A spark comes from the front of the car.

"Hurry, Clay," I cry out.

All at once, the front of the car ignites, and Cane lifts me to drag me away. Clay pulls Gregor from the car. Royce appears and helps Clay rush to get Gregor to safety away from the flaming vehicle. The car explodes just as we take cover in the lobby of the building.

When Cane releases me, I rush to Gregor and throw my arms around him. I can't stop sobbing. He kisses the top of my head and wraps one arm around me.

"It's okay, baby. It's okay," he murmurs. "Let's get you to the hospital."

"Me?" I pull away to look up at him in confusion.

"Baby, your legs and palms are bleeding."

I look down and sure enough, my leggings are covered in blood. The sting from the tiny cuts starts to register in my brain. I look at him and his bleeding head, then his arm that I'm pretty sure is broken or at least dislocated.

"I'm fine. We need to get you to the hospital. What were you thinking?"

"Protecting my family at any cost," he says with a weak smile.

I nod. "Yeah, okay. I got it," I say and close my eyes against the tears.

Gregor

I groan as I turn my head and open my eyes. Cee is tucked into my side, holding me closely. I smile even as I wince against the pain.

My body aches, but I'd do it again if I had to. When I saw that car headed for Ally I didn't stop to think. I ran the light and placed my car between her and the danger headed her way.

I promised Cee I'd take care of her and Ally, and I will. We tried to handle things quietly. I think now it's time to make a little noise. I told Clay at the hospital that it was time to set things in motion. I have my answers and I understand everything going on.

King is in no way subtle, but that's a risk I'm willing to take to make sure things are handled. For Cee, I'd shift the world on its axis. That means taking care of Ally's mess.

I brush a lock of hair from Cee's face. Her bandaged hand flexes on my chest. I think it pained me more to see her hurt than to have a dislocated shoulder and fractured wrist.

She said she loves me. I know those words gave me the strength I needed to help Clay pull me out of the car. I wanted to hear them again to make sure she really said them.

"Go back to sleep," she mutters.

"I want to watch you," I reply.

She lifts her head and gives me a sleepy smile. "I'm not going anywhere. You need to rest," she says with a smile.

My heart swells. I hear the words and the depth of their meaning. I've been waiting so long to take this breath. She's mine. I can see it in her eyes. The walls are no longer in our way.

"I love you," I say as I watch her face.

She lifts her hand to cup my jaw. Her eyes search mine for a few moments. I realize I'm holding my breath when she speaks.

"Sid told me she's pregnant. It made me realize something as I stood there. I've been so upset with you over what never was. Now here we are with a chance to have it all and I've been blocking us both from having what we want most.

"I was just about to tell Sid that when that car started speeding toward Ally. I... I have too much to lose without you. You're the only one I want to live through this messy life with. I trust you, Gregor, and, baby?"

"Yes, gorgeous."

"I'm staying because I want to. I love you with everything I have."

I tug her down to capture her lips. I kiss her with all the words I can't form to say. This is my happily ever after. This woman is what I've needed in my life.

I break the kiss and look her in the eyes. Taking a deep breath, I go to ask one of the hardest questions of my life. Yet, I need to ask.

"Yes, we can start expanding our family," she says before I can get the words out.

I feel like my face splits as my smile takes over. I wrap my good arm around her, holding her tight. I say a prayer of thanks because I know I had divine help to get my woman back.

"I love you with everything I am. I will never hurt you again," I promise.

"I know, babe. I know."

CHAPTER FIFTY-TWO

Til Death & Beyond

Chloe

Three months later…

I stand beaming up at my husband. We did it. We've said our vows again in front of everyone. I love this man more than I ever have.

Now that I know what my sister had been hiding from me, I know he did the right things to keep me from behind bars. All in all, I know this man would do anything to keep me happy and my sister safe.

"I love you," I purr as he leans in to kiss me.

He kisses me passionately as he holds me tight. My life flashes before my eyes. We lost so much time, but we've been making the time we do have worth it.

"I love you too," he says against my lips. "Always have, always will, Mrs. Hennessy."

"Mommy, Mommy," Chloe calls as she comes running toward us.

My heart squeezes. It does every time she calls me that. She's been doing so for a few weeks now. I've been in a much better headspace.

Dr. Keller has helped a lot. However, the playroom has worked its magic as well. We have our own language in there.

I bend to pick Chloe up. "Hey, sweetie," I coo once she's in my arms.

She cups my face. "Mommy is pretty, right Daddy?" she says as she turns to Gregor.

"Yes, baby. Mommy is pretty. She's the most beautiful bride I've ever seen."

"You're not bad yourself," I say to him with a smile.

"How about I dance with my family?"

He takes Chloe into his arms and wraps his free one around my waist, guiding us out to the dance floor. I look up at him with a face-splitting smile.

"This. This is everything."

"Too an eternity of *this*," Gregor murmurs and kisses my nose. When he pulls away, Chloe palms his cheeks and kisses his nose like he did mine. I laugh and wrap my arms around them.

This is my family, my forever.

We're Next

Chloe

Four months later…

I wring my hands together as I pace the waiting room. I'm not only nervous for Sid—her water broke in the middle of the wedding. I'm nervous about the reaction I'll get when I share my secret with my husband.

I've only known for a few days. With the wedding and my second show at the Soho gallery, we've all been so busy. It never seems like the right time to tell him.

"She's going to be fine," Gregor murmurs in my ear as he comes up behind me to wrap me in his arms to stop my pacing.

I melt into him, savoring his embrace and heat. I never thought I'd be here. We've come such a long way.

"I can't wait to be on the other side of this. You swollen with my child, bringing our baby into this world," he says.

I smile and turn in his arms. His eyes soften as he looks down at me. My husband is one fine-ass man. I'm glad he fought for me when it counted.

"What do you hope we're having?" I ask and bite my lip.

"I'd be happy with a boy or a girl. A girl means we'll just have to try again," he croons.

He pauses and his brows knit. I watch as the wheels turn. I can't keep the smile off my face. I roll my lips and nod at him.

"You're pregnant?" he whispers in awe.

"Yes," I say softly.

He cradles his arms around my head, tugging me into his shoulder. He rocks from side to side as he holds me tightly. I can feel the emotions rolling off him.

"God, I love you so much. I want to be there for everything. You're going to have to pry me away. Thank you, baby. Thank you so much."

"For what?" I ask, my words muffled by his shoulder.

"For staying," he chokes out, releasing me to look into my eyes. "For being one of my greatest treasures and now, adding one more."

"*Well*, I can't say I didn't have motivation," I tease.

"You haven't touched a dime." He chuckles.

"How do you know?"

"I'm your husband. I know everything."

"You didn't know I was pregnant." I laugh.

"Maybe I did, maybe I didn't." He shakes his head, a huge grin taking over his face. "We're next."

"I guess you're right. Cally was in such a rush to get here." I grin.

"True."

"But I may have or may not have overheard a little something about someone else."

"*Chlo*," he groans.

I laugh before kissing my husband. The secrets around here never stay buried long, but something good always comes from them.

ABOUT THE AUTHOR

Blue Saffire, award-winning, bestselling author of over thirty contemporary romance novels and novellas, writes with the intention to touch the heart and the mind. Blue hooks, weaves, and loops multiple series, keeping you engaged in her worlds. Blue writes for her own publishing company Perceptive Illusions as Blue Saffire as well as Royal Blue.

Blue and her husband live in a house filled with laughter and creativity, in Long Island, NY. Both working hard to build the Blue brand and cultivate their love for the artists. Creative is their family affair.

Blue holds an MBA in Marketing and Project Management, as well as an MED in Instructional Technology and Curriculum Design. She is also an NLP Master Practitioner.

ACKNOWLEDGMENTS

Do you see that? It's blood, sweat, and tears. LOL. This one took a minute... again. This book is an emotional roller coaster for me on so many levels every time I touch it. Gregor and Cee had a tough story to tell, and I needed to find the balance in it. I knew right out of the gate it wasn't going to be easy, but I love the final results, again. I got my alpha male and female. She got her healing on her terms and he got his woman.

Thank you so much for your support and for sticking with me as I make my way back. I know I have a ton of things going on in my life, but you all stood by me and let me take my time. That means so much. I have so much more for you guys.

Writing a book requires a piece of my soul. Each one is an offering. I have to find the right pieces to give so that I have peace. Your willingness to allow me to do that and come on the journey is cherished in a way you just will never understand.

I thank God for this gift to be able to place you as a reader into the life and feelings of two fictional characters and take you to new places. To Him be all the glory. I thank God for blessing my words and keeping me through every step.

Next! *I'm going to come back to this series after I run through a few more on my list. Hold on, I got you.*

Wait, there is more to come! You can stay updated with my latest releases, learn more about me, the author, and be a part of contests by subscribing to my newsletter at
www.BlueSaffire.com
If you enjoyed *A Million To Stay*, I'd love to hear your thoughts and please feel free to leave a review. And when you do, please let me know by emailing me TheBlueSaffire@gmail.com or leave a comment on Facebook https://www.facebook.com/BlueSaffireDiaries or Twitter @TheBlueSaffire

Other books by Blue Saffire
Placed in Best Reading Order
Also available....
Legally Bound

Legally Bound 2: Against the Law

Legally Bound 3: His Law

Perfect for Me

Hush 1: Family Secrets

Ballers: His Game

Brothers Black 1: Wyatt the Heartbreaker

Legally Bound 4: Allegations of Love

Hush 2: Slow Burn

Legally Bound 5.0: Sam

Yours 1: Losing My Innocence

Yours 2: Experience Gained

Yours 3: Life Mastered

Ballers 2: His Final Play

Legally Bound 5.1: Tasha Illegal Dealings

Brothers Black 2: Noah

Legally Bound 5.2: Camille

Legally Bound 5.3 & 5.4 Special Edition

Where the Pieces Fall

Legally Bound 5.5: Legally Unbound

Brothers Black 4: Braxton the Charmer

My Funny Valentine

Broken Soldier

Remember Me

Brothers Black 5: Felix the Watcher

A Home for Christmas

Be My Valentine

Coming Soon...
*The Ones Left Behind Book 3: Work Husband
Series*
Ox Book 5: The A**hole Club
Kelex 6: The A**hole Club

Work Husband Series
Unexpected Lovers
My Best Friend's Wish

The Lost Souls MC Series

Forever
Never
Always

Check out Blue Saffire exclusives on the
BlueSaffire.com website
Dom
The Fixer
Lost

**Other books from Evei Lattimore Collection Books
by Blue Saffire**
Black Bella 1

Destiny 1: Life Decisions
Destiny 2: Decisions of the Next Generation
Destiny 3 coming soon...

Star

**Other books from Royal Blue Gay Romance
Collection written by Blue Saffire**
Kyle's Reveal
Beau's Redemption

Work Husband Series

Lost Souls Series

⭐Forever: Book 1-Brick
⭐Never: Book 2 -Gutter
⭐Always: Books 3-King
Again: Book 4-Cage
Before 4.5- Thor
Sometimes: Book 5-Jackie
Lifetime: Book 6-Grim
Still: Book 7-Kevlar
Once: Book 8-Diggs, Axle, and Sugar
Now: Book 9 -Tracks
When: Book 10-Holden